LEMONS AND LIES

ALSO BY ALEXIS CASTELLANOS

Guava and Grudges

LEMONS AND LIES

Alexis Castellanos

BLOOMSBURY
NEW YORK LONDON OXFORD NEW DELHI SYDNEY

BLOOMSBURY YA
Bloomsbury Publishing Inc., part of Bloomsbury Publishing Plc
1359 Broadway, New York, NY 10018
50 Bedford Square, London, WC1B 3DP, UK
Bloomsbury Publishing Ireland Limited, 29 Earlsfort Terrace, Dublin 2, D02 AY28, Ireland

BLOOMSBURY and the Diana logo are trademarks of Bloomsbury Publishing Plc

First published in the United States of America in September 2025 by Bloomsbury YA

Library of Congress Cataloging-in-Publication Data
available upon request
ISBN 978-1-5476-1408-0 (trade paperback) • ISBN 978-1-5476-1409-7 (e-book)

Book design by John Candell
Typeset by Westchester Publishing Services
Printed by Integrated Books International, United States of America
4 6 8 10 9 7 5 3

This one's for Reed. None of this
would be possible without you.

Please note this story contains depictions of parental abandonment, trauma from that abandonment, and mental health struggles. As these may be upsetting themes, please take care and read at your own discretion.

CHAPTER ONE

I did not think I would be spending my lunch hour sitting on a toilet eating a limp ham sandwich in my senior year of high school. I thought I would be sitting next to my twin brother, Adrian, at the prime lunch table next to the bank of windows, surrounded by all the people I've hung out with since middle school. Instead, I'm in a gray-speckled bathroom stall staring at the recent graffiti additions.

The distant roar of the cafeteria bleeds through the door, and the pungent scent of ammonia is making my unappetizing meal an even worse experience. But I've decided that spending my entire lunch break sitting on a toilet is better than the embarrassment of sitting at my cousin Miguel's lunch table with *his* friends—or worse, trying to sit with my brother.

I'd *thought* I had my own friends, until Adrian made it very clear that those people were *his* friends. Since Adrian isn't talking to me, no one else in his group is talking to me, either. Adrian Morales is practically a king at this school, and even though

I'm his twin sister, my position gives me no leverage now that he's decided I betrayed him. And by betrayed, I mean held him accountable for stealing a doughnut recipe from our family's rival and playing it off as his.

The men in my family are *such* drama queens.

I take another bite of my sandwich and have to hold back a gag. It isn't getting any better with time. The bread is soggy, and it has a weird smell that I'm almost positive is a result of being in a bathroom and not entirely the ham's fault. Either way, I shove it back in its paper bag to give to my dog, Leo, when I get home.

Now to wait out the last of the lunch break. I pull out my mini sketchbook and continue to work on my latest doodle, another promotional illustration for my family's bakery. We're best known for our dessert burrito, which we've turned into a mascot called Gordo. Last week my dad asked for an illustration of Gordo playing football for a cross-promotion with homecoming in a few weeks.

I'm just about done with the helmet when I hear the growing sounds of voices and clicking heels. Someone is ranting, loudly, and stomping toward the bathroom, so I quickly pull up my feet and backpack to hide my presence and wait.

I hear the door swing open, followed by the familiar voice of Rose McGinnis.

"If it wasn't totally a crime, I would have flung myself across the table to fight Ginger," Rose says.

"I've never met a more entitled person in my life." I recognize the second voice as Ana Maria Ybarra. "Except maybe Adrian."

I cover my mouth quickly and try to choke down my sudden laugh. Last year, I would have come to my brother's defense, especially since the insult came from the mouth of an Ybarra, our family's former sworn enemies. But Ana Maria and my cousin Miguel somehow managed to bury the hatchet between the Moraleses and Ybarras this summer through . . . the power of *love*. Gag.

They do make a cute couple, though, which makes up for how cloyingly sweet their whole romance is.

"After everything she put Gage through last year, I can't believe she's going around pretending like it was nothing," Rose continues, still seething over whatever interaction brought them to the bathroom. "She cheated on him! He does not owe her anything!"

"I feel bad," Ana Maria says as she turns on the faucet. "He barely comes around the table during lunch anymore."

"He says he's using all the time he has to study and make up for last year's grades so he can get back to being valedictorian, but I know part of the reason is because she won't leave him alone. I bet she thinks she can win him back in time for homecoming."

Before Miguel came to town, the social circles between Ana Maria and me did not cross, so I don't know a lot about Gage Magnussen beyond the fact that he has been at the top of our class since freshman year. He had a straight shot to valedictorian until his girlfriend, Ginger, cheated on him, causing an end-of-junior-year spiral that resulted in the smallest GPA drop. But that drop was enough to knock him from first and put someone else at number one—that person being Adrian. Last year this unexpected win had him on top of the world, and I know he's giving it his all to keep his spot.

"There has to be something we could do to get her to leave him alone," Rose muses while Ana Maria splashes some water before turning off the faucet. "I could catfish her and pretend to be Gage, just to turn around and break her heart in revenge."

"I think you need to take this energy and use it to memorize your lines for the musical," Ana Maria suggests.

"Okay, maybe I don't have time for a whole catfishing operation, but I'm sure someone else in the Debate Club would be happy to take the reins," Rose continues.

"I don't think catfishing is the right way to use anyone's time, Rose."

"Ugh." I can't see her, but I know Rose is likely slouching dramatically in protest. "Way to take the fun out of revenge, Ana."

"I thought we all learned our lesson when it came to things like enemies and revenge?" Someone pulls paper towels out of the dispenser, throws them in the trash, and opens the door. "I need something from my locker before lunch is over. There was—" But the rest of their conversation is cut off as the bathroom door slams closed.

I wait a full minute before dropping my feet back down. We're closing in on the last ten minutes of lunch, when everyone rushes to use the bathroom before fifth period starts, which is my cue to get out of my stall before anyone spots me.

Slinging my bag over my shoulder, I slip out as quickly as possible and power walk my way to the exit. A group of sophomore girls nearly hit me in the face with the door, giggling and shrieking about something and barely noticing my near collision.

I had always felt a little invisible before, always in Adrian's shadow, but this is next-level.

With my ego dragging on the floor behind me, I push my way through the door. I'm all of three steps out when a cold hand grips my wrist and pulls me the opposite way down the hallway.

CHAPTER TWO

Caught you!" Ana Maria is grinning like a maniac, her reptilian grip tight around my wrist. This was in a nightmare I had once. I manage not to scream this time, but it's close. Ana Maria in real life isn't as scary as she was in my nightmares. She's really too twee to be scary at all.

"I think we need to reconsider the peace treaty between our families," I say, slipping my wrist from her grip. "It was better back when you didn't attack me and just ignored me."

"Oh, come on," Ana Maria says with a hefty eye roll. "I wouldn't have to wait outside the bathroom door to jump you if you just ate lunch with us like you did at the start of the year."

When my brother made it clear that siding with my cousin after Doughnutgate meant that I was cut from his life, I was left on my own. And I quickly learned that I didn't have much other than Miguel, who was happy to welcome me to his lunch table.

But just like Adrian and his goonies weren't my friends, Miguel and Ana Maria's group weren't, either.

No one intentionally made me feel weird, but the more I sat with them week after week, the worse it felt. Until the idea of sitting in a bathroom stall seemed better than sitting in the cafeteria, where it was like everyone could see straight through me—or rather, didn't see me at all.

"I can't handle all of that Debate Club energy," I say flippantly.

"And you think I can?" Ana Maria returns. "We need some more calm vibes to balance out the table."

"We both know that's not why you're here. Miguel sent you." I cross my arms over my chest and stare down at her in challenge.

I can see Ana Maria consider her options before finally admitting, "Okay, yes, I did have to talk him out of barreling into the girl's bathroom, but that doesn't mean that I don't care, too. You work in the food industry, you know how unsanitary it is to be eating on a toilet, Valeria."

She's right. Which is probably why I've only managed to eat a single bite of anything I pack before I get too grossed out. But what if I do go back to sitting with them, and in a couple weeks or months Miguel and Ana Maria break up? Will Miguel still be welcome with the Debate Club? Where would I go then?

"Listen, I'm not sure—"

"Valeria," Ana Maria cuts me off, "I get not wanting to sit with us. But you have to stop hiding in the bathroom. It's got Miguel all worried, and he has me literally going into every bathroom on campus during lunch to find you. He's driving me crazy."

"I'm not hiding," I argue, just to argue, because I know that I am, in fact, hiding. I just hate that I've been caught.

"Is there any teacher you like? A classroom you can spend your lunch in?" she suggests, ignoring my pathetic attempt to brush off her accusation.

I can't help the bark of laughter that escapes me at her question. Me? A teacher's pet? I doubt most of my teachers know who I am beyond being the disappointing other half of star pupil Adrian Morales.

While my twin has coasted through every honors, AP, and college-level course he's taken, I've been just getting by in all my classes. I'm never doing so poorly that I'm seen as a problem student (with the exception of sophomore year Geometry, which I did end up failing, but there were extenuating circumstances then) but I'm certainly not the kid raising their hand. My tactic is to sit somewhere in the middle, where I can be perfectly unnoticeable.

So, no, I don't have a classroom I can hide in during lunch. Out of context, I'm not even sure some of my teachers would recognize me as one of their students.

"I'll come back to the table," I tell her, not wanting to admit that the toilet was really my only other option. If our school offered off-campus lunches, this wouldn't be a problem at all. I could sit in my car or take a drive to the park, where I could sit on the hood and eat a ham sandwich with the briny smell of the sea and some geese to keep me company.

"Oh, what a relief." Ana Maria visibly relaxes at this news. Miguel must have really been worried. Or just really annoying.

It's wild how much my cousin has been able to change all our lives through the simple act of falling in love. Last year, Ana Maria would have probably been happy to see me on the outs with my brother and relegated to toilet lunch. But the concern in her eyes right now is real, and not just because Miguel made her do this.

Granted, their epic love story is also the reason I'm on the outs with my brother. Ana Maria was at the center of Doughnutgate. Adrian stole her recipe and passed it off as his own to our father. Papi was more than happy to see his son taking an interest in the family business, and Adrian was practically glowing from the praise. I swear he's like a solar-powered lamp that charges solely on attention. When Miguel found out the truth about the recipe and confronted my brother, all hell broke loose. And worst of all, Papi was *disappointed* in Adrian.

I think that's what has my brother holding so tight to this grudge. Not because Miguel punched him, or because he got caught as a liar, but because he fell in our father's esteem. And that probably hurt him the most.

Ana Maria hooks her arm around mine and pulls me back toward the cafeteria, a pep in her step now that her work is done.

"Listen, the Debate Club kids grow on you after a while," she assures me. "You can even play with them by throwing out some random statement that isn't true and they're like a swarm of fish. They jump over each other to be the first to correct you, and then they'll turn on each other."

"I think we have different ideas of fun," I say, shivering at the idea of being at the center of a swarm of Debate Club fish.

Ana Maria sighs and continues to pull me back to a place I had been determined not to return to. Proof that my will isn't as strong as I like to think it is.

CHAPTER THREE

The second-worst part of senior year, after spending lunch on a toilet, is that my final period of the day is Algebra II.

Not only is math my worst subject, but I'm the only senior in a class full of juniors because I'm the stupid Morales twin who failed Geometry my sophomore year.

That was the first school year without having our mom at home. She wasn't *gone* gone, just on an extended trip to Miami to take care of her ailing mother, but adjusting to her absence was difficult. Between Abuela's doctor visits and the different time zones, it was hard to schedule family phone calls as often as we would have liked. Most Sundays we managed to get Mom and Abuela on a video call for check-ins—calls spent listening to Adrian go on and on about making the football team and getting top grades in English and whatever other impressive feats he was up to.

It wasn't easy not having Mom around. There was an adjustment period where we learned to get by as a unit of three instead of four. The schedule at the bakery kept Papi so busy that he was never home in time to make us dinner, leaving Adrian and me to scrounge around the kitchen most school nights. Without having his number-one cheerleader in his corner every day, Adrian became defiantly determined to be the best at everything. There were the looks we got, the whispers about our family that went around until Adrian's biceps grew twice in size and became a reliable threat to anyone running their mouths. And I learned that family is just a word.

But we held on to the promise that once Abuela was settled in a nursing home, Mom would come back and things would go back to normal. Except Abuela refused the nursing home, and Mom's trip was extended . . . indefinitely. We found new ways to get through life at home. Dad got us a dog, as though picking up a yellow lab's steaming turds was some kind of consolation for not having our mom around. Adrian got into a sport where he could tackle people to take out whatever repressed emotions he was feeling, and I perfected the art of being invisible. If no one could see me, no one could expect anything of me.

Then Abuela died, a quick cremation and no funeral. And Mom stayed in Miami. There was Abuela's house, full of junk, to take care of. There were legal issues that I never totally understood, distant relatives claiming ownership of something, and debts that were left unpaid. Mom insisted that she needed to stay in Miami to take care of everything. That's when the video calls started to go unanswered, when trips back home were promised but never seen through due to some unexpected circumstance or another. After all that, life started to crumble a little bit.

Papi threw himself into the business, all his work paying off when the bakery blew up on social media, leaving him to work overtime to accommodate the new popularity. For Adrian, the answer was to be bigger and better to get our mom's attention back on us.

And I was left to grapple with the fact that one of the few people in this life who was meant to love me unconditionally didn't. But what was scariest is that as bad as the truth felt, I think I preferred life without her in it.

All of that resulted in needing to repeat Geometry my junior year.

"I have your exams from last week graded," Ms. Metsker announces after the final bell rings, holding a stack of papers in her arms. "I see you all are finally grasping quadratics, which is good because midterms are looming around the corner. Who wants to solve the question on the board while I pass your exams back?"

Two hands toward the front of the class shoot up. They should know better at this point. Ms. Metsker never picks the eager to solve the bell work. Her eyes glide right over the front row and zero in on me, hunched over at a desk deep in the far corner.

I must look as miserable as I feel, because Ms. Metsker decides to take pity on me and turns her attention to Ethan Lawson, the kid who reeks of weed and seems to be asleep but manages to always give the right answer.

"Ethan, why don't you give that equation a go?"

Ethan gives a lazy nod and lumbers toward the blackboard. Ms. Metsker begins to pass the tests back, doling out praise to the students who did well and warning others. I watch Ethan jot what appears to be chicken scratch on the board as the rest of the class begins to chat quietly. Before Ms. Metsker has even finished passing back exams, Ethan is done and flopping back into the desk in front of me.

"Excellent work, Ethan!" Ms. Metsker says when she glances over her should to check his answer. "You could try to write more neatly when you're doing work for the class, though."

Ethan grunts and Ms. Metsker turns down our aisle. I'm the last person to get their exam back, and at this point the quiet whispering has turned to a gentle roar.

Ms. Metsker drops my exam on the table and doesn't even have the decency to flip it upside down to keep my grade private. Instead, it lands right side up, the ugly red F with accompanying red marks flashing like a signal to let everyone know what a loser I am.

"Talk to me after class," Ms. Metsker says quietly, and it's clearly not a request.

I grimace and give her a weak nod as I snatch the papers and flip them, unable to take the sight of my own failure.

The rest of class passes in a blur. Ms. Metsker goes over the questions from the exam that most students got wrong, but I can't focus over the buzzing in my head.

When the last five minutes of class roll around, the kinetic energy of the room gets dialed up by a thousand. Zippers are snapping shut, papers are shuffling, shoes are tapping anxiously under desks, and I've torn off most of the skin around my fingernails. When the bell rings, the class rushes out the door, eager to enjoy the crisp, sunny afternoon. We're on our last stretch of good weather in the PNW, and everyone is eager to enjoy it while it lasts.

I take my time putting everything back in my bag before I drag my feet to Ms. Metsker's desk.

"Ms. Morales," she says, looking up at me from her seat with a friendly face that can't quite manage to hide her disappointment. As a teacher, I think she's fine. She's a Black woman somewhere in her thirties, wears homemade math joke T-shirts, and manages to get a rowdy room of teenagers to respect her on most days. But that doesn't help to soften the blow of what she says next. "I'm going to give it to you straight: you're heading down a path where you do not graduate high school this year."

I bite my lip and break eye contact with her, unable to take the shame that those words make me feel. I'm not *good* at school, but I'm not normally *this* bad. It's just that since senior year started, my usual routine has been turned upside down. I don't have Adrian to turn to for homework help—or anything else, for that matter—and my aunt has inserted herself into every part of our lives, where she's not entirely welcome. I've been distracted and unfocused and I've been able to fake it everywhere except here.

"You *need* to pass this class to graduate, Valeria. I want to help you get to that podium, but you're going to have to put in the effort, too."

I'm biting down harder on my lip, trying not to give in to the tears that are threatening to fall.

"Valeria, please look at me," Ms. Metsker says firmly. When I reluctantly drag my eyes up to her, she nods. "Do you want to graduate?"

"Yes," I say immediately. High school has never felt like the joyride it seemed to be for my twin. Coasting in his wake was the only way I could get through it, but now that I'm on my own it feels like torture. I can't go through another year of this just because I can't make sense of Algebra II. "What can I do to fix my grade?" I ask.

"I can offer a retake of this last exam, but only if you start peer tutoring. If that's not enough to help you, we'll have to consider different options, but I spoke to your Geometry teacher from last year and we're confident you can improve your grade. If you can turn your performance around by midterms, you won't be in danger of failing this semester anymore. But this only works if you go to tutoring."

"I'll do the tutoring," I say without hesitation. I have enough to deal with at home, I don't need to add *failing my senior year* to the list. "Where do I sign up?"

"Go to Mr. Robertson's classroom, he hosts the Math Club this afternoon. Any member that has passed Algebra II will qualify as a tutor. I'll schedule your retake exam for Friday. And you'll need to earn at least a B on your midterm in order to pass this semester. Do you have any questions?"

How did I let things get this bad? Why can't school come as easily to me as it does to my brother? Can I just bury my head in a hole and pretend this never happened?

But Ms. Metsker isn't here to help me with my existential dread. I give her a limp smile and shake my head no before slinking out of the room.

I take the back hallways to Mr. Robertson's classroom. I make it there without catching anyone's attention, and my escape is so fast that I run into students still milling about the classroom despite it being past the end of the day. A group are gathered around the desk with Mr. Robertson, a graying white man with a pot belly and a deep love for die-cut classroom decorations.

"You need to take care of the exponents first," he says as he scribbles over a student's notes.

"But what about—" the sophomore whose notes he's working on begins to protest, but something must click from what Mr. Robertson is writing in his notes. "Oh! That makes so much more sense."

The other students peer over the table to watch the explanation unfold, and they all seem to have a collective light bulb moment. I hope this is a window to my future self, a future where a kind math tutor blows open the doors of Algebra II in my mind.

I set my backpack down on a table, catching Mr. Robertson's attention.

"Oh, hello!" he says, straightening up and turning to greet me. "Are you here to join Math Club?" He glances down at his watch. "We usually start fifteen minutes after the last bell."

And right now it's only five minutes past. I give him a weak smile and shake my head.

"No, I'm not looking to join the club. Ms. Metsker said I could come today to find a student tutor?"

Mr. Robertson returns the pencil to the student and walks over to my table. His mouth is screwed to the side like he's trying to find the best way to give me bad news.

"I'm actually not sure if anyone is available to help. I don't like to let my students get too overwhelmed with tutoring assignments in case it causes them to fall behind, especially with midterms right around the corner," he explains.

My heart begins to pound in a concerning gallop, a *tha-thump* that threatens to break through my chest. This is not how this was supposed to go.

"I need a peer tutor in order to retake the test I failed for Ms. Metsker's class," I explain, hoping a sob story will help loosen his rules.

"What's your name?" he asks, since I've never taken any of his classes.

"Valeria Morales," I say, and I can see on his face when he makes the connection to my brother. His brow furrows a bit, confused and then surprised.

"Okay, Ms. Morales, I'll look over everyone's schedule and see if we can squeeze you in." Mr. Robertson turns back to his desk and bends over, clicking around and opening a spreadsheet. While he works to find a hole in someone's schedule, a new group of students roll into the classroom, all laughter and shuffling steps.

"Yo, Mr. Robertson!" a gangly junior calls out in greeting as the group dumps their bags on various tables and gets settled. I glance over their faces nervously, worried some Debate Club kid is double-dipping in the school clubs, but I don't know any of these students.

"Please don't sit *on* the tables, Mr. Anderson," Mr. Robertson says without looking up. I watch the teacher anxiously as he clicks around, but I know my fate is sealed when he looks up at me with a frown.

"I'm sorry, Ms. Morales, right now no one has an opening in their schedules. But things change week by week, so if you still need a tutor, you should check in next Friday."

"But my makeup exam is on Friday, I can't—"

"Are you looking for a tutor?" a girl who came in with the group looks up from her phone at me. She's all round, bright blue eyes and fake freckles speckled across the bridge of her nose.

"Yeah," I say slowly, not entirely wanting to admit it.

"Mr. Robertson, you could always ask a certain *someone* who is refusing to rejoin the club this year despite winning the AMC award three times in a row," she says with a smile that has a gleeful edge. She turns to face me. "Gage Magnussen ditched us this year even though we've been in Math Club together since we were freshmen. He made some lame excuse about studying, but that makes no sense because Math Club *is studying*. We just sit here and solve fun math problems." I don't call her out on her oxymoron. "He's a really great tutor, too. If he agrees, I'm sure Mr. Robertson will count it as official peer tutoring, right?" She looks over her shoulder at the teacher.

"Sure," Mr. Robertson says, "if you can convince him, he's certainly a wiz with algebra."

What was supposed to be an easy process to get help has now become *a mission*. How am I supposed to convince Gage to use his spare time to help me when I don't even know the guy beyond him being my brother's academic rival? If anything, he'll be *less* likely to help me.

"Are you sure there is no one else available?" I ask, not able to keep the note of pleading from my voice. "Even just for this week?"

"I'm afraid not."

When I think about the future, I've never had a crystal clear vision of what it would look like. Adrian has dreams of being a D1 athlete with an academic scholarship at a nice state school, Ana Maria wants to go to culinary school in Paris, Miguel wants to study film at UCLA . . . but me? The future has always seemed like a concern for later, something I'll get to when the time comes. I'll apply to college somewhere probably, walk the stage at graduation with Adrian, major in something basic like communications or advertising or English, and then work in corporate America, not because I particularly want any of these things, but because that's what people do. This is the script for life I've been reading from.

But now this future I had taken for granted is in jeopardy. What was only a vague, blurry outline of what could be after high school graduation is going up like smoke, making me face a future I had never considered. One where I'm held back, the yawning expanse between my twin and me growing wider than ever before. I can't let that happen.

At the end of this week I'll be retaking my test, and if I don't get a tutor now, I'll be on my way to flunking it, again. My only option is to track down Gage Magnussen and convince him to teach me math. It can't be harder than Algebra II, right?

CHAPTER FOUR

My family lives in a 1970s split-level home with a two-car garage and a driveway long enough to fit four cars. The garage has never once contained a car so long as I've been alive. It's always been my father's workshop, filled to the brim with appliances in need of repair and furniture he's building for the bakery.

Growing up, our mom and Papi shared the driveway without problems, one car to each side. Mom had left her car behind and Adrian claimed it as soon as he got his learner's permit, even though Papi insisted we needed to *share* the car. Last year I finally saved up enough to buy what some might consider the most decrepit vehicle in Port Murphy, but the jangling sound it makes when I drive has grown on me.

Three cars were annoying to juggle; we always had to make sure we put our keys by the front door when we got home so a car could be moved whenever someone needed it out of their way. And since I went most places with Adrian, my car was usually the one blocked in.

Then Tia Isa and Miguel moved into the basement, with their two cars. If Adrian hadn't stolen Ana Maria's recipe and caused the blowup between him and Miguel, the car situation would have done it.

What was once a manageable system of leaving your keys by the door was no longer functional. Suddenly, no one left their keys by the door. They ended up in the pockets of jeans at the bottom of the hamper, covered in slobber and hidden in Leo's toy box, or displaced in the fourth dimension.

Overnight street parking earns you a ticket, even if you are doing so in front of your own home, so we are forced to play car Tetris every day, and someone always ends up straddling the sidewalk to fit on the driveway.

I love having my cousin around, but if he and my aunt don't find their own place soon, I'm not sure how much longer this can go on.

This is all part of the reason why I carpool with Miguel most days, with Adrian sulkily getting into his car by himself in the mornings. Luckily, my short delay today, caused by my impending high school failure, wasn't enough to catch Miguel's attention. He usually drags out every minute he can spend with Ana Maria after the last bell. They even made their own film appreciation club to spend more school-sanctioned time together, time her dad couldn't overrule because it had "educational value," but I know they just sit in a room to watch movies and eat snacks that Ana Maria makes.

When I find my cousin, he's at his locker, but instead of the usual company of just Ana Maria, his Debate Club friends are there with them—including my current target: Gage Magnussen.

"Come on, dude," Noah Brinkley whines, his attention on Gage. "Don't back out of movie night! We're screening the short film we worked on this summer."

Gage drags a hand through his messy, tawny hair and grimaces. I'm a little surprised that my cool, big-city cousin ended up getting close with the Debate Club guys, especially Gage. I don't know him very well, but he's always seemed closed off and so serious for a kid in high school. He's the guy who'll get voted most likely to succeed, and if he were still dating Ginger, they would definitely have been voted Prom King and Queen. They'd been dating since freshman year and were always like the mom and dad of our class.

But that all changed when Ginger cheated on him and they had their blow-up breakup at the end of junior year. He seemed to rally well enough this summer, where he showed up at pretty much every party looking perfectly fine, but now that school has started again, he just looks . . . sleepy?

"I really wish I could, Noah," Gage says apologetically.

"Give the guy a break," Miguel cuts in, throwing an arm over Gage's shoulder in an attempt to break up the tension in the group. "You have that gala thing you have to help your parents with, right?"

"He's done that every year," Noah points out.

"Yeah, well, Ginger always helped me with it, and that's obviously not happening anymore," Gage says, shrugging off my cousin's arm. "I have to get going. I really am sorry, Noah."

If his friends can't convince him to spare some time to hang out, how am *I* going to convince him to spare some time on tutoring me? The sinking feeling in my stomach grows worse. A reality where I don't get a tutor in time and end up failing algebra suddenly becomes a lot clearer to me.

Gage turns around abruptly, and I hardly get a chance to move out of the way. A quarter inch shy of six feet, I'm not easy to bowl over, but Gage clips my shoulder with just enough speed to get me to lose my balance.

His eyes widen in surprise and his hands shoot out to steady me.

"Sorry," he says, blue eyes scanning me as though it were probable that I received some kind of serious injury from our collision. Everything about his features is sharp and angular, at odds with the soft look of concern on his face.

"No problem, I'm good," I assure him, feeling grim. He gives me a tight-lipped smile before heading back off toward the parking lot.

Little does he know, my future now rests on his shoulders. And I need to find a way to convince him that doing so is worth his time. I can't even convince Adrian to put the toilet seat down.

"Is anxiety contagious?" I ask, wiping at my shoulder where I made contact with Gage as I approach my cousin. "That guy is wound tight."

"You can thank your brother for that," Noah snaps at me.

"Whoa," Miguel cuts in. "Not cool."

I hold my hands up in surrender. "Hey, I'll never stop you from calling my brother out on being an asshole. Just don't drag me into it," I say.

"I think we can all agree that Ginger is the more reasonable person to blame in all this anyway," David Tsao says.

"Sorry," Noah mutters, shrinking under Miguel's irritated

gaze. "I'm going to head out. See you tomorrow." He nods at the group before heading off, David trailing behind him.

"He's been in a bad mood all week. He's still upset Rose broke up with him," Miguel explains. He gives me a pointed look. "Which you would know, if you came to lunch."

"Ugh, please, I've had a terrible day, can we not do this now?" I beg.

"Your day would probably have been a lot better if you ate lunch at our table," Miguel persists.

"I already told your girlfriend that I won't eat in the bathroom again," I tell him. "Please, let's just go home so I can shower off this day and watch some reality TV."

Miguel sighs and slams his locker closed before we head out to the parking lot. Since he has the nicer car and he says my driving makes him carsick, Miguel drives on the days we carpool together. I don't mind because his car has seat warmers that I always set on high as soon as I get in.

When we get home, Miguel parks behind his mom's car, which is parked behind my car. The second column of cars, where my brother and dad park, is empty. Adrian is at football practice and Papi is probably at the bakery.

We go our separate ways once we're inside the house, Miguel down to our daylight basement and me upstairs to my room. The responsible kind of student would probably open up her computer and look up YouTube videos on Algebra II subjects and digital tutors or something.

But I'm not that girl. At least for today, I just want to live in a world where I'm not failing math. Tomorrow I'll try to come up with a plan to convince Gage to be my tutor, but today I just want to wallow. I spend hours star-fished on my bed with my laptop on my chest, playing the most mind-numbing reality television I can find. I've pulled the blackout curtains shut on my windows so I can truly just melt into my bed for the remainder of the day.

But Tia Isa has to cut into my solitude.

My aunt's familiar knock rattles against my door, cutting through the on-screen catfight I am watching.

"Dinner's ready, come help set the table."

Since moving here this summer, Tia Isa has tried to "fix" our household. She sees the hole where my mother was, the hole my family has steered clear of for the last two years, and has decided it is her duty to fill it.

But we'd all left it empty for a reason.

"Coming," I grumble, not wanting to leave my safe cocoon. Family dinners have been icy since the catastrophe this summer, and everyone is too stubborn to do anything about it.

Adrian is too proud to admit he was wrong, Papi is too disappointed in him to let it go, Miguel is unwilling to forgive without an apology, and Tia Isa is desperately trying to pretend everything is fine. And me? I'm trying to eat my dinner as quickly as possible to get away from the table.

But to be fair to my aunt, the one good thing she's brought back into this house is excellent food. Because while our dad runs a bakery and spends much of his time working on recipes, when it comes to eating at home, it's either leftovers from the shop or buttered noodles and PB&J sandwiches.

Since Tia Isa and Miguel have moved in, it's been an endless feast of Cuban meals. Fricase de pollo, ajiaco, ropa vieja, tamales cubanos, fufu, and so much more. When I walk into the kitchen tonight, I see she has a pot of congri on the stove and a dish fresh from the oven that looks like boliche. The deep fryer is on the counter, which means she's made mariquitas from scratch with her homemade mojo sauce.

I pull out the plates and begin to set the table when I hear the garage door creak open, signaling Papi's arrival.

"I'm home!" he calls out. There's a *click-clack* of nails on wood as Leo, our hopelessly dopey Lab, runs across the house to greet Papi.

The idea of getting a dog two years ago had been a welcome one, but it was not an easy decision. Adrian wanted a big, scary-looking dog, something like a rottweiler or Doberman. I wanted something cute and cuddly like a spaniel or a beagle. We went back and forth arguing about the kind of dog we were going to get until Papi called a draw and came home with some kind of yellow Lab mix.

"Do you think Adrian will make it to dinner tonight?" Tia Isa asks me as she carries the boliche to the dining room table. "I texted him, but he never responds."

"Probably not," I say, because Adrian hasn't made it to dinner most nights since school started. He always claims that he got held up at football practice, but I know he's just trying to avoid the dinner gauntlet.

"He has an away game this week, doesn't he?" Papi asks, crunching on a mariquita he stole from the kitchen as he enters the dining room.

"It's on the calendar on the fridge," I remind him.

Miguel appears from the basement shortly after that, and we

begin our usual dinner-table song and dance, all choreographed by my aunt. How was school? How are college applications going? Did you remember to schedule your senior pictures? Even though I respond with one-word answers, Tia Isa keeps going.

The front door slams shut halfway through the meal, and Adrian appears through the dining room archway, clearly not expecting to see everyone at the dinner table. His timing is off tonight.

"Adrian!" Tia Isa says brightly. "You made it just in time. Sit down and serve yourself."

Not one to turn down food, Adrian silently goes to the kitchen and begins to fill his plate.

"How was practice?" Tia Isa asks.

Adrian ignores her as he scoops rice. Tia Isa's composure cracks a bit, the slight twitch at the corner of her mouth giving her away.

"You know, the football boosters got in touch about their upcoming fundraiser—"

"Why would you be talking to the football boosters?" Adrian finally responds, glaring at our aunt across the table. I can see Miguel tense up beside me in anticipation of what comes next.

"Well, your father is busy with the shop, so I thought I'd—"

"I have a better idea," Adrian says, dropping his fork and looking Tia Isa dead in the eye. "Why don't you take all that thinking and find a way to move out of your little brother's basement and leave us the fuck alone."

"Adrian!" Dad snaps.

"Don't talk to my mom that way," Miguel practically growls

as his mom throws an arm across his chest, as though Miguel might leap across the table and strangle his cousin. And not without reason, given the brawl that happened this summer in the middle of the living room.

"I am trying—" Tia Isa starts, but Adrian is ready with another insult.

"Why don't you *try* finding a job and getting—"

"ENOUGH!" Papi roars in an authoritative voice he rarely uses. "You have no right to speak to your aunt that way, Adrian. This is *my house* and *I* get to decide who stays here and for how long. Tienes que cambiar tu actitud inmediatamente si quieres seguir jugando tu juego de football."

Adrian opens his mouth, likely an attempt to stick his foot in it, but Dad cuts in before he can start.

"Go finish your dinner in your room, Adrian. Estoy *harto* de tu mierda esta noche."

Adrian rolls his eyes and picks up his plate, making sure to kick back the chair so it squeals against the floor as he gets up. We all watch in silence as he trudges up the stairs before Papi looks over at his sister, embarrassment clear on his face.

"I'm sorry, Isa," he says, sounding defeated. "Please don't take anything he says to heart."

If I'm being honest, I think Tia Isa could take a *little* bit of it to heart. I don't love the way Adrian expresses his disdain at having our aunt live with us, but I do wish she would get up on her feet a little quicker so things at home could go back to normal. Or at least I'd like her to stop trying to insert herself into the role of the mother we're not looking for.

Tia Isa waves off her brother's apology.

"I've heard worse," she says, and it makes me feel bad for the thoughts I just had, because I know she means it. She definitely heard worse from the shitty husband she is in the middle of divorcing. "So, Valeria, do you have any fun plans for the weekend?"

What, me? The girl who has no friends and has to eat her lunch on a toilet and is likely failing out of high school? Do *I* have any thrilling plans this weekend?

Now I'm back to resenting her.

CHAPTER FIVE

I spend the next day on the lookout for one Gage Magnussen. Six foot two with a boyish charm that will probably fade once he grows into his gangliness, what sets him apart from most guys in our class is the fact that he usually dresses like a retired math teacher: khakis, a buttoned-up plaid shirt, round wire frame glasses, and, in the winter, sweaters that look like they were lovingly knit by a grandmother somewhere but, knowing his family, are likely just purchased from some designer line.

Since we don't have any classes together, I look for his distinctive head of tawny locks in the hallways all morning, but I don't spot him in the hordes of students milling about between classes. It really shouldn't be this hard to find one person on a campus this small.

Once lunch rolls around, I have no choice but to join Miguel's table and hope Gage is there. If I'm lucky, I can find a moment to talk with him away from the rest of the group. The last thing

I need is for the school's overachievers to hear I'm failing a class they all aced a whole year ago.

Unlike Adrian, who takes up space in the cafeteria, Miguel's friends choose to fight God and eat lunch outdoors. Instead of a cozy, climate-controlled, and *dry* cafeteria, they set up shop at one of the picnic tables under the awning outside.

At the start of the school year, I warned Miguel that his little Southern California butt was going to freeze in a couple of weeks. But he brushed me off and assured me he was made of stronger stuff. The stronger stuff is currently curled up in his seat, fleece zipped up to his chin, puffer piled on top, and beanie pulled down to his eyebrows.

"It's only fifty-five degrees out here," I say in dismay as I take the empty spot across from him. Gage is unfortunately nowhere to be seen, but the rest of the Debate Club guys are seated around us in T-shirts, and one guy is even wearing shorts. "How are you going to survive the winter?"

"We need to toughen him up," Noah says, throwing an arm around Miguel's shoulder. "We should do the polar plunge on New Year's Day."

"Please leave my delicate flower alone," Ana Maria cuts in, picking Noah's arm off Miguel. "If you start talking about winter now, you'll scare him off."

Noah and some of the other guys continue to tease my cousin about his delicate constitution, but I'm already moving on to my mission: find Gage.

Ari Adler, another member of the Debate Club and well-known gossip, happens to be sitting to my right. I don't know her very well, but if I come up with the right entry question, maybe I can get her to reveal Gage's location without garnering unwanted attention.

"Is the weather why Gage gave up on sitting with you all out here?" I ask as I pull out my ham sandwich.

Ari glances over at me, surprised that I'm speaking to her. Her eyes dart to Miguel and Ana Maria, as though to make sure it really is *her* I was talking to.

"Oh, no, I swear that guy is half penguin," Ari says once her gaze returns to mine. "Even in January when it gets miserable out here and we all go inside, he loves sitting in the cold. The dean usually has to come shoo him indoors for his own safety."

"So is he just not in the Debate Club anymore? Has another club stolen him away during lunch?" I say, trying to lead her back in the direction of his location.

"He's holding on to the title of president with a vise grip after all that drama with Lor last year, *on top* of what Ginger did. He just spends his lunch doing homework and extra credit and all that other stuff so that he can knock that ass—" Ari's eyes go wide as saucers when she realizes she was about to bad-mouth my twin to my face. I raise my eyebrows and smile a little at her reaction. "So that he can, uh, so he can be class valedictorian."

After that, Ari clams up, either embarrassed to have had that slipup or scared that she might do it again. I'm not getting anything else from her, so I let it go and eat my lunch quickly. There's not many places a grades-obsessed nerd could be on this campus, and I think I know where to start.

By the time I finish my ham sandwich, the table is loudly arguing the merits of using the pour-over method of brewing coffee versus a Moka pot. David and Noah are shouting over each other, and Rose is cheering them on as Ana Maria plugs her ears. One of the deans supervising lunch has their eyes on the table, and I know this is my opportunity to slip away while everyone is distracted.

I play up gathering all my garbage and stand up from the table with my math binder tucked under my arm. I toss my trash in the can on the farthest end of the quad, near the doors to the main hallway. Checking over my shoulder at the table, I see Miguel try to break up the argument by standing up and pushing the two guys away from each other.

Taking my chance, I hurry through the door and sneak into the hallway. To my left is the roar of the cafeteria spilling from the open doors. I can see the bank of windows Adrian's table sits against and spot him holding court like he always does. He has that lazy, smug look on his face that makes you think he gets everything in life handed to him. And while that may be true about some things, I know my brother has worked his ass off to be at the top of our class.

When we started middle school, some confused or misinformed or malicious school employee placed my brother and me in ESOL, a program meant for learning English as a second language. Our incoming paperwork had the last name *Morales*, and under the question of languages spoken at home, my parents had filled it out truthfully: Spanish first, followed by English. My abuelos were around a lot more back then, and we spoke with them almost exclusively in Spanish.

For the school, that was enough to believe that we couldn't speak English well enough to be taught alongside our peers. To say our father threw a fit would be an understatement. He tore those office employees to shreds. Without ever getting to know us or our family, they assumed because Adrian was Cuban American that he would be brutish and dumb, and he has always had to work twice as hard as our peers to prove himself. The assumptions about me didn't start until puberty hit, and I've managed to curb stomp those comments by wearing baggy clothes and messy hair.

But that doesn't change the fact that when my brother fights so hard for the things he wants, he never thinks of the fallout. He's never concerned about who he hurts in order to get what he wants. So while part of me wants him to beat out Gage for valedictorian, I also want to see him lose it. Just to see him hurt a little bit. Because while going through life for me seems like a series of gut punches that make me see stars, Adrian doesn't even blink when he gets hit.

Adrian Morales is impenetrable, and I've always used him as my shield. But I'm on my own now, thanks to him. So I think I need to take a page out of my twin's book and fight for what I need, consequences be damned.

And what I need right now is to track down Gage.

I can't say the library is a part of the school I've been to a lot. I'm usually in and out, pulling a book for a paper, which usually then gets lost under a pile of sketchbooks in my bedroom, which then makes both the paper and the book get turned in late, which then lands me with a C average and a library fine. There might even be a sign in the librarian's office with my face on it that says, "DO NOT LEND HER BOOKS."

I'm not sure what I was expecting lunchtime in the library to be like, but I'm surprised by what I find when I walk in. Without the looming stress of a research paper or late fees, the library is actually a really nice space.

It sits on the back corner of campus facing the Olympic Mountains. All along the west wall of the room is a line of windows with a spectacular view of the mountains reaching up to the sky before being swallowed up by the clouds. Circular tables are clustered by the windows, and various groups of people are sitting around quietly chatting or reading. There's even a leather couch tucked up against the north wall, where one student is openly napping. It seems as though speaking isn't necessarily discouraged, but everyone is keeping their conversations quiet. And is that . . . music? The librarian has some kind of lo-fi playlist sounding through the speakers, adding to the overall calming environment.

Why was I eating in a gross toilet stall when *this* was here all along?

And then I see him. There, tucked away in the back corner, is Gage Magnussen.

He is, as expected, wearing a blue flannel shirt, and his wire frame glasses have slipped all the way to the tip of his nose. He seems engrossed in whatever it is he has open on the desk in front of him, his pen moving furiously across the page. His backpack is hung across the back of his chair, a generic bag covered in a slew of embroidered patches: the microphone logo for the Debate Club; our killer whale mascot, Neptune; and a whale patch that says "Respect the Locals."

Not sure where to start, I take the plunge and slip into the empty seat next to him. He's so absorbed in his work, he doesn't even notice my sudden appearance. On closer inspection, I can see that the notebook he has open is made up of graph paper, with dozens of small graphs and diagrams. I can't make out a single thing. This is definitely the person to turn to for math tutoring.

"Hey, Gage," I say, making sure not to speak too loudly. I'm still convinced a librarian will spot me and hunt me down for a fine I didn't know I had left unpaid. But from Gage's reaction, you'd think I'd taken a bullhorn to his ear.

He jumps a full inch off his chair in surprise and lets out a startled sound. I watch in fascination as the back of his neck flushes red once he realizes what he's done. He looks around quickly to make sure no one saw or, worse, got it on video.

"Sorry about that," I say, in a whisper this time. "I didn't mean to startle you." I can't help the edge of a laugh that creeps into my voice.

"Valeria?" he says, like he still thinks this is all part of an elaborate prank.

"In the flesh," I reply. "What are these drawings?" I ask, jerking my chin toward his open notebook.

Gage looks down at the notebook like he's surprised to find it there.

"These are my AP Physics notes," he says before looking up at me with a skeptical expression. "Planning on stealing them to give to your brother? He spent the entire class flirting instead of taking notes today."

"Why does everyone always think I'm out here doing my brother's dirty work?" I snap. I cross my arms over my chest and lean back in my seat, trying to brush off the irritation. Gage doesn't really know me, I can't be all that mad at him. But his joke, if it was that, still stings.

"Sorry," he says immediately, wincing a little. "You're right, I shouldn't take my feelings about your brother out on you." He runs his hands through his hair and leans back in his seat, angling his body to face me better. "We don't really talk, so I was just a little surprised. As evidenced by my screech."

"That was not a screech," I assure him. "It was more like a very manly yowl."

"Ah, even better." He watches me for a moment and an uncomfortable silence stretches between us. "So, did you just come here to ask about my AP Physics notes?"

"No," I admit. "I just didn't know how else to start a conversation with you."

"Why would you want to start a conversation with me?" he asks, sounding perplexed.

"I'm failing math," I blurt out, instead of saying the rehearsed speech I have been practicing in my head all day. I drop my gaze, my turn to be embarrassed.

"Oh," he says in surprise, and I'm not sure how to read that response. Judgment? Pity? Surprise that I'm not as clever as my twin?

"Ms. Metsker is letting me retake an exam this Friday if I get a peer tutor, but when I went to Math Club yesterday Mr. Robertson said that everyone is booked up because I guess math is kicking everyone's ass and I can check back next week, but that's not very helpful, but then one of the Math Club members mentioned your name and how you're usually in the Math Club and Mr. Roberston said he would count you as a peer tutor if you agreed and I just had to ask you, so I've been trying to hunt you down to ask you to please, please, please be my math tutor."

I finally clamp my mouth shut and take a deep breath, hoping he is able to make sense of the jumble that just came out of my mouth.

"I'm sorry, but I had to step back from tutoring this semester to focus on getting my own grades back up," he says gently, and I want to laugh. If he doesn't get his grades "back up," he'll be salutatorian instead of valedictorian. If I don't, I don't *graduate*, and I get left behind, my twin off to whatever amazing college he decides to go to while I stay in Port Murphy to repeat another year of high school, like the worst version of *Groundhog Day* ever. I don't know exactly what I want to do after senior year, but it certainly isn't staying back to do it *again*.

"I promise I wouldn't ask if you weren't my last hope," I tell him. "I already had to take Geometry twice, so if I don't pass this class I won't get the third math credit I need to graduate. I'm not looking to fight you or my brother for valedictorian, I just want to get my diploma at the end of all this."

Gage's brows knit together, and this must be what he looks like when he's trying to solve some complicated equation. Is he trying to figure out how to let me down or how to fit me into his schedule?

I think he's come to some kind of decision when he leans toward me a little bit and opens his mouth. His knee bumps against mine and he doesn't seem to notice our sudden point of contact because he remains focused on my eyes. But before he can say anything, a voice cuts through our little bubble.

"Gage!"

CHAPTER SIX

Our school isn't very big, so while I might not know everyone, I definitely know *of* everyone. And I know all about Ginger Davis and the chaos she wrought on Gage's life last spring.

My brother wouldn't shut up about Ginger and the cheating scandal that brought down Port Murphy High's golden boy. He seemed to relish knowing all the details of how it went down and was more than happy to share them with me.

The full story goes something like this:

The Magnussen and Davis families are close, both being from the wealthy set in town and working in law. The Magnussens own their own law practice and hired Ginger, who is essentially pre-pre-law, as an office assistant for a couple days a week after school.

Last spring the Magnussens also hired an intern from the local community college. With Ginger spending her afternoons at the office and Gage spending his at Debate Club or Math Club or whatever other college application bait he does after school, the couple wasn't spending as much time together junior year.

The details are murky on what exactly he saw, but last April Gage caught his girlfriend cheating on him with the intern. They broke up, Gage wore sweatpants to school for two weeks straight, and Ginger went on to date the other guy. Gage seemed to be in some kind of fog during that time, not caring that his grades were slipping and that all his hard work would be lost to my brother.

By the end of the school year it seemed that he had recovered, back to plaid and khakis. Ginger had ended things with her new beau by the start of summer break because it turns out guys in college who try to date girls in high school are actually terrible and not someone you should date.

And now it seems like she wants Gage back, judging by the way she's sauntering over to our table.

"I've been looking everywhere for you!" she says with a megawatt smile, planting her hands on the table and leaning over *just* enough to show a hint of cleavage.

Gage's knee is still pressed against mine and it seems like that's plugged me into him somehow, because I can *feel* the tension grip his body at Ginger's approach. The relaxed, calm guy I had been talking to is gone and instead there's someone wound so tight he seems on the verge of bursting.

"I've been busy," Gage says. I'm frozen in place, unsure of what to do. This doesn't seem like the kind of conversation I should be part of.

"You've made it nearly impossible to track you down." She sighs dramatically. "Your parents wanted me to talk to you about the charity auction."

Oh, and did I mention that after the cheating scandal, his parents fired the intern but kept Ginger?

"I told my parents not to bother you. I don't need your help," he says evenly, but I can hear the barely reined in frustration burning at the edge of his voice. "I'm handling it."

"Of course, but I was chatting with the manager at the co-op the other day and he said you hadn't reached out yet. We usually have all the businesses secured by now. You're clearly running behind, so why don't you let me help? We can start contacting people after school today." She says it so simply, so matter of fact, that I know she thinks he won't argue with her.

Gage takes a deep breath. It's clear he wants nothing to do with Ginger right now, but she isn't taking no for an answer. Suddenly, I see an opportunity. The only way I'm going to get Gage to help me is if I'm able to offer him something in return, and I doubt he'll take embarrassing stories about my twin as payment. But I'm willing to bet he'll accept a way to get Ginger off his back.

"Actually," I cut in, leaning in closer to Gage, letting my whole leg press against his, "there's no need for your help."

Ginger's eyes cut to me for a moment, taking quick stock. I can see the calculations running behind her eyes. I'm usually someone you don't want to mess with, someone whose twin brother is at the top of whatever high school polygon we all exist in. But everyone knows things are fractured between me and Adrian, so what kind of threat level does going up against me get now? Even I'm not sure at this point.

"This isn't really something just anyone can do," Ginger says. "It requires spending a lot of time together, and I'm sure you have plenty of other things keeping you busy this year." I can hear plainly what she's not saying out loud: this is a job for a *girlfriend.*

A-ha. Thank you, Ginger Davis, for the brilliant idea.

"Oh, *I know,*" I return, slipping my hand across the back of Gage's shoulders. I lean in close, paying attention to his body language. If he tenses or flinches or gives me any indication that he doesn't like where I'm going with this, I'll back down. I'll come up with another excuse. I'm not here to make his life more miserable, I just need a math tutor.

But to my surprise, Gage leans into the touch, helping me paint the perfect picture of a happy couple. I'll take that as my green light. Ginger pulls back from the table and crosses her arms, a clear sign that she's feeling at least a little threatened by this charade.

"I figured since we were already dating that it would make sense for me to help him run the auction. You know my dad owns a bakery downtown, so I have a bunch of connections with local businesses, and we already have plenty of people interested in making some really cool donations this year." If I've already dug myself a hole straight to hell, what's a few more shovels full of bullshit? "So we don't really need your input, but it was so nice of you to offer."

Ginger purses her lips and glares at me. The one avenue she had to get back into Gage's life has been cut off, but I'm not scared of her. I have bigger problems in my life, and this five-foot-two bottle blonde doesn't even make my top ten, even if she is glaring daggers at me right now.

"If that's all . . . ?" I ask, tipping my head to the side in a question and resting it on Gage's shoulder. During this standoff between Ginger and me, he's reached around my chair and is resting his hand across the back, further tethering us together.

I've left Ginger speechless, because instead of replying with some kind of witty retort, she just spins around and glides out of the library, trying to look unbothered. Once the library doors shut behind her and we're out of her sight, I slide back into my chair and release Gage from this impromptu performance.

"I'm not sure what just happened," Gage finally says, pulling his arm from the back of my chair and turning to face me head on. "But thank you."

"You're welcome. Now, before Ginger interrupted us, you were about to insist you couldn't tutor me because you're so swamped, correct?" I say.

"I mean, yeah," Gage says, and the confirmation makes my stomach drop. One wrong move and I won't get a tutor, leading to a domino effect where I fail math, flunk out of high school, and watch my twin cross the graduation stage without me, furthering the wedge of distance between us to a point of no return, leaving me with a giant question mark for a future. I *have* to sell Gage on my idea.

"Well, now you don't have to turn me down because I just offered you a solution to all your problems."

"And that solution is?"

"Being your fake girlfriend and helping with this auction thing," I say in a mock whisper.

Gage blinks. "I'm sorry, I'm not connecting the dots here."

"It's a mutually beneficial agreement. I don't want anyone

to know that I'm failing and need a tutor, so you being my boyfriend is the perfect cover. You want to be left alone by Ginger and your parents, so me being your girlfriend is the perfect cover for you. I can keep Ginger away from you and take this auction prep off your plate. I wasn't kidding when I said I have connections—I grew up going to those retail association meetings downtown. They love me." I pause and try to give him my most convincing smile. "It's a win-win scenario for the both of us."

Gage leans back in his seat and rests his head on clasped hands as he looks up at the ceiling tiles of the library. He seems to be weighing my proposal, and I wonder how much of this is for show. I felt the relief in him when my leg pressed against his, giving him that little bit of support he needed to get through an interaction with Ginger. My idea would *work*.

"What would the fake dating entail?" he finally asks. I consider his question. Gage has only dated one person, and his track record with her was fairly straightforward: they attended school dances together, they rarely showed PDA, and they always had lockers next to each other.

My track record? Empty. No one has ever asked me out or tried making out with me in a closet at a party or anything like that. I've gone to dances with dates, but the dates were usually one of Adrian's single friends and it was always a *strictly* platonic deal. I have my suspicions that Adrian has made threats to anyone who has tried to get near me, and his power is too great to be ignored.

"I've never dated anyone before, so I think we're working

with a blank slate here. We can just say we're dating and let everyone else make their own assumptions. Having study sessions and planning this auction will probably be more than enough to convince everyone."

"What about homecoming? It's just a few weeks away," he points out.

"Are you asking?" I say with mock delight.

"Uh—" Gage sputters nervously.

"No dances," I assure him. "I have two left feet."

Gage nods, looking relieved. I'm not sure whether I should be bothered by just how relieved he looks to find out he doesn't have to go to a dance with me. I may not look it, but I do clean up well.

"And what about your brother?" he asks.

"Oh, that's the part that makes this thing so romantic!" I insist, getting back into my saleswoman persona. "Imagine it," I say, swiping my hand in the air before us as I set the stage for him. "You always expected that you wouldn't like me, that I was the same as my brother. But when you reached out to me for a donation for the charity auction—a Cuban feast hosted at the restaurant with a dessert menu by the up-and-coming Ana Maria Ybarra and live music—you got to know me better and realized I was *different*. Not only was I witty, charismatic, carefree, and beautiful, I was someone you wanted to spend more time with, even with everything in your life being as chaotic as it is right now."

"Is that seriously something you could get donated?" he asks, skipping over the backstory of how he fake fell for me.

"Oh, definitely. My dad is a firm believer in community

engagement and loves having any opportunity to bring out his guitar. And after the whole Morales-Ybarra feud ended this summer, my dad and Ana's dad have these jam sessions at the bakery. Plus, my aunt supposedly has a really great singing voice, so I'm sure my dad would be more than happy to put something together."

"And what about other donations?"

"We could probably swing a romantic dinner at Locicero's, a day at the spa from Olympic Wellness, the bookstore could do one of those, like, shelf-named-after-someone things? And I know Michelle at the florist downtown would be up for donating her services in some capacity. I know Ginger mentioned the co-op, but the new manager there, Peter? He's a real stick in the mud and probably wouldn't offer up much. But Ana's mom is the manager at the Wild Poppy Bed & Breakfast and could probably get a two-night package donated. My dad is also close with the guy who runs Blue Mills Farms, and they could donate a trail ride—"

"Okay, you've proved your point, you're well connected in town," Gage says on a laugh, waving his hands to dispel my donation tirade. "You'll be way better at this than I ever was. I could never bring myself to be charming enough. Ginger was always the one sweet-talking people into making donations."

"Are you kidding me?" I reply, a little outraged on his behalf. "You're plenty charming, Gage. You've certainly charmed the Math Club, who were all very upset that you decided not to join them this year."

"I don't know about—"

"*And*," I cut him off, "you've charmed everyone in the

Debate Club. And you charmed my cousin! Him and the guys are all deeply distraught you won't grace them with your presence at lunch, you know."

"And I must have charmed you, too, then, right?" he says, and I feel like a record scratch plays in my head once I register what he said. My mouth hangs opens as I struggle to come up with a response. "I mean, I must have," he continues. "Since you decided to date me? Because your story only covers why *I* would date *you*. Not why you would agree to date me."

He has a good point. After years of never dating anyone at school, what made me say yes to Gage Magnussen?

"Well," I say, trying to recover from my system reset, "I think you have it. You charmed me and I couldn't resist. It's your compelling Debate Captain allure and that big skull full of math and equations."

"Are those the only things you know about me?" he asks, the corner of his mouth curling up in a smirk. "That I'm in the Debate and Math Clubs?"

"No," I hedge, trying to think up anything else I know about him. I decide to deflect. "And what do you know about me?"

"Well, you're a great artist. The mural you painted at the bakery is awesome, and you designed that little burrito guy and his doughnut girlfriend, right?"

My mouth hangs open in surprise. I did, in fact, design the bakery's mascots: Gordo the dessert burrito and, after we started selling Ana Maria's doughnuts, the doughnut mascot Anise. And when we started getting all that social media attention, Papi wanted to spruce up the interior a little, so I offered to paint a mural. But it's not well known that I'm the one behind our branding.

Gage takes my open-mouthed surprise as confirmation and continues.

"And now that you're out of your brother's shadow, you seem a little lost."

Okay, rude. But true. And a little unsettling that Gage, a guy I've hardly spoken to, has been able to see me so clearly, despite my best attempts to be invisible.

"Have you been reading my diary?" I accuse, covering my embarrassment with a joke.

"You keep a diary?" he asks, brows rising in surprise.

"No," I admit. "Well, do we have a deal or not? Because I really need a tutor and this is my last hope."

"You've made me an offer I can't refuse, Ms. Morales," Gage says. "I can tutor you during lunch this week. I'll make sure you're ready for that exam."

I exhale in relief, his promise lifting the weight that's been dragging me down for days.

"Let's shake on it," I insist, reaching out my hand between us.

Gage takes hold of my hand instantly, giving it one good shake. We're officially fake dating now and I'm hopefully back on track for graduation this spring. The future seems a little less bleak, and for the first time in days, I feel a bubble of hope rise in my chest.

CHAPTER SEVEN

Gage asks to see my first exam so he can see how I did and where we need to focus our work. It is beyond embarrassing to hand over the papers riddled with red marks, but Gage's expression stays neutral.

"What's the verdict, Doctor?" I ask anxiously as he scribbles down some notes in his illegible handwriting.

"Diagnosis: not terminal. You can easily bounce back from this. I'll make sure you're ready for the retake." He sounds so confident, so sure of not only his abilities but of mine. I'm not even that confident about myself.

"Great. So now let's go over my half of the deal." I ask him some questions about the auction, when the deadlines are and how many donations they usually get. He has to dredge up emails from last year to answer my questions because, just like Ginger said, he hasn't gotten very far on his own. The auction is held as part of a gala, which is in four weeks. Gage's parents have a planner handling most of the event, but the auction is solely

Gage's responsibility, so we'll have to start speaking to businesses sooner rather than later.

The bell rings as we're wrapping up. Gage packs his notes and I remember that I left my backpack at the table with Miguel. I'm about to run out of the library with only a quick goodbye, but then I freeze.

"I don't have your number, which is not very girlfriend-y of me," I say quickly before we both stand from the table.

"Easy fix," Gage says, pulling out his phone and unlocking it before handing it to me. I look down at the perfectly organized screen, complete with hour-by-hour calendar at the top and apps organized in labeled folders. I've put my future in the right hands.

I quickly add my name to his contacts, making sure to add three heart emojis, and shoot off a text to my number.

"See you tomorrow, same time, same place?"

"Same time, same place," he confirms, sliding his phone back into his pocket.

I dash out of the library, earning a dirty look from the librarian (another point against me and perhaps another Wanted sign will go up in the back room), and run back to the lunch table. Most of the people have already cleared the quad, but some people with classrooms nearby are standing around and chatting.

Much to my dismay, Miguel is sitting on the lunch table with my backpack at his feet. He has his arms crossed and he's glaring daggers at me.

"I didn't hide in the bathroom!" I shout at him as I jog over to the table. "I had to go to the library."

"You can *read*?" Miguel asks in fake surprise. I give him a punch to the shoulder, not holding back. Miguel and I are nearly the same height, and even though he played competitive mermaids at his school in Los Angeles, when we're on land I can definitely take him. "Jesus," he says, rubbing the spot where I socked him as I snatch my bag.

"I was actually meeting Gage. I'm helping him with that charity auction he does for his parents' gala thing," I say, testing the waters with this confession.

Miguel's brow climbs nearly to his hairline in surprise.

"What— How— *When*?" he sputters, unsure of what question he should be asking in this scenario.

"Listen, my next class is on, like, the other side of campus. I'll see you after school!" I turn on my heel and escape before Miguel can string together enough words to ask a question.

When seventh period rolls around, I walk into Algebra II with my head held high.

"I found a peer tutor, Ms. Metsker," I say when I reach her desk.

"Oh, excellent!" Ms. Metsker says with a genuine smile. "The tutor will log the tutoring hours with Mr. Robertson and you can have your retake this Friday afternoon."

"Perfect," I say with a smile before going to my usual desk at the back of class. I'm riding the high of successfully getting Gage to help me, and I feel better than I have in weeks. My life is slowly getting back on track, and soon I can go back to worrying about the other concerning things in my life, like the growing chasm between me and Adrian and the overall twisted family dynamic at home that grates my nerves on the best of days.

But when class starts and Ms. Metsker starts going over the next chapter, my confidence wanes.

"All right, today we're getting started on polynomials!" Ms. Metsker says with genuine excitement. And as much as I want to share in her excitement, I'm still struggling to understand *trinomials*, how I am supposed to follow this polynomial business?

I can already hear the buzz that starts in my head when I get overwhelmed, some part of my brain shutting down. As Ms. Metsker continues to write on the chalkboard, a scramble of numbers and *x*'s and . . . is that *Greek*? I know I'm in trouble.

I struggle to follow along all class, starting off by copying everything Ms. Metsker has written on the board, but after a while I get lost in my own notes and give up. When the bell rings I'm nearly ready to tear out my own hair and have moved on to just doodling Gordo in the corner of my notes.

I'm not sure Gage knows what he signed up for.

With the pep in my step gone, I head over to Miguel's locker, where most of the Debate Club is hanging out. They're all gathered in a tight circle as I approach, and Ana Maria is a few feet away, leaning against the lockers and watching the Debate huddle with anxious eyes.

"What is going on with them?" I ask as I rest my shoulder on the locker next to her.

"You don't know?" she asks. "It's about you."

For a moment my heart stops and I think everyone has found out about my impending high school failure, but then I catch sight of Gage in the middle of the huddle looking harassed.

"Oh, no," I breathe.

"Yep. Gage dropped the bomb that you two are dating—which, by the way, I will need the details on how *that* happened—and now Miguel is playing the role of overprotective father and Noah is acting the jealous ex because he's mad Gage apparently made the time to start dating you but not to go to his movie premiere."

"What should I do?" I ask her as the group continues to talk over each other.

"Save him from this torment, maybe?" she suggests. "Or maybe prove that he's not lying about dating you, because I'm guessing that's what most people are thinking."

I wasn't expecting to have to perform this fake dating charade so soon, but at least it's a handy excuse to take Algebra II off my mind. I drop my backpack on the floor next to Ana and walk up to the guys.

"I don't see why this is such a big deal— " Gage is saying, trying to quell the fervor that has worked up around him.

"The *deal*?" Avery Daniels squeals. "I heard once that one of the guys on the soccer team said something about Valeria in the locker room and it got back to Adrian and he ended up getting kicked off the team *and* with a black eye. You're too pretty for a black eye, Gage!"

"My cousin isn't going to give him a black eye," Miguel says, and for a second I think he's going to be reasonable about this. "But *I* might if you're just using my cousin to get back at Ginger as some kind of rebound thing."

"Oh my God!" I shout, shoving aside a despondent-looking

Noah and squeezing my way next to Gage. "Can you please stop harassing him?"

I don't know how to act like someone's girlfriend, but holding hands seems like a good start. I reach for Gage's hand, if only to lend him a little of my strength and to sell us together. He holds on to me tightly, giving me an affirming squeeze.

"I— Why— You—" Miguel starts, but he can't seem to string together enough words to say anything.

"You can head home without me," I tell Miguel, pulling Gage away from the Spanish Inquisition. "Gage and I are going to hang out for a little bit, and he'll drop me off."

Not letting anyone get in a word edgewise, I pull Gage over to my abandoned backpack, where Ana Maria is still leaning against the lockers.

"Good job," she whispers with a small thumbs-up as I pass by. I shoot her a grateful smile and pull Gage out of the hallway.

He sags with relief when we push through the doors and out into the misty, gray afternoon. Our school is close enough to the sound that the air has that briny smell to it, mingling with the pine scent from all the trees surrounding us. Gage takes one heaving gulp of that air, not letting go of my hand as we make our way toward the parking lot.

I realize I have no idea what car he drives, so I just follow his lead down the gravel paths that make up the student lot. Neither of us has said anything since the hallway, but instead of feeling awkward in that silence, I feel oddly comfortable. Gage isn't expecting anything from me, and I'm not expecting anything from him because, honestly, I have no idea what I'm doing. I was just trying to save him from an uncomfortable moment with friends that was, ultimately, my fault.

Gage pulls out his car keys and points down a row of cars.

"That one's mine," he says, pointing at a Subaru Outback that looks like it's taken care of, unlike my poor car, which has given in to that salt air and has begun to rust *everywhere*. It has a bumper sticker with a crab and the text "Crabs Are Inevitable" that I'm choosing not to question. He must be the male equivalent of a horse girl but for marine life, and I'm not looking for a lecture on crabs. "Was that a coverup, or are we really going to hang out?"

"I mean, if you have the time this afternoon, we can get a head start and talk to some businesses downtown," I say, but then I remember the bags under his eyes and the general air of stress and feel like I need to walk it back. I let go of his hand and wave mine in the air in some kind of erasing motion. "But don't feel pressured! I know you have a lot going on right now and I really don't want this setup to be an extra burden on you, I want this to be a fair deal between us, so if you can't today, I'll find my own way home."

Gage brushes away my flapping hands with a laugh. "Don't back out on our deal just yet, Valeria."

"I'm not!" I argue.

"Good, because I just stood down your cousin, who was ready to throw hands because *someone* told him you were hanging out with me to help with the auction."

"Oh God," I moan. "I didn't think he would go and harass *you* about that."

"Yeah, well, he caught me and started asking me a lot of

questions and I just told him we started seeing each other, which then became a whole thing, as you saw."

We're standing next to his car now, both of us against the driver's side. I turn and press my back against the door and stare up at the gray expanse of sky over us.

"I really didn't think it would be that big of a deal. People date all the time. Hell, my brother is seeing someone new, like, every month. I thought this could just be a, like, under-the-radar thing. Casual. No big deal."

"Unfortunately for us, we have surrounded ourselves with a bunch of not-so-casual-have-to-make-a-big-deal-out-of-everything people. But this will blow over soon enough, I'm sure," Gage says. "In the meantime, we have businesses to get to, right?"

"Right," I say with an affirmative nod. There is only one thing in my life right now that deserves my attention: passing Algebra II. Everything else is just noise. I can deal with noise. I can't, however, deal with math, so I need to get this plan in order.

I'm not sure if what I'm feeling right now is confidence, but it's something like it. Hopefulness, maybe? Because despite the uncomfortable situation my fake dating scenario put Gage in, he still wants to help me. So if he won't give up on me when things get hard, I won't give up on him.

CHAPTER EIGHT

I know downtown Port Murphy like the back of my hand. The main street sits two blocks west of the water, tree-lined with banners hanging from the light poles and charming facades from the 1800s still intact. There's a co-op, an antique shop with the best collection of cuckoo clocks, a used bookstore, several restaurants, and a crystal shop where you can get your cards read by the town psychic, who accurately predicted the day Queen Elizabeth would die. Down by the water there's the bed-and-breakfast where Ana Maria's mom works and a small waterfront park with a gazebo and a large flock of geese you should avoid if you're wearing blue.

And the business owners in this town *love* me. I was the cute little kid who was always underfoot during community meetings, with pigtails and a gap tooth. The old manager at the co-op would always give me a free cookie when we were grocery shopping, and Michelle at the flower store always does my dance corsages for free.

I may be at risk of failing my senior year of high school, but I have this town wrapped around my finger. I am going to pull together the best list of donations the Magnussens have ever seen.

"Where should we start?" Gage asks as he turns out of the student lot.

"Let's go by block," I suggest. "If we start on second street, we can hit Michelle at the flower shop, Diana at the bookstore, Cece at Olympic Wellness if she's free, and then end the day with a snack at the bakery. On the house, of course," I assure him.

"Have you ever done this before?" he asks, his voice flat and hard to read. I bristle immediately.

"Think I can't do it?" I ask, not able to keep the acid from my voice. "I may not be as smart as Ginger, but I'm certainly more—"

"That's not what I meant," Gage says, his grip tightening on his steering wheel, cutting me off before I can say anything bad about his ex-girlfriend. "I wasn't asking because I don't think you can do it, I was asking because you're so confident going into this."

"Oh," I say, backing down. I don't normally care whether someone thinks I'm smart or not. I never wanted to be the overachiever my twin is, with all the attention and expectations that come with it, but this math situation hasn't exactly been great for my self-confidence. Gage is the only one who knows what's going on, and I guess I'm worried he'll think less of me because of it.

Luckily, he keeps the subject on fundraising, probably sensing my discomfort. "I've been dragging my feet because I'm terrible at talking to people about stuff like this," he says. "Ginger was always the one who could get them to throw in something extra or get a reluctant business to participate. I was just there because my name is on the gala."

"What exactly is the gala for?" I ask, realizing I probably need to know more about it before I can get people to donate to it.

"It's part of the fundraising efforts for my parents' law firm. Every year they pick a cause to raise money for. Last year it went to an organization that helps people pay bail. This year their focus is on global vaccines and health care. They always have a speaker come in to discuss the topic at hand, and in addition to the auction there is usually some kind of entertainment. It's black tie and they invite everyone in town with money burning a hole in their pocket."

Port Murphy may be a small town on the Olympic Peninsula, but plenty of people who got rich quick in the early days of tech in Seattle took their money and settled down out here. We have a fair mix of the haves and have-nots in town, regular blue-collar folk working trade jobs mingling with remote tech workers or folks who were able to retire at forty-five from cushy tech jobs and now just work as "consultants," which sounds like a fake job to me.

"It actually sounds like an awesome event," I say. "I think plenty of the business owners would be happy to donate for that cause. I know Michelle is already very active at the local hospital and is really passionate about health equity." I jot down some quick notes on my phone and start a new spreadsheet with a list of businesses we should contact.

We stop at a red light and Gage leans over to see what I'm putting together. "Honestly, I think I'm getting the better side of this deal," he says with a smile, settling back into his seat.

"How quickly you forget the shakedown from my cousin!" I say on a laugh. Miguel has been playing up protective older brother with me since Doughnutgate this summer. I think he feels guilty that I lost my twin to this fight between them, so he has set himself up as my protector in Adrian's absence.

"I will take that any day of the week if it means you take this auction prep off my plate," he tells me.

"I wouldn't say it's *off* your plate," I tell him. "There's probably a spoonful left on there, considering the gala is in your name. I need you there to prove that I'm not just going around town stealing donations for my own use."

Traffic is starting to pick up as we make our way to downtown, but Gage manages to snag a street parking spot and nails the parallel park in one try. I bet he's never dinged his car on anything before, or had to use Bondo and nail polish to hide said ding from his dad or anything outlandish like that.

We start today's tour at one of my favorite shops in Port Murphy: Pacific Gardens, a flower and plant shop on the corner of Second and Main. The actual storefront has a small footprint, with the majority of Michelle's stock outside under the green-and-white-striped awning in an explosion of plants and flowers. There are tiers of bright blooms along the front window, stunning heritage roses and dahlias the size of my head, and decorative branches and greens. She has dozens of plants for sale, too, ferns and calatheas and philodendrons of all kinds.

Inside, Michelle is working behind the counter on one of her signature ikebana arrangements, building something that looks more like a sculpture than it does the average bouquet.

"Hi, Michelle!" I call out as we enter through the open front door.

"Valeria!" Michelle cries out in greeting, dropping the rose she was cutting and stepping out from behind the counter. She pulls me in for a hug, her smile warm and friendly. Michelle is a middle-aged Japanese woman who immigrated to this country around the same time as my dad. Although their family's reasons for leaving their countries were different, Michelle and my dad (and Ana Maria's dad, too) all shared something that not many other people in this small town did. She always did her best to stay out of the drama between our families and is now very pleased that we've put the rivalry behind us. "What brings you here this afternoon? Is it homecoming already?"

"Almost," I tell her, "but that's not why I'm here. You know Gage Magnussen, right?" I ask, stepping aside to introduce my partner in crime. Michelle looks up at Gage and gives him that same warm smile.

"Of course I do," she says, giving him a polite nod.

"And you're familiar with his family's charity auction for their annual gala, right?" I ask, pulling up the link to the gala's website on my phone to show her.

"Oh, yes," she says, glancing at my phone before returning her attention to Gage. "I believe I donated something a few years ago, when that girl was organizing it."

"Well, I'm the girl organizing it this year," I say proudly, "and I want to highlight all the wonderful local businesses that

Port Murphy has with this auction." I give Michelle a quick rundown on the charity this year for the gala, and I see her eyes light up with interest. "We don't need any promises right now, but I wanted to ask if you might be interested?"

"I'd love to donate something!" Michelle says. "I could donate some tickets for my flower arranging classes, too."

"That would be amazing!"

"When would the donations need to be finalized by?" Michelle asks.

I look over at Gage and poke him gently in the ribs.

"Oh, uh—" Gage says haltingly. "In two weeks?"

"I'll follow up with you via email," I add on quickly, "with more firm details. This was just meant to be an informal introduction."

"Oh, you're all grown-up!" Michelle cries out, pinching my cheek for good measure. "You must be working hard on those college applications. I'm sure something like this looks great on them."

My smile falters for a moment at the reminder that college may not be in my future, not if I can't get my algebra grade up. And even if I do, no school would give a student like me the scholarships I need to afford a degree in the first place.

"I bet it does," I agree, struggling to keep my smile in place. I'm saved from more talk about my unlikely future when a customer strolls in, a man looking harried and desperate. "I'll let you get back to work, Michelle. Thank you for your time!"

"Of course, sweetheart," Michelle says, squeezing my shoulder once before stepping aside to greet her new customer.

Gage and I scuttle out of the shop, even though I'm kind of interested in sticking close by to eavesdrop on the man, who is clearly looking to buy an apology gift for a romantic partner.

"Wow, you got her to commit to donate in, like, less than five minutes. People really do love you around here," Gage says.

"Don't sound so surprised," I joke, but Gage starts stammering anyway.

"No, no, that's not what I meant—"

"I know I may *look* scary," I cut in, giving him a hard time because the way the tips of his ears are turning red is kind of cute.

"You don't look scary," he rushes to assure me.

"No? What do I look like, then?" I challenge him. "Use one of those fancy speech-and-debate words. Or better yet, an SAT word."

"Uh, you're—adroit," he stumbles. "Is the bookstore next?"

"Wait—" I call after him as he rushes into the bookstore. "Did you just call me a *droid*?"

We continue to each of the businesses on the block, introducing ourselves and asking about their interest in donating. Gage is quiet and only speaks when I push him to, but overall the introductions go well. I mark off everyone we speak to on my new spreadsheet and make notes about our conversation before moving to the next store.

By the time we finish with all the shops on the block and get to the bakery, my throat is dry and my stomach is rumbling.

"Do you want your usual?" I ask him as we step into the shop, the familiar scent of butter and garlic enveloping me. Pitbull is playing on the speakers, which means that one of our younger employees is working behind the counter today. The shop is full of the after-school crowd, kids with only enough money to order a fountain drink and a side of fries but enough time to kill that they end up taking over the tables for hours.

"I have a usual?" Gage says in surprise.

"Yeah, almost everyone does," I tell him. "You usually order a Cuban sandwich, no pickles, and a café con leche with an extra shot of espresso."

"Wow," Gage says, and I can't tell whether he's impressed or weirded out.

"I'm not stalking you," I assure him. "We have a small menu and I've worked here since I was fourteen. I can pretty much correctly guess what any local will order nine times out of ten."

"Nicole Valleys," he says suddenly, and for a moment I'm totally thrown. Then I catch on to his game.

"The Cuban Chop salad, extra avocado."

"Dallas."

"In the morning, an iced dirty chai and a cheese pastelito. In the afternoon, if it's raining, she gets café con leche with avocado toast, and if the sky is clear she gets a frita."

"Mark Evans."

"He doesn't eat pork so he doesn't come here, but I did see him order a café con leche once."

"Natalie Yu."

"Have I not proved my point yet?" I ask.

"You have, but now it's a fun game for me."

"Well, I need food and water before I list off anyone else's order by memory. Are you having your usual or not?"

Gage sighs and nods, ushering me ahead to the cashier. I'm considering ordering one of our specials for the month, a new initiative between Papi and Ana Maria. Right now they've come up with a rotating selection of tostadas, a combination of the classic buttered and pressed Cuban bread and tartines. This month we have a sizzled shallots, Cuban chorizo, and avocado with plenty of lime zest for the savory option. Our sweet option has caramelized persimmons, queso cubano, candied walnuts, and a drizzle of spiced caramel and flaky salt.

Our menu was good before Ana Maria, but I have to admit since she's joined forces with our dad it's gotten so much better. We sell out of her doughnuts every weekend, and the locals have been loving the new specials.

I order the sweet tostada and then guide Gage over to the table farthest from the fries-and-soda crew.

I hand Gage his cup and we walk together to the drink station in the back. I think he might go for the soda for the caffeine, considering his espresso problem, but he surprises me when he goes to the water dispenser.

When he twists the valve, nothing comes out.

"Oh, it's empty," I say quickly, inching closer to him so I can pull up the giant stainless steel dispenser. "Uh, let me just grab the thing."

"You're not on the clock," Gage points out as he steps back to give me more room.

"A Morales is always on the clock if they're inside the shop."

I fill up the water in the kitchen and waddle back to Gage with a full dispenser. One good heave and it's back up on the table, full of fresh water and ice. I glance around out of habit to make sure nothing is running low.

"Oh! We're out of lemons," I say, not sure whether he puts

them in his water. Either way, I should refill them while I'm here.

"I really don't need—"

I ignore him and grab the empty container, hurrying into the kitchen and pulling the bin of fresh wedges from the fridge. I return with a topped-off container and proudly present him with the lemons. "Here you go!"

But instead of saying a polite thank you, picking up the tiny tongs on the counter, and serving himself a wedge, he stares at the container in confusion, brows drawn and mouth pursed.

"Those are limes," he says, looking up at me and back down at the container.

"Yes," I agree, setting them down on the table because standing there holding them up to him was starting to get weird. "As promised. Fresh lime wedges."

"You said lemons," he says, a small quirk at the corner of his mouth as he turns and serves himself one. "I wasn't sure why you were going to bring me lemons when this restaurant only ever has lime slices, despite my mom's persistent request that you offer both."

"Oh," I say, finally understanding his confusion. "Bilingual problems," I explain. "My brain refuses to recognize the fact that the word 'lime' exists. In Spanish, 'limón' means both lemon and lime, and my brain treats 'lemon' the same way. Everyone always talks about how great being bilingual is, but they never tell you the downsides," I say with an exaggerated seriousness in my voice.

"Ah, I see," Gage says. "I thought I was getting some kind of backdoor citrus deal in exchange for our, uh, situation."

"You're making our deal sound way more nefarious than it actually is."

"I'm okay with letting things get a little nefarious," he says with a teasing smile that takes me by surprise. "How can I negotiate for some lemons out of this?"

He's wearing khakis, I tell myself. *There is no way that him asking for lemons can be this hot if he is wearing khakis.*

"I'm sorry, but I'm going to have to stand firm on this one," I tell him, feeling weirdly anything but.

CHAPTER NINE

After we finish up our food at the bakery, I direct Gage through the winding roads of my residential neighborhood. Roads curve into each other and end in cul-de-sacs, featuring rows of untouched mid-century homes. In the 1950s there was a small population boom in this area, with a new paper mill offering plenty of work and, later, a hospital. The houses in my neighborhood are middle-class split-level homes with big yards and basketball hoops mounted above garage doors.

I imagine Gage lives on the other side of town, near the water, in one of those hideous modern homes full of beige interiors with lots of gray and cedar paneling on the exterior and no friendly cul-de-sacs.

The sun is setting as we coast down the quiet streets, and the change between daylight and dusk is minimal today. I know I should miss the sunshine, but I think there's something romantic about gray skies and misty rain. It's so moody and mysterious outside when the weather is like this, adding a sense of drama to everyday life. Sunshine is so boring and redundant; it comes with no surprise thunder or howling wind, just a higher chance of skin cancer.

"That's me," I say, pointing at my house, surprised to see all five cars tucked into the driveway. I'm never the last one home. It's either Adrian, held up at football practice, or our dad, hard at work trying to get the second location of Morales Bakery up and running. "I had fun this afternoon," I tell him, and I'm not sure why I felt the need to say it.

But Gage smiles as he pulls to a stop in front of my house. "I did, too," he says. "I'll see you at lunch tomorrow?"

"Yes, I'll come pencil in hand and ready to learn," I promise.

Gage pops the trunk for me and I pull out my backpack, throwing him a final wave before making my way up to the front door. I can see the light on in the garage, which means Papi is likely working on one of his recent projects. He's been trying to cut down on costs for the new shop by buying some things secondhand and fixing them up himself. The latest project is a set of booths that badly needed reupholstering, and I can already hear the *snick* of the upholstery stapler from the driveway.

Inside, the smell of garlic and cumin wafts from the kitchen. From the front door I can hear Tia Isa singing along to Beny Moré's "Cómo Fue" in a surprisingly sultry alto. Papi wasn't kidding when he said she could sing. I peek my head into the kitchen, where my aunt is belting passionately as she does dishes while a pot of something delicious-smelling simmers on the stove. She doesn't notice me, and I decide to keep it that way, sneaking my way upstairs. But I'm thwarted by Adrian, who is barreling down the stairs, making a beeline straight toward me.

I expect him to brush past like he's done since the summer, but Adrian is zeroed in on me right now. I look around anxiously, unsure why I've suddenly got all his attention.

"Yes?" I ask nervously, readjusting my backpack strap as Tia Isa wails the line *"No sé explicarme qué pasó."* Adrian glares me down.

"I can't believe you," he growls, pointing an accusatory finger in my face and shaking it around. "Picking Miguel's side over mine this summer I could let pass—"

"Clearly not," I mutter, considering this is the first time he's started a conversation with me since Doughnutgate.

"—but going and dating my *worst enemy*?"

"Oh my GOD," I shout, frustrated by how over-the-top dramatic the men in my family can be. Adrian has never *once* called Gage his worst enemy. Academic rival, maybe. But today it's suddenly a Shakespearean-level feud. Now that we aren't hating the Ybarras anymore, it's clear Adrian is trying to fill that void with someone else. "You're acting like I'm dating a guy who took a hit out on your family or something."

"But that's *exactly* what's happening, don't you see? He's only dating you to try and get under my skin so he can knock me down from number one."

My mouth hangs open in shock. For the first time in my life, I'm doing something that has *nothing* to do with my twin. I'm solving my own problems and making my own friends, but somehow it's still all about Adrian in the end.

"You didn't even consider that, did you?" he asks, looking pleased with himself for revealing this dark, secret truth to me.

"No, I didn't," I snap back. "Because *I* was the one who asked *him* out."

Now Adrian is the one sputtering to find a response. He didn't expect that from me.

"I don't understand," he says finally.

"What? The concept of me doing something without your approval?"

"Don't act like this is about me—"

"Oh, then please tell me what this insane confrontation is about?" I yell at him, and at this point the music in the kitchen cuts out and I know Tia Isa has heard us. But Adrian doesn't care.

"Listen, just because you asked him out doesn't mean he's not doing this to get at me. Gage is a sore loser and—"

"Adrian! Me dating Gage has *nothing* to do with you!" I'm tempted to admit to possibly flunking out of high school just to get him to drop this, but I know that admission would only serve to open a whole other can of worms that I'm not ready to handle.

"You can't know that!" he shouts back at me as Tia Isa steps out of the kitchen with a wooden spoon in hand.

"What's going on out here?" Isa asks as she walks up to us. I watch as Adrian visibly tenses at her approach.

"None of your business," he snaps at her over his shoulder. Isa frowns and sucks in a deep breath, as though my twin's response were a physical blow. "This is between me and my sister."

"No, it's not," I cut in, "because I am not entertaining whatever this is right now, Adrian. I have things to do."

"Mark my words, Valeria," Adrian says. "Gage will break your heart. He's not over Ginger, the only reason he would date you is to get under my skin."

"Adrian!" Isa shouts in horror as I stare down my twin. "You can't say things like that to your sister." My eyes cut to my aunt, who really has no place in this conversation. Why is she even trying? Why is everyone getting into my business right now? Before this summer, I flew under the radar in my family, and I liked it that way. Now everyone is inserting themselves in places they're not welcome, and I am *over it.*

"Why are you butting into this?" Adrian snaps. "Don't you have your own family problems to solve?" he says, hitting our aunt where it hurts most.

Isa purses her lips and just stares at Adrian. She nods to herself, just a small shake, before turning around and heading back into the kitchen.

"Don't be so harsh with her," I tell him, quieter now so I won't be overheard.

"Don't act like you don't feel the same," he tells me.

"Just because you *feel* a certain way doesn't give you license to be an asshole," I tell him.

"Whatever. But when this whole thing with Gage goes to shit, don't act like I didn't warn you."

I just smile at him in response. I'm going to look forward to proving him so very wrong when this is all over.

CHAPTER TEN

I end up skipping dinner that night, despite my aunt checking on me and asking me to join them, and wake up late the next morning. I lie in bed for a while, hoping to miss Adrian in the kitchen, and when I hear his car start in the driveway, I rush downstairs and grab the first thing I see on the counter for breakfast. Today happens to be one of those lucky mornings when the kitchen is full of day-old pastries from the shop. Papi doesn't always bring home leftovers like this, but when he does it always feels like a little treat.

I'm tearing into my pastelito de guayaba when I hear Miguel race up the stairs from the basement.

"Morning," he says to me, still bleary-eyed from sleep. I can tell he had trouble sleeping last night because he pulls the cafetera from the cupboard and sets to making some Cuban coffee. "Want some?" he mutters in my direction.

"Sure," I say with a full mouth, waiting for his brain to power on. In a minute he's going to remember how we left things yesterday and he's going to start it back up.

I can tell the moment it happens. He's watching the cafetera on the stove, waiting to spot the first sputters of coffee, when his head snaps up. He looks at me with narrowed eyes for a moment.

"That wasn't a dream, was it?" he asks.

"Nope," I say, tearing off another bite of pastelito.

"Ana Maria told me I was being an asshole," he tells me, and he pouts a little when he says it. "She's never said that to me before."

"Well," I say, giving him a hip check to move him away from the stove so I can take the cafetera off the heat. I pour a little of the fresh coffee into a stainless-steel foaming pitcher and add some sugar. "You kind of deserved it."

I set the cafetera back on the stove to finish brewing and grab the frothing stick to make espuma. Traditionalists will tell you that you have to mix the coffee and sugar with a spoon, but lazy teenagers will tell you an electric handheld frother works just as well.

"Sorry," he says. "You don't realize how much machismo you accidentally inherited until your baby cousin gets her first boyfriend."

"Two months!" I shout at him. "Being two months younger than you does not make me your *baby cousin.*" I'm choosing to ignore the bit about "first boyfriend" because acknowledging that fact to lady-killer Miguel is downright embarrassing.

"Uh-huh," he says, clearly not caring about my complaint. "Just like a baby cousin to complain about being called 'baby cousin.'" I roll my eyes at him.

"Let's have our coffee and go, we're going to be late," I tell him, grabbing the cafecito cups from the cabinet and pouring us each a healthy serving. Miguel clinks my cup and we throw back our coffee in a single shot before running out the front door.

As we make our way onto campus, it's clear that the news about Gage Magnussen dating someone new has spread like wildfire. Dallas, one of my brother's ex-girlfriends, is making eye contact with me as she whispers to her friends. I feel like an animal at the zoo.

"I can say this because it also applies to me," Miguel says, stopping at our lockers and turning to face me. "But I feel like our family tends to attract an inordinate amount of drama. It's not even an exaggeration to say the entire class is talking about you and Gage."

"Ugh," I say, slamming my head against my locker with a groan. "You're supposed to tell me that those whispers are all in my head and that everyone is *not*, in fact, talking about me behind my back." I flip around and glare at my cousin.

"Would that I could, but I can't lie to you, baby cuz. You're the talk of the town."

"What town?" Rose appears behind Miguel with Ana Maria.

"Our town. Valeria and Gage are the hot topic, and she can't take the heat," Miguel accuses.

"I can take the heat," I complain. "I just don't know why everyone is so interested."

"Oh, I know," Rose pipes up. "Gage's breakup was one of the wildest things to happen last year, and everyone thinks that—"

"He has found happiness again!" Ana Maria cuts in, stepping

on Rose's toes. She tries to make the stomp covert, but Rose wails in protest and makes the whole thing very obvious.

"What are people actually saying?" I ask nervously. I know what my cousin and brother thought, but I didn't want to listen to their opinions because it all came from a place of familial machismo. But it's entirely different knowing we're interesting enough to garner the whole school's opinions.

I'm not sure how to feel about that. Our relationship may be fake, but my classmates' perception of me is quite real. But I suppose if no one ends up guessing the real reason behind our relationship, none of their opinions really matter?

"Just stupid stuff," Ana Maria tries, but at my glare she raises her hands in defeat and nudges Rose.

"Well," Rose starts. "It's not all bad. Some people just think Gage is using you to piss off your brother, but anyone who really knows Gage knows he wouldn't do that. Some people also think the opposite, that you're trying to sabotage Gage to get back into your brother's good graces. And while I would have one hundred percent believed that about you last year, as I was morally obligated to as an honorary Ybarra, I know you wouldn't do that, either. And then . . ." Rose trails off, glancing at the floor nervously. "Some people think you're a rebound and that Gage isn't over Ginger."

Rose doesn't qualify that rumor, which means she must think it has some merit. I saw Gage with Ginger yesterday. He was uncomfortable and closed off, but that doesn't mean he can't still have feelings for her. Love is complicated, and she was his first love. If this were a real relationship, it's possible Gage could be using it to get over or even get back at Ginger.

But it's not a real relationship. So it doesn't matter how he really feels about Ginger.

What matters is me passing Algebra II.

The first period bell rings then, giving me a valid excuse to cut this conversation short.

"Everyone at this school needs a hobby," I say casually, as though Rose's revelations don't matter to me at all. "Or something else to talk about. Rose, is there some kind of enemies-to-lovers scandalous relationship you can start so I can get the heat off me?"

"I'll see what I can do, but the only enemy I have left is your brother, and I'm not really keen on that," Rose says.

"But it would make quite the story," Miguel points out.

"Veto!" Ana Maria shouts.

"Double veto!" I echo.

CHAPTER ELEVEN

At lunch, Gage is ready with notes and a mini whiteboard, apparently unbothered by the whispers following him around campus. We start from the first module, making sure I have a full grasp of each concept as we move on. He also comes with a stack of papers and documentation for the gala, along with access to an email address so I can start following up with the business owners we spoke to.

With our heads pressed together in the back corner of the library, it's enough to get most people to continue speculating about our relationship. Ginger unknowingly does her part in our charade by glaring daggers into my back whenever I walk by, and that ends up being more than enough fuel for the gossip mill without me trying to climb Gage like a tree between periods.

By the time we get to factoring and quadratics on Thursday, Gage and I have a tutoring system down. We're speeding through the lessons and I'm feeling ready for my retake on Friday.

I'm also feeling more comfortable around him. He's an easy

person to hang out with, his energy soft and warm and so unlike the other men in my life. He's also very, *very* good at tutoring.

"You're picking up on this stuff really quick," Gage says as he takes a bite of his sandwich with one hand and wipes the mini whiteboard clean with the other. "It just seems like those early lessons didn't stick, and catching up since then has been the problem."

"Yeah, well, senior year has not been easy," I tell him, looking down at my page of notes. I consider how much to tell him. Do I want him to know the real reason I fell behind so badly this year? For some reason I want Gage to have a good opinion of me, to think I'm more than a failing nobody. "You know my brother isn't speaking to me, right?"

"Miguel did mention something about that," Gage says. He doesn't look overly curious about this nugget of information, or hungry for the truth behind whatever gossip he's heard. He just looks willing to listen.

If I were to try to talk to Miguel about this, he would just spend the entire conversation complaining about Adrian. If I tried to explain to my dad what's going on, he'd just wave it off as regular teenage behavior.

I'm not sure anyone I know would just *listen* to me. But Gage is offering me that right now, so I take him up on it.

"Well," I sigh, deciding to just go right into it. "There was this huge family fight this summer and Adrian was hurt that I didn't pick his side, even though he was definitely in the wrong. And his response was to just . . . ice me out. It wasn't so bad those last few weeks of summer, but by the time classes started I realized . . . my entire social life revolves around my brother. And with him cutting me off, he essentially cut me off from everything and everyone at school." I peer up at Gage through my lashes to see how he responds to this revelation.

His brows are furrowed, and he still has those bags under his eyes from too little sleep, but he doesn't look at me with pity. Instead he looks a little mad.

"I tried to just, I don't know, push through it. But it sucks, you know? People I thought were my friends dropped me because my brother said so. And as a result I kind of . . . checked out a little bit. I was able to catch up with most of my classes because it's easy enough to fake it with English or art class, but math? It was like this snowball effect. Every week things were getting worse and worse, and eventually I just decided it was easier to ignore it than to address it. Until I was informed I'm on my way to failing high school." I sit back in my seat and sigh. "I can't do another year of this."

"Sounds like what happened with me last year," he says, his voice soft and careful. "Depression just slithers in and turns your life upside down before you can even register it's there."

Depression? Is that what he thinks I've been going through? I thought it was just deep, crippling embarrassment that had me frozen in fear. But my brother ditching me isn't so different from a breakup, I suppose. Gage and I are both missing someone deeply, even though they hurt us.

"When everything happened with Ginger, I felt disconnected from life. I knew things were getting bad, but it was like watching it happen to someone else. But I still knew, logically, that it was happening to me. I just couldn't bring myself to do anything about it, which left me lying awake at night."

"Do you still have trouble sleeping?" I ask, as though the answer isn't written on his face.

"Oh, definitely," Gage says. "You wouldn't believe the things I've tried in order to get myself to fall asleep. Acupuncture, meditation, those weird sleep playlists on YouTube, running a mile, sleep mocktails—you name it, I've tried it."

"I'm sorry, did you say 'running a mile'?" I ask.

"Oh yeah." He nods. "Exercise at night is supposed to help make you sleepy, but I just end up feeling *more* amped up after a run."

"Well, next time you can't sleep, call me," I tell him.

"Really?" Gage asks in surprise.

"I can tell you a story so boring it'll put you straight to sleep," I promise. Since he's managed to make Algebra II suddenly make so much more sense in the span of two days, I think he deserves a little more from my end of the bargain. Why not help him fall asleep?

A surprise laugh escapes Gage at my offer. He's so serious most of the time, but his face really does light up when he smiles. His lips part just slightly, showing the tips of his front teeth, and his sleepy eyes brighten just a little bit. I want to make him do it again.

"You know, I think I'll take you up on that one of these days," he says. The shrill ring of the bell cuts through our conversation, and the library around us bursts into motion. Gage and I pack up our things and wave goodbye as we head off toward different ends of campus.

Despite our lunch study date going so well, I'm feeling less confident after dinner that night. I have my notes from my sessions with Gage open and my old exam on my bed, but I don't know if I'll be able to pass my retake tomorrow. Do I *really* know how to graph quadratic formulas? Or is everything I think I know actually wrong?

The *x*'s and the numbers and mathematical symbols start to blur together and I'm half-convinced I don't know what I'm doing. I switch from my normal playlist and pull up a studying playlist on YouTube that's supposed to make you feel like you're in an ancient, dark library. I'm hoping the music change will trigger some switch in my brain and help me focus, but half an hour in and I'm still staring at the practice questions Gage worked on with me today.

I throw myself back onto my bed despondently and stare at the ceiling. It's well past midnight, most of the house is asleep, and if I don't fall asleep soon, I'm going to be running on fumes tomorrow.

Picking up my phone, I pull up my contacts and scroll down to Gage's name. Is he asleep? Is he lying in his room spiraling about Ginger? He hasn't taken me up on my offer of an anesthetizingly boring story, and we only really talk during lunch. I've spent my last couple of afternoons on my own, making the rounds at some businesses to chat with people about donations or working at the bakery. Would it be weird for me to call him?

Dread is pooling in my stomach, and at this rate I think I'll spiral myself into flunking straight out of high school. I tap his number and call.

I shut my eyes tight, as though seeing whether he answers my call or not would be worse than just hearing it. But not two seconds into my call, the ringing stops.

"Hello?" a groggy-sounding Gage answers the phone.

"Oh my God, you were asleep," I babble immediately, sitting straight up in my bed. "I'm so sorry, pretend I didn't call—"

"Valeria! Valeria!" he says, trying to catch my attention over my panicking. "You didn't wake me up, it's okay."

"I didn't?" I say in surprise. "It sure sounded like I did."

"No," he laughs. "I just sound like this when it's the middle of the night and I've been working on homework for hours. I promise you did not wake me up."

"Oh, okay, good," I say, falling back onto my pillows. "I feel less bad now."

"Were you calling to offer me up one of your boring stories? I've actually been falling asleep *accidentally* while working on stuff. I wake up in the morning at my desk with pen marks on my face and a crick in my neck."

"Oh, that explains that little blue mustache on your upper lip today."

"Please tell me you're joking," he says, sounding a little mortified.

"Of course I am. I wouldn't let my fake boyfriend walk around campus looking like ballpoint-pen John Waters."

"Who?"

"Don't worry about it," I tell him. "I called because I've managed to convince myself I actually didn't learn anything with you this week and that I'm going to fail my retake tomorrow and it's just going to be downhill from there, no turning back, straight to flunk town for me—"

"Whoa, whoa, whoa," Gage says in that same calming voice from before, like he's talking to a spooked horse. "Slow down. I see now why you called."

I let out a pained sound in response.

"What's going on?" he asks patiently.

"I'm looking at our notes from today, and I'm worried I won't actually remember how to do any of this stuff without you and your little whiteboard next to me."

"But you said things were going better in class, too, right?"

"Yes, with my notes and textbook open."

"Even so, you couldn't say that last week, with your notes and textbook open," he says evenly.

"Okay, but—"

"No matter what, you're going to do better on this test than you did the first time. And we'll keep working together to get your grade up. You're not going to flunk town," he assures me, and I laugh at the sound of him saying "flunk town."

That giggle manages to ease something in me, and the panic that's been slowly building feels like it's been deflated.

"I'll make sure you're ready for that retake tomorrow. But you're going to have to go to sleep. And eat a lot of protein for breakfast. Feed your brain and all that."

"Is that why my brother eats, like, five eggs for breakfast every morning? Has that been the secret to academic success all this time?"

"I prefer the smoothie route for the added fiber, but probably, yeah," he says seriously.

"That has to be the nerdiest way to talk about food," I laugh. "I normally just grab whatever is easiest and follow it up with a granola bar after second period."

"Do you want to hear what my exam prep routine is?" he offers.

"Sure, couldn't hurt."

"Okay, well, first I try to go to bed at a decent hour, but I see the ship has sailed on that for tonight. Before going to bed, I put on headphones and find a binaural beat playlist. Some studies show that listening to them can help improve quality of sleep, and the night before an exam I'm willing to do anything for an extra edge. I set my alarm for six a.m. sharp, and when I wake up I do some stretches to warm up my body. I follow that with a well-rounded breakfast. Smoked salmon, spinach-egg-white omelet, and a bowl of berries and nuts. And coffee, which has been shown to improve test scores. Then I go to school and just trust myself. I put in the work, and ultimately the exam is out of my control. You have to learn to accept that."

"You didn't mention a single carb," I complain.

"Did you not hear the part where I said what really matters is just trusting yourself?"

"Yeah, sure, trust myself," I say quickly. "But skip carbs in the morning?"

"I didn't say that! Sometimes I have muesli with my berries."

"I'm sorry, I'm just really stuck on this breakfast thing. My people have bread for breakfast that is made with *lard*. And we slather it in butter. My dad makes a breakfast sandwich that's just Cuban bread, butter, and bacon."

"Has he gone to a cardiologist?" Gage asks with genuine

concern. Then he realizes how off topic we are and tries to wrangle the conversation back toward his point. "Valeria, breakfast doesn't matter right now. You need to go to sleep."

"Can you tell me a boring story?" I ask. Well, beg, really.

"I can read to you from my Latin textbook," he offers.

"Latin? Your language elective is *Latin*?"

"Valeria," he says in that warning tone, sensing that I am trying to derail us again. "Turn off the lights and lie down."

"Okay, fine," I mutter, leaning over to turn off my bedside lamp. Plunged into darkness, I pull my blankets up to my shoulders and settle into bed. I put Gage on speaker next to my pillow and stare up at my ceiling. "I'm ready."

Gage clears his throat and begins to read aloud.

"Ciceronis in aedibus." His voice is scratchy and soft as he reads. "Ac domino familae amantissima erat." I close my eyes and let the words wash over me, the deep cadence of Gage's voice helping to slow down my thoughts and ease my mind toward rest. "Sed natura morosior, quod vitium aetas provecta auxerat."

The Latin quickly turns into a gentle hum at the back of my mind as I settle deeper and deeper into my pillow. I don't know if I fall asleep first or Gage stops reading, but eventually, everything disappears and sleep takes me.

CHAPTER TWELVE

I try to follow Gage's exam prep morning schedule, but I wake up well past six a.m. with no appetite for smoked fish. I decide to try to make a smoothie with what we have on hand, but my options are limited, and I have to excavate a freezer-burned bag of blueberries from a deep corner of the freezer.

In my panic to have a healthy breakfast, I end up not having enough time to put a real lunch together. Gage isn't going to be happy when he sees the lackluster fuel I've brought, but I hope he appreciates my attempt with the smoothie.

At lunch, I get to our table before he does and pull out my notebook and food. If I eat it all before he gets here, then he won't see what I brought and judge me for it. I take out a pouch of tuna fish, an expired packet of trail mix, and five cherry tomatoes. I open the tuna pouch, hoping to get the worst of the meal done with first.

I've never liked tuna, but it's one of those foods Adrian likes having in the pantry for his jock lunches. I could never get over how *fishy* cooked tuna is, and I never liked tuna salad. But maybe straight tuna from the pouch would be better?

One whiff of it, though, has me gagging loudly at the table.

Nope, can't do it.

"Was that you?"

I jump a mile high at the sound of Gage's voice behind me.

"Oh God, you scared the hell out of me!" I hiss at him.

"Well, you scared poor Ms. Cunningham at the front desk with that sound you just made. Are you okay?" He bends over to get a closer look at me, sticking his face in front of mine. I swat him away quickly.

"I'm fine, I'm fine," I assure him, trying to covertly slide the tuna fish away while he sets his bag down.

"Is that your lunch you're trying to slide off the table?" he asks me, a smiling edge to his voice.

"Okay, fine, you caught me! I was just gagging from the smell of tuna, because you had me convinced that I needed to eat fish to pass this retake today, but turns out I still hate tuna, so all I have for lunch now is this." I wave at the cherry tomatoes and trail mix, which is strangely powdery from age.

"I think you took the wrong thing away from our conversation last night," Gage says.

"I guess I can go get whatever they're serving in the cafeteria?" I say, ignoring him. "My belt is made out of leather, I can chew on that for the protein?"

"I can do you one better," Gage says, pulling his bag up into his lap.

"No, no! You're about to do that gallant thing and give me your lunch, aren't you?" I whine. "Stop it, you can't do that."

"I am not giving you *my* lunch," he says, pulling out his usual lunch bag and setting it aside. Then he reaches back into his backpack and pulls out a second identical lunch bag. "I made you brain lunch."

"You made me *what*?"

"I told you about my brain breakfast, but I didn't tell you about brain lunch." Gage opens the bag to reveal a perfectly packed meal. In the middle there's a sandwich made of wheat bread, cut in half and standing on its side to reveal the bright orange-yellow of chickpea curry salad. In the side compartment there is a small salad with dressing on the side, apple slices, and a mini brownie. "This is the lunch I make on the days I have big exams."

"I— You—" I'm at a loss for words as I stare down at the carefully made lunch. The lunch he made *for me*. "Why?"

"I figured you were going to be too frazzled to make a proper lunch this morning. We've been eating together all week, Valeria, and even on your best day I wouldn't label any of your meals as nutritionally well rounded."

I gasp in outrage. But he's not wrong. On most days, I just pack the same ham sandwich and random odds and ends from the kitchen. It could be a banana. It could be a giant lemon poppy seed muffin. Or it could be none of those things. On Wednesday I had half a block of cheddar cheese and an apple. Gage had watched in horror as I took one bite of apple and then another bite of cheese straight from the block.

"So, as your tut—I mean, boyfriend," he says, eyeing a person walking by our table. We've been openly working on math together in the library all week, but we haven't really captured the interest of the library crowd. We always pick the table in the farthest corner with the fewest people near it, and working on classwork together seems like a couple-y enough thing to be doing. But still, we're not going to openly be calling our relationship what it is, in case someone overhears. "As your boyfriend," he tries again, "I thought it was my duty to pack you your own brain lunch for your exam this afternoon."

Gage just smiles at me, looking relaxed and calm, like he hasn't just done the sweetest thing ever. If this is what fake dating the guy is like, what must actually dating him be like?

"And," he continues, turning the lunch bag to the side to reveal a zippered compartment, "I snuck some chocolate-covered espresso beans in here for you. You can eat some after last bell so you get the caffeine boost for your retake."

"You're making me feel like you're offering me performance-enhancing drugs, Gage," I accuse, opening the zipper to peer at the drug in question. As promised, there is a reusable baggie filled with chocolate-covered espresso beans. They all have a variety of coatings, from dark to white chocolate and in-between colors indicating some kind of flavor combination.

"There is nothing in the student handbook that says anything about consuming caffeine before an exam," Gage says matter-of-factly, like he really read the student handbook cover to cover, more than once. "Let's eat our lunch and then we can get started on reviewing everything for the retake. Sound good?"

I nod eagerly before tearing into the lunch he made me, which turns out to be better than anything I've ever made for myself. You'd think being raised in a restaurant, I would have picked up some cooking skills, but the ability for and interest in cooking passed over both me and my twin. I did, however, inherit the love of good food. It is an unfortunate combo, having an advanced and elevated palate but only having the will to learn how to boil water.

While we eat, I update Gage on my progress with finding donors for the auction, and as I name donation after donation, I can practically see the weight of the gala being lifted from his shoulders. We've both come into each other's lives at the perfect moment, saving each other from our accidental spirals.

And when he pulls out his whiteboard and starts writing equations, the *x*'s and *y*'s that were turning into mush on my papers last night suddenly make sense again. We go over all the questions I got wrong on the last exam one more time, and he gives me a five-question pop quiz that I pass with flying colors.

"You're going to nail it," Gage says with confidence, a confidence that is so strong it bleeds into me. I'm going to do well because Gage Magnussen made sure I would do well, and Gage is no failure. With him on my side, I will pass math. I'm sure of it.

I ride that high all the way until the last bell. After class, Ms. Metsker heads over to my table with a stapled exam in hand. The room is still clearing out of students, the distracting sounds of zippers and slamming lockers swirling around me as I watch her approach.

"Mr. Robertson let me know that your tutor logged in time every day this week, so you're cleared to do this retake," she says as she rests a hip on the desk across from me. "I'm so happy you took my offer seriously and put in the work. I've also noticed an improvement during class this week. You've really turned over a new leaf, Ms. Morales."

She says my last name in that irritating way English speakers do sometimes, all garbled up into one syllable. But I can't even be irritated at that, because her praise is genuine.

"Thank you for giving me the opportunity to do a retake," I say.

"I'm glad you took me up on it. I don't like to see any of my students fail."

I try not to flinch at the "f" word, the fear of flunking out of school still simmering in the back of my head despite all the positive strides I've taken this week. I think I might hold on to that fear until I shake hands with the principal and snatch my diploma from her hands on graduation day.

"Well, the room is cleared out. While I go and close the door, you can get set up," she tells me as she steps away to close the classroom door.

I clear off my desk and quickly reach into that zippered pouch for the chocolate-covered espresso beans. I crunch down on four simultaneously. While my fingers dig around in the compartment to reach for another handful, I feel something else. Curious, I open the pocket wider and find a very nice mechanical pencil. I pull it out to inspect.

It's got a retractable eraser, a grippy cushion, and has been topped off with lead. A final exam gift from Gage. With a small smile, I set the pencil down next to my graphing calculator. When

Ms. Metsker returns to my desk, I'm swallowing down the last of the coffee beans and ready to get this exam over with.

"You'll have thirty minutes to take the exam. Same exam rules apply here. I'll be at my desk doing some grading if you have any questions." She holds up the exam. "Ready?"

"Definitely."

CHAPTER THIRTEEN

I did it!"

When I turned in my retake to Ms. Metsker—with no time to spare because I spent all my extra minutes going back and double-checking, triple-checking all my work—I was struck by a euphoric sense of relief and giddiness.

Taking that exam had felt *good*. I knew what I was doing. There were a couple questions where I tripped up initially, got confused by the prompt and turned around by my own math, but instead of panicking, I took my time. If something was taking too long to click, I moved on, coming back to the question after I had given myself some time to reset.

Suddenly, my future stretched before me and it looked good. I could pass this class. I could graduate. I will have a future beyond these cinder block walls.

There was a slight dip in euphoria when I watched Ms. Metsker go through my exam and start grading. I watched her nervously as she went through answer by answer, making marks

I couldn't see and flipping through papers. It only took her a couple minutes to grade my exam, with a final tally and circled grade on the front page.

She held it up with a big, bright smile, showing off the B-minus marked at the top.

I had to run and tell Gage immediately. He needed to know that his hard work had paid off.

And I know exactly where Gage would be spending his Friday afternoon. There is a speech-and-debate tournament tomorrow, and he has practice with the team in Mr. Shah's classroom. I could text him, or leave him a voice note, but with him so close by, I needed to just run and tell him.

So, without preamble, I threw myself through Mr. Shah's classroom doors and barreled toward Gage.

"I did it!" I cry out again, practically launching myself into his arms. Noah, who is standing next to him with a pen shoved into his mouth, jumps at my sudden arrival and bites down hard on the pen with a yelp.

Gage, frozen in what must be a mix of surprise and confusion, still manages to wrap his arms around me and returns my hug without skipping a beat.

"You already got your grade back?" he whispers in my ear, his breath brushing across my skin and making my baby hairs dance. The deep timbre of his voice vibrates across my skin and freezes me in place. I hadn't told anyone I was retaking an exam, and he was making sure that secret is kept. Meanwhile, I had just catapulted myself into his arms in front of all his friends and he was taking it in stride.

"B-minus," I whisper against his neck in a quiet rush. Gage's arms squeeze me tight in response, and I smile against the collar of his shirt. "I'm sorry for interrupting," I say loudly, for everyone to hear, and begin peeling myself from Gage. A rush of cold air fills the space between us, and it serves as enough of a shock to end my euphoric episode altogether.

"I, uh," I start, trying to come up with a reasonable excuse for my dramatic entrance, "got a really great donation in for the auction!" Neither truth nor a lie, just a spin on a fact. Cece at Olympic Wellness had agreed to offer two facial packages for the auction this morning.

Noah is still coughing after nearly choking on his pen, and Rose is watching me with a knowing expression. It seems like the club meeting hasn't quite started, because some of the members are lounged about the room and one seems to be making hot tea with a kettle they must have brought from home.

"We haven't started yet," Gage assures me. "Want to step out for a second?"

"Yeah," I say with a nod.

With a guiding hand on my shoulder, Gage leads me out of Mr. Shah's classroom and into the empty hallway.

"You see? You knew what you were doing after all," he says once we're a few feet away from the classroom door. He has his arms crossed and a pleased expression on his face.

"I genuinely thought that I could never catch up with this class. That even with tutoring it would be an uphill battle to pass."

"I already told you, you can do this stuff. You just had a rough start, and now that we've gone back over stuff from the beginning of the year, you're back on track."

"I don't want to get too excited," I say carefully. "I still have to get a good grade on my midterm, but this is a pretty good start." I take a deep breath and release it, letting all the stress of the last week go with it. "I couldn't have done it without you, Gage."

The corner of Gage's mouth kicks up, a pleased look on his face.

"I, um, made you something. As a thank-you," I tell him, turning to dig around in my backpack so he can't see the embarrassing flush on my cheeks.

During my art period today, I had taken the time to make Gage a Victorian-style letter. It's an intricately folded piece of paper, and with every step of the unfolding process, it reveals a new art composition. Using markers, I filled the paper edge to edge with illustrations, from dancing donuts to crabs, with the final illustration featuring a cartoon Gage being crowned as the Best Guy Ever. It's hardly enough of a thank-you for someone who is single-handedly saving my future from falling into a black hole. But at least it's something.

Once I find the letter in my bag, I shove it into the empty space between us. He takes it gently and takes his time inspecting it. "It's a Victorian puzzle letter," I explain as he fingers the edge of a fold. "I thought you'd appreciate the challenge."

"It's beautiful," he says, sounding a little distracted as he tries to figure out how to pry the thing open. "Is that Gordo there in the corner?" He points at the little anthropomorphic burrito gesturing toward the bit of paper that unlocks the first fold. "This is incredible, Valeria. These drawings are so tiny and detailed."

I'm grateful I'm not actually a redhead (the hair dye stains on our bathroom floor are irrefutable proof I'm not), because I'm sure I would be bright red right now after hearing that sincere compliment from Gage.

"Oh," I say, trying to brush off the swirl of surprise and delight the words have brought up. "Those are just little doodles. Nothing special."

"Come on, Valeria," Gage says, glancing up at me with a surprisingly stern look on his face. "Your art is fantastic."

"Okay, enough of this," I say, trying to hide how flustered I am by pushing his hands away. "You know, it's a bit rude to open a gift in front of the person who gave it to you. Look at that once you're home," I tell him.

Gage follows my orders with that knowing smile of his and gladly changes the subject.

"How do you plan on celebrating your results?" he asks.

"I hadn't even considered celebrating," I admit. "I was going to head downtown and talk to some businesses. I have the paperwork ready for donors to sign. I figured if I failed, working on the auction would take my mind off things."

"And if you passed?" Gage prods.

"I hadn't thought that far," I admit. "Work on the gala stuff anyway? If I'm actually on my way to graduating now and want to apply to college, I'm sure working on this thing will sweeten up my application." Back at the flower shop, Michelle had thought this whole thing was a bid to spruce up my college applications, and maybe now it could be.

"How practical and boring," Gage says. "I'm shocked."

"Maybe you're rubbing off on me," I joke, giving him a playful shove with my elbow.

Gage's eyes crinkle, and he looks a little devious, some thought passing through his mind, but before he can say anything, his eyes jump to the classroom door.

It pops open and Rose steps out.

"Sorry, Gage, but are you going to be much longer?" Rose asks, and she looks guilty as she says it. She clearly didn't want to interrupt our conversation. "I can get things started if you need some time?"

"Go," I tell Gage quickly, giving him a gentle push on his shoulder. "I've taken up enough of your time, go play-fight with your friends."

"That's a terrible way to describe Debate Club," Gage admonishes me.

"If you say so."

Gage huffs out a laugh and surprises me by closing in a step and wrapping his arms around me. Now I'm the one caught in a surprise hug, but I don't hesitate. I wrap my arms around his middle and give him a tight squeeze.

"I'm really proud of you," he says. He leans back to look down at me with one of his goofy smiles, the kind that looks a little sleepy and relaxed. Before I can think of anything to say, he's pulling away and jogging back to the classroom.

I press myself against the brick wall to try to settle myself, my nerves still jittery after the exam. I feel warm and fluttery, some kind of strange side effect of scholarly excellence that I have never experienced.

But now that Gage has fulfilled part of his end of this deal, I have to go do my part. I have an inbox full of emails from local businesses and contracts to deliver this afternoon. Two deep breaths and then I'm pushing myself off the wall and heading out to my car. All the usual after-school traffic has thinned out, and I manage to get to downtown in record time, parking in my spot behind the bakery.

I'm determined to do this charity auction stuff right, so I've put together an entire binder filled with all my relevant paperwork so I can look like I know what I'm doing. Is half of the binder filled with blank paper to fill it out and make it look more stately? Yes, and it does leave quite the stately impression.

I stop by the bakery first, dipping into the fridge in the back and taking out some of our prepackaged guava lemonades. These are another recent addition to the menu, thanks to Ana Maria, and so far a crowd favorite. And I think they might just be the perfect thing to help me grease the wheels about town.

Olympic Wellness is first on my list, where I find the owner, Cece, dusting the shelves on her front window, our eyes making contact between boxes of serums and a bouquet of dried flowers. She rushes to unlock the door and welcomes me into her oasis.

Most people refer to this place simply as "the spa," and for good reason. As soon as I walk in, the sound of calming music washes over me, the room smelling of salt and lavender and eucalyptus. There are gauzy curtains and dried florals and a stick of incense burning in the corner.

"Valeria!" Cece says, wrapping me in a warm hug as soon as I step foot through the door. She looks exactly as you might expect: wavy strawberry blond hair that cascades down her back, a wardrobe clearly stolen from Stevie Nicks, and Birkenstocks.

"I brought you some lemonade," I tell her, pulling back and

taking one out from my tote bag. “I know it’s cooling off outside, but it’s still a nice treat.”

“Oh, you’re so thoughtful, thank you!” Cece says, taking the lemonade with both hands and setting it down on her counter.

“I want to thank you again for your generous donation to the auction,” I tell her, pulling out my binder and taking out her contract. “Since the value of your donation is over five hundred dollars, we can guarantee you special placement in the program and feature your logo and business name on other promotional materials.”

“Wonderful! You know,” Cece says, taking the contract, “the Magnussens have never reached out to me before about participating in the auction. I’m not sure if it’s because of my witchcraft or because they don’t take skin care seriously, but I’m so happy to be supporting a good cause. They’re lucky to have you.”

I wish Gage were here to help me parse through *that* response. I can’t wait to tell him about this later.

“You know,” she says again, filling out the contract as she talks, “people think because it’s cloudy here all the time that they can’t get sun damage, but they’re wrong! Oh, Valeria.” She looks up from the papers. “I have a new sunscreen that just came in, it’s excellent. You should take a sample.” She turns her attention back to the paperwork. “Is that everything?” she asks, flipping through the papers one more time before passing them off to me. I give them a quick look-through before smiling up at her.

“Yep, we’re good,” I assure her. “I’ll follow up via email and make sure you get final approval on ad placement for the program. And please reach out if you have any questions or concerns.”

"Oh, and—" she says, reaching behind the counter to fetch a small box. "Here's that sample I promised. Keep it in your bag and make sure to reapply throughout the day," she instructs. "And take one of these," she says, reaching behind the counter and pulling out a container of lip balm. "It has SPF, too," she assures me, and I'm starting to worry that if I stay here any longer, she's going to pull out a parasol from behind the counter and try to give it to me.

"Thank you so much, Cece," I say, backing away before she can foist more sun protection on me. "I'll be in touch!"

I back out of Cece's shop, the chimes over the door tinkling as I head down the street. Two blocks away from Olympic Wellness is the bike shop I've been trying to get a hold of this whole week to no avail. I figure an in-person visit, with lemonade, is due.

As a famously not-outdoorsy family—due in part to one disastrous camping trip when Adrian and I were five where Mom fell in a river and broke her ankle, Adrian woke up screaming because a raccoon was clawing at his tent, and everyone got poison oak—we've never been inside the bike shop, and I'm not too familiar with the owner.

When I step into the shop, the calm serenity that befell me at Olympic Wellness is torn to shreds. The speakers inside blare metal music, and the smell of rubber and dirt assaults my senses. I'm on edge as soon as I walk in, the bikes and tires hanging from the ceiling as either decor or surplus stock making me anxious about any sudden earthquakes.

The owner, Darren, isn't behind the counter or anywhere in the front of the shop. I'm about to back out, putting this on the list for later, when I hear a familiar laugh coming from the direction of the workshop. It stops me in my tracks and I listen, trying to place it. I know I've heard it before, and something about it has my hairs standing on end.

I slip through the tight aisles toward the back, where the door to the workshop is wide open, and the two people chatting are in full view.

Ginger is sitting on the edge of a table, ankles crossed and head thrown back in a laugh, blond hair tumbling in artful waves over her shoulder. She looks as pretty as a picture, and I'm not the only one who thinks so. Across from her is Ian, the owner's son, squatting down on the floor where he is working on a bike, wrench in hand but focus totally on Ginger. Ian is two years younger than us, tall as a string bean with sharp cheekbones and a grown-out mullet. Dark grease stains cover his pale face, but it does little to hide the rosy blush to his cheeks.

"I'm so glad you get it," Ginger says. "It's for his own good, really."

My skin prickles at her words, and even though I haven't overheard anything else, I *know* this is about Gage. Ginger has been up to something here, because she has no other reason to be at this shop flirting with a sophomore.

"Trying to save the planet?" I call out from the doorway. My voice surprises Ian enough to make him fumble the wrench, the sound of it clanging against the concrete, loud and ringing. But Ginger doesn't bat a lash; her eyes just track up toward me with a somewhat feral gleam.

"Excuse me?" she says slowly, deliberately.

"I mean, why else would you be in the bike shop if not to trade in your car for the more eco-friendly option?"

"I, uh," Ian cuts in, saving Ginger from answering as he stumbles up from the floor. "I better get back to the front," he says. I step into the workshop to let him pass, then turn to Ginger.

"What?" she says, not looking even a little cowed.

"Why are you here, Ginger?" I ask.

Ginger pushes off the ledge of the table and wipes the seat of her pants before picking her bag up from the ground.

"That binder's cute," she says in the most patronizing way possible. "You know, you don't have to play so hard at being smart. I'm sure Gage has other reasons for liking you."

Whatever confidence I still felt after passing my exam, after having Cece sign the paperwork, is drained away immediately by Ginger's words. I try not to show it, to keep my head up and spine straight, but her words are like a blow to the solar plexus. I can't even come up with a pithy comeback before she's breezing past me and out of the bike shop.

I take a few seconds in the workshop alone, taking deep breaths to calm myself so I don't send my *cute binder* hurling at one of the bikes.

When I finally make it back out to the shop, Ian is sitting behind the counter playing a game on his phone.

"Hey, Ian," I say, dropping my binder on the counter. "I've been trying to get a hold of your dad this week but haven't heard anything."

"He's out of town," Ian says without looking up.

"Do you know when he'll be back?" I ask, and Ian answers with a shrug.

"Is there a manager I can talk to in the meantime? I want to ask about the Magnussen charity auction. I know the shop donated some bike rentals last year."

"Oh, that?" Ian says, still not looking up. "We won't be donating this year."

"Really?" I say, getting a little frustrated. "And why would that be?"

He just shrugs again.

"Does it have anything to do with whatever Ginger was here talking to you about?" I push. The tips of his ears grow bright pink, but he doesn't respond.

"Did she talk you into something?" I ask, now concerned that she might be going around to businesses and trying to sabotage me.

The bell above the door dings as a middle-aged man pushes his bike into the store. Ian jumps off his seat in record time and rushes to help the customer.

"Good afternoon!" he calls out eagerly, startling the man with his exuberance.

It's clear I'm not getting anything else out of Ian, so I push past him and out the door. If Ginger is trying to undermine me, I just need to work faster and harder to get ahead of her.

CHAPTER FOURTEEN

All night and into the next day, I'm still riding that post-exam high despite Ginger's best attempts to bring me down. Tia Isa's conversation at dinner doesn't irritate me, Adrian's glib comments don't bait me into an argument, and waking up early for an eight-hour shift at the bakery doesn't faze me.

I'm behind the counter with Emma, a twenty-something who landed in Port Murphy after graduating college because she "wanted to be close to the hiking trails" and who always smells like camphor. She's white with blond hair that has highlights from being in the sun and not the salon, a septum piercing that she flips up while she works, and a minor in Spanish, so she's halfway decent at pronouncing everything.

"It looks like things are slowing down a bit," I tell her after ringing up a customer. "I'm going to go take my break."

Emma just nods and continues wiping down the counter. I head toward the back, where Ana Maria is working in the kitchen alongside our usual staff. She typically comes in on the weekends to work with my dad on seasonal menu items, but he's been tied up at the new location, working with contractors over some "plomería de mierda" that's resulted in two busted water pipes.

I squeeze past our line cooks toward where Ana Maria has her station set up.

"What do you have up your sleeves this time?" I ask her as I fill up a deli container at the sink.

"I've given in to the masses," Ana tells me without looking up from the caramel she's babying at the burner. "Calabaza Spice."

"What!" I cry out in delight. "Be still my beating heart, you're turning pumpkin spice Cuban?"

"Well, the doughnuts already have pumpkin in the dough," Ana says. "And anise, while not technically in pumpkin spice, is a warming spice. So it makes sense to do it. But I will have you know I'm doing it against my will. Your dad made me."

I laugh at how despondent she sounds over the idea of making a pumpkin spice flavor for her doughnuts. I think it actually sounds really good, so I step in closer to inspect what she's made so far.

"Are these the doughnuts in question?" I ask, pointing at a tray full of deep brown figure-eight donuts covered in spiced sugar. Before she can answer, I've pried one off the tray and taken a bite out of it. "Oh my God," I say through a mouthful of the most delicious doughnut I've ever had. "Ana."

She finally looks up from her caramel to stare at me, terrified by my reaction.

"What is it? Are they terrible?" she wails in panic.

"Ana," I say again, taking a moment to swallow before I continue, "this might be the best thing you've ever made."

"Really?" Her expression wobbles like she might break into tears. "I wasn't sure if the flavor was coming through enough."

"These are perfect," I assure her. "Has my dad tried these? He's going to flip, they're so good!"

"Not yet, but he is hoping to sell some at the fall festival on Monday. I know—" Her eyes widen and her attention turns back to the pot. "Fuck, the caramel!" She pulls the pot off the burner and quickly grabs a whisk before adding an entire stick of butter. It hisses and spits as she stirs the butter in.

"Val!" Emma calls from the front, using a nickname literally no one uses except for her. "Someone is asking for you out front!"

That's strange. No one ever comes to look for me at work. There was a brief period when an older guy kept asking for me whenever he came by the shop, bringing me gifts and knickknacks that I felt very uncomfortable getting. He happened to ask for me one day when my dad was working front of house, and since I wasn't there that day, I'll never know exactly what happened, but we haven't seen him around the shop since.

So I really have no idea who to expect.

"I'm having another one," I tell Ana, snatching a doughnut before heading back to the front. When I push through the revolving door, spiced sugar dusted on my lips, I'm surprised to find Gage sitting on a counter stool at the table against the front window. He doesn't see me at first, his attention on something outside while his fingers drum mindlessly across the tabletop.

He must have come here directly after his speech-and-debate tournament because he's in a perfectly crisp suit. Gage is usually wearing what could generously be called nerdy chic. It's never so unfashionable or dated that he looks like some kind of stock character, but it's also decidedly different from what the rest of the guys in our grade wear. You'll never catch him in a band tee or ironic jorts, but he also isn't wearing sweater vests or patterned bow ties.

Gage in a suit is something altogether different. This is like the grown-up version of his everyday khakis and button-up plaids, a vision into the future where he follows in his parents' footsteps and works at some fancy law firm in Seattle. The suit isn't any off-the-rack number, either. The sleeves are hemmed to the perfect length, the shoulders fit smoothly across his wide back, and there are no imperfect bunches or bulging seams.

I'm still staring at him, appreciating the subtle plaid pattern to his suit paired with a vertical-striped shirt—who knew he would be a pattern mixer?—when his attention turns toward me and he catches me mid-ogle.

"Hey!" he says with a smile, either ignoring or not noticing the fact that I've just been starting at him silently for thirty seconds with sugar dusted all over my face. I quickly wipe off my lips and walk up to the counter. "Sorry to stop by without notice, but do you have a minute to talk?"

Despite his pleasant expression, a stone drops in my stomach at his words. Does he have to back out of our deal? He did help me pass my retake exam, after all. Is he getting back together with Ginger? Did someone find out about the *fake* part of our relationship?

"Sure," I say, mustering up my best fake smile. "I was already on break anyway. Come on back," I say, opening the small swing door to let him in behind the counter.

"Is this legal?" he asks as he steps up to the counter. "I've never been in the back of a restaurant before. Don't you have to be an employee or wear a hairnet or something?"

"You'll be fine," I promise. "We'll just step into my dad's office."

Once he's behind the counter, I lead him through the kitchen toward the office. When Ana Maria looks up and spots Gage, she raises her eyebrows at me suggestively. Before she can say anything, I push Gage through the office door and close it behind us.

The Morales Bakery office is just a glorified closet. It has shelves with boxes that are filled with paperwork and receipts and newspaper clippings. In the middle of the room is the desk, outfitted with a work computer and one of those rubber band bouncy balls. There are two chairs in the room, one behind the desk and one in front of it, which is where I lead Gage and prompt him to sit down.

I take the seat behind the desk and immediately feel like I'm about to interview him.

How would you rate my performance as a fake girlfriend?

Do you think I can actually pass Algebra II?

Why do you look so good in a suit? It's not right.

"Sorry for the drop-in," he apologizes again. I wave his concern away.

"It's totally fine. You're welcome to drop in whenever. As my fake boyfriend, you are guaranteed free food from the bakery. It's one of the perks." I gesture toward the kitchen with my thumb. "You should grab one of the doughnuts Ana Maria is working on before you head out."

"I'll remember that," he says. He looks down at his lap and fiddles with the hem of his jacket.

An awkward silence stretches between us, Gage staring down and me watching him avoid eye contact. This is probably the first time since I've started hanging out with Gage that we've had a sudden lapse of uncomfortable silence between us, and I'm not sure what to do. I definitely don't want to push him, but I also don't want to sit in this dim office with him in awkward quiet.

"How'd the tournament go?" I ask, trying to pry him back into conversation. "Tens across the board? Blue ribbons?"

"Seventy-five bucks and a piece of paper with my last name spelled wrong," he says. "But Port Murphy High stole the show. Rose made an impassioned plea for why human cloning should be legal, and I had to defend zoos."

"Congratulations, I think?"

"Well, the tournament is part of the reason why I'm here," Gage says. "My parents were there."

He leaves it at that, like I should know what that means. We stare at each other across the desk, and he scrunches up his face before continuing.

"They happened to hear from someone that we're dating, which turned into a whole thing when I brought up that you're helping me with the auction," he says. I frown, not sure why his parents would be upset that he was getting help. "They were hoping you could come to dinner tonight."

Oh. I understand now. His parents don't trust me, probably don't think that I have the skills necessary to help Gage with something like this. Underachiever Valeria can't be expected to do anything as good as her twin. I forgot how much it hurt when things like this happen. When I push to do something outside my comfort zone, something new and untested, and before I start I'm already a step behind because no one believes in me.

"To . . . what? Vet my donation-getting skills? Do I need to bring a résumé? Perhaps a cover letter?" I say, and I can't manage to keep the bite out of my tone.

"I know, I know," he says, running his hands through his hair in frustration, leaving it standing up on end. "I'm sorry. They're more concerned about the fact that they don't know you, not that you don't know what you're doing, I promise. I told them about the donations you've gotten and the connections you have. But they don't feel comfortable having a stranger work on this."

Which is why they had been pushing him to get Ginger to help. As irritated as I am by his parents, I know that this is something I have to do as part of our deal. And does it really matter what his parents think of me if I'm just here to get a tutor?

"No, it's fine, I get it," I say, waving him off. "I get off work at three, and I don't have any plans tonight, so it shouldn't be a problem." I take a deep breath and try to push past the bubbling irritation inside me. When I let that kind of resentment simmer, I tend to get in worse trouble. "I'll put on my most trustworthy outfit and charming face." Although it won't look as nice as his tailored suit. "Wait, there isn't some kind of dress code for dinner, is there? Like closed-toed shoes only and skirts three inches below the knee?"

"Do you think my family is part of British royalty?" he says with a laugh.

"I don't know! Your parents throw an annual gala!"

"I assure you, dinner at my house is probably no different than dinner at yours."

But that doesn't reassure me at all.

CHAPTER FIFTEEN

Gage offered to pick me up for dinner, which I eagerly agreed to because the rattling sound of my car pulling up the Magnussens' driveway is not the first impression I want to make with my fake boyfriend's parents.

When I get home, I rush upstairs to start getting ready. I tear through my closet, trying to find my best old-money outfit. My everyday clothes look like something a seven-year-old boy might wear, oversized shirts in bright colors and baggy shorts. But buried deep in the closet is what I like to call my Clothes Graveyard.

These are the things my mom bought me and forced me to wear. Frilly dresses, pleated miniskirts, satin fabrics, and pops of lace. And bows. So many bows. None of these things appealed to me, but I had been her little doll growing up. She loved putting me in matching sets as a baby, complete with coordinating bow.

The thing about most dolls, though, is that they don't go through puberty. They don't tear bows out of their hair or jump in the mud and destroy a dress. I don't think my mom appreciated that about this particular doll.

I don't know why I've kept these for so long. I could have donated them or thrown them straight in the trash. But thankfully, for this one night, I haven't. One of these outfits would work just fine for dinner at the Magnussens'.

I pick a beige dress with a tiny red rose pattern and pair it with a bright red crocheted cardigan. The sweater won't keep me dry in the spitting rain that's been going since this morning, but it'll make me look like I'm a put-together kind of person. And it will help to disguise how tight the bodice of the dress is across my chest.

I'm not exactly the same size I was freshman year of high school, having gained a few inches both vertically and horizontally. But the back panel of the bodice is stretchy, with just enough give for me to squeeze in. It also has enough give for my boobs to squeeze *out* in a Regency romance–esque display of cleavage. Hence, the cardigan.

I dig through my jewelry box, full of random things like three of my baby teeth and a rock my abuelo insisted was from his home in Cuba, and pull out a simple gold chain. I don't bother changing my earrings, keeping in the same small gold hoops I've had since I was little.

Then I tidy up my binder and update the spreadsheet. It's color-coded and has rows for value of the donation, suggested starting bid, and all the contact information for the businesses. I print out the spreadsheet and tuck it into a folder to give to the Magnussens. If this *is* an interview to prove I'm the girl for the job, I want to be prepared.

Gage texts me when he's turning into my neighborhood, and I double-check myself in the mirror before running downstairs.

In the dining room, Papi and Tia Isa are sitting at the table, going over a stack of documents. When they spot me on the staircase, they brush the papers aside and look up at me in unison.

"No corras por las escalaras, Vale," Papi admonishes me. "You'll fall and break your leg one of these days."

"Don't worry, Pedro, I don't think any of your kids inherited your clumsiness," Tia Isa says affectionately. Papi is terribly clumsy, which has never been a good quality for someone who works in a kitchen. "We ordered pizza, it should be here soon."

"I'm actually going to a friend's house for dinner tonight," I tell them.

"Oh, that's nice," Dad says, and there's a sense of relief in his tone that tells me he's noticed how checked out I've been this year. Which is weird, because I feel like I've hardly seen my dad at all since school started. "Text me when you're heading home, okay, mijita? And remember you offered to help out with festival prep and everything."

Dad was thrilled when I offered to help at the Fall Festival booth. Students have the day off from school and free entry to the festival this Monday, which means that neither Adrian and I nor the other teenage employees of the shop are ever willing to help that day. But being the newly friendless loser that I am, I'd promised last month to lend a hand.

"Lo recuerdo," I say as I step into the dining room to give each of them a kiss on the cheek in goodbye. As I lean in to Tia Isa, I don't miss the covert move she does with her forearm to disguise the stack of papers under the sleeve of her sweater. As if

I would be curious about their business when I have so much of my own to worry about.

Walking this time instead of running, to appease my dad, I head out the front door down to the driveway and hide under the eaves of the roof to stay dry while I wait. After a couple seconds, I hear a car turn down our street, and just as soon headlights are blinding me as Gage pulls up into the driveway.

He has a new ornament dangling from his rearview mirror, an octopus holding a microphone in one tentacle and a guitar in the other. Part of me wants to ask him about this aquatic interest of his plastered all over his Subaru, but part of me prefers to keep it a mystery. That way, I can make up my own stories about him in my head, like imagining that an octopus documentary is his favorite movie. Or that he's a merman.

I make a run for his passenger side, holding my arm above my head to try to ward off as much rain as possible. Pulling open the door, I slide into the seat, seat warmers already on, and close the door.

"Hey," I greet Gage as I toss my purse down by my feet and pull on my seat belt. "Thanks for the ride."

"Anytime," he says.

Once I'm settled in my seat, I look up at him, pulling a wet strand of hair out of my face. He's no longer in the tailored suit from this afternoon and is back in his usual uniform. Today it's a pair of black slacks and a chunky knit sweater with a collared shirt underneath. It's not quite casual and not quite dressed up, which means I think I nailed the dress code.

"You look really nice," he says. "The royal family would approve."

A *honk* of unexpected laughter escapes me at his joke. It's loud and sharp and takes us both by surprise. The honk turns into a rolling laughter that pulls at my abs and makes my eyes tear up a little bit. Gage is laughing, too, bigger and louder than I've ever seen him laugh before. We go on like this for a minute, our laughs pushing each other on and on until finally I cry out.

"Stop!" I say between laughs. "I can't take this anymore, my abs are killing me!"

"I've never heard someone make that sound before," he says, *still* laughing.

"No!" I cry out, grabbing on to his shoulder and giving him a couple shakes. "You have to stop laughing or else I will make that sound again!"

"But I *want* to hear it again," he argues.

I throw myself despondently against the passenger door, and Gage's laughter finally fades out.

"Okay, okay, I promise I'll stop," he says, pulling on my arm to get me to sit up again. "I think we both needed that."

"No kidding," I agree. "You made me so nervous for this dinner with the way you came into the shop today."

"I'm sorry, I was projecting," he says, backing out of the driveway. "To be honest, I've been so stressed out, between classes and Debate Team stuff and this gala, and my parents don't help, with their constant check-ins." The words come tumbling out of him all at once, as if that one tiny confession has burst open the floodgates. "I'm taking AP classes, dual enrollment college courses, competing with the Debate Club, running the silent auction, and trying to squeeze my way back to valedictorian, and the moment I start to feel the strain of all that work and try to take a break, they start acting like I'm slacking off. That's why I'm not doing any of the Math Club stuff this year," he explains.

"Because being in the Math Club is . . . slacking off?" I say, failing to understand.

"In their eyes, yes. It's not in line with my career plan—or rather, *their* career plan for me. Math Club is 'wasted energy,' as my dad called it last year. Never mind that it's the one club I genuinely loved being in, something I found on my own and—" He cuts himself off, taking a breath before continuing. "The point is, whenever they get on my case about something, I get really stressed. I'm sorry I'm putting all that on you for tonight."

"Nah, don't worry about it. We got this," I lie. Clearly Gage needed to get all that off his chest, but it's only made me more anxious. Because I'm not in the National Honor Society like Ginger, or taking a million AP classes like Ginger, or paving a path to a brilliant future like Ginger. Instead, I'm just struggling to finish high school with only a dim vision of what my future could be.

And is that the kind of person they would trust to help with their gala? I hold on tighter to my binder, hoping that proof on paper will be better than whatever proof I personally lack.

"They are looking forward to meeting you," he goes on. "Morales Bakery has to be their favorite restaurant in town."

"Wow, that's high praise," I say, trying to brush off my unease. "Except for the lime thing, right? Your mom is strictly a lemon-in-her-water kind of person?"

"She says limes are bitter," he says, and hearing that, I'm suddenly nervous about what the actual food part of this dinner might entail. I've been spoiled at home lately with Tia

Isa's delicious meals—I mentally prepare myself to eat and compliment bland white food.

Moving the conversation away from his parents, Gage tells me about his debate tournament that day and Noah's superstitious competition prep. He takes the back roads to his house, leading us through parts of town I've never seen. We turn down a road that cuts through two empty fields that once had cattle, but I can tell he's heading toward the water, exactly where I expected him to live.

As I'd guessed, Gage lives in one of those modern monstrosities, all gray angular shapes and pops of warm wood to give the otherwise lifeless facade some vibrancy. It has a retaining wall around the property with cascading plants, a wisteria vine curling around a trellis above the garage doors, and big, wide, open windows.

Gage pulls into the driveway and presses the button on a garage door opener. His garage seems to be fully functional, with space for three cars and your regular garage storage.

Now that I'm seeing the house and its neatly organized garage and the very fancy electric car parked next to Gage's, the panic begins to creep back up.

I clutch my binder to my chest and open the passenger door. Gage jogs around the front of his car to meet me on my side as I get out. He presses his hand to the small of my back as he leads me into the house.

"Remember, this is more about me than it is about you," Gage whispers, his nose brushing the hairs at my temples. "I'm not worried about you anyway, because you're very charming when you want to be," he tells me.

"I am?" I say in surprise.

"When you *want* to be," he repeats. "As far as I can tell, you *rarely* want to be, but when you turn it on, you really turn it on." I'm saved from coming up with a response because he opens the door into the house and we nearly run into Mrs. Magnussen.

She's a petite blond woman with a long face and Gage's same milky complexion. Her hair is styled in a sleek, long bob, and she's wearing a flowy white blouse with striped slacks. She looks just as put together as she always does, with minimal makeup and expensive bracelets on her arm.

"Oh, Gage! You're back sooner than I thought," she says as she hands him the giant paper bag she had been holding with the Locicero's logo stamped on the side. "Would you mind throwing that in the recycling? I'll help your friend in. It's so lovely to see you, Valeria."

Gage's hand leaves the small of my back, his sudden absence sending a shiver down my spine. Mrs. Magnussen smiles at me with her perfect teeth and gestures for me to step into the house.

"Thanks for having me, Mrs. Magnussen." When I'm with family or family friends, the usual greeting is a kiss on the cheek. It's almost second nature for me at this point to greet most adults by pressing my cheek to theirs with a loud smack of my lips. For a second I stumble, my body confused from the panic-laden drive here, and I step in toward Mrs. Magnussen. But then the astringent smell of her expensive perfume hits my nose and I realize that a kiss on the cheek is probably not how I should greet her.

My stumble results in me tripping over the small step out of the garage, my binder flying out of my hands and fluttering to the ground.

"Oh!" Gage's mom cries out as I grab on to the doorway to right myself. "Oh, honey, did you trip?" she says in surprise, and I feel the heat climb up the back of my neck. Somewhere behind me, the recycling lid slams shut. Her eyes move to the spilled papers on the floor in front of me, and I quickly kneel to gather it back up.

"Didn't see that step," I say as I shove my papers back in. Off to a great start! Why am I so jittery? Gage offers me a hand and helps me stand back up. He places that guiding hand on my lower back again and leads us out of the utility room and into the kitchen.

"Make yourself at home," Mrs. Magnussen says breezily as she guides us from the kitchen into the open-concept living room. "I have dinner heating up right now, and we'll be ready to eat in a few." I can already smell the familiar oregano-and-basil scent of Locicero's signature red sauce. On the counter a salad has been moved from the to-go container into a wooden bowl that looks hand carved and expensive. There's an open bottle of red wine next to a glass that Mrs. Magnussen picks up.

I'm not sure what making myself at home here would entail, but considering Gage is ramrod straight next to me as we stand next to the kitchen island, I assume I'm already playing the part.

"Where's Dad?" Gage asks.

"Finishing up a call," his mom says, waving in the direction of what I assume is the office or grand library or whatever it is rich people have in their houses.

"Can I help set the table?" I ask, eager to have something to do other than stand here.

"No, honey, thank you," Mrs. Magnussen says. "What are those papers you brought?" she asks, eyeing the binder I have in a death grip.

"Oh," I say, thumbing my finger across the edge of the papers, "Gage said you'd want to talk about the auction tonight, so I brought some documentation of our progress so far."

"Well, that's something," Mrs. Magnussen says with that same perfect smile. "Working on this charity auction really is like a second job. The time Ginger and Gage spent on this the last few years really is astronomical! But they really got it down to a science last year."

"I wouldn't say that," Gage cuts in.

"I'm just saying it's a lot of work! And it's not the best to bring in someone new at this point."

Gage's mom is talking about this charity auction like it's some high-level client at her law firm that needs the Cadillac treatment.

"Mom—" Gage says, so sternly and so quickly that I jump in surprise.

"Smells great in here!" Mr. Magnussen calls out as he enters the kitchen, breaking the tension bubble. For now. "That call left me *starving*. Let's get this show on the road." Then he catches sight of me, and his brows jump up like he wasn't expecting me there. "Oh, welcome!"

"Valeria," Gage supplies. His dad shoots him a quick glare before turning his business smile back on me.

"Of course, from Morales Bakery. Welcome, Valeria. Why

don't you grab that salad and we'll all make our way to the dining room?"

Mrs. Magnussen pulls the take-and-bake lasagna out of the oven, the top level of bubbling cheese blistered and golden. At least I don't have to worry about the food being bad. Unfortunately, I still have to worry about everything else.

CHAPTER SIXTEEN

So, what are your plans?" Mr. Magnussen asks as he serves himself some salad. The question is open-ended, but the way he says it, I know what he means. What are your post-graduation plans? What are your higher education plans? What are your career plans? How does *your* future compare to that of my sparkling son's?

We're seated in the dining room, which is just as sterile and beige as the rest of the house. There are no personal touches in the room, or in any of the house that I've seen so far. Just beige and more beige and one indoor olive tree that has seen better days.

The table has a glass top, so I can't even restlessly jiggle my leg without being noticed. There's a chandelier that looks like a diagram of something out of the periodic table and dining chairs that are more aesthetic than they are comfortable. Mr. and Mrs. Magnussen are sitting on either end of the long table, perched like the king and queen of the home.

"I'm not sure," I say, thinking that it's likely the easiest answer I can come up with that isn't a lie. I can't set my sights to postgraduation until I make sure that *graduation* is actually happening.

"Valeria is an amazing artist," Gage cuts in. "I was going to ask her to help design the signage for the gala. She does all the graphic design work for the bakery."

"See, now, that's an excellent idea," his mom says, and I jerk in surprise. As polite as she's been since I've been here, she hasn't exactly been warm or positive. "That would be a much more reasonable use of Valeria's time. Why don't you have her just do that and bring Ginger back in for the auction?"

And there's the kicker. I look over at Gage in mild panic. I'm supposed to be making his life easier, a shield from being put in proximity with Ginger while he's still hurting. But it feels like I've made things worse. It was bad enough he didn't want Ginger involved, but bringing in someone like me to help? It seems to have only agitated his parents more.

"Mom, I already—"

"You know, Mrs. Davis was asking about Ginger helping out with the gala," Mr. Magnussen adds. "Ginger already knows that auction backward and forward. I know things ended badly between you two last year—"

"They didn't just 'end badly,' Dad," Gage snaps. "She cheated on me."

I shove a bite of lasagna into my mouth, wishing I could melt into the floor and escape.

"Don't use that tone on your father," Mrs. Magnussen

quickly defends her husband. "You need to stop letting your feelings get the better of you, Gage."

Silence stretches across the table for a moment, the clatter and scrape of our silverware the only sound in the room. I suddenly miss my family in a profound way I'm not sure I've felt before. I would much rather be at our scratched-up dining table, with the well-worn rug bursting with colors and the family pictures on the credenza, dealing with Adrian's passive-aggressive attitude or Tia Isa's constant meddling, than *this*. Even with our problems, at least the emotion, the love, is still there. At least it's *allowed*.

"Ginger will *not* be helping with the auction," Gage says in an even tone. "Because Valeria has already been helping me. If you actually gave her a chance or looked at what she has booked so far, you'd see she's been handling it. And I would also ask that you respect the fact that I am dating *her*, not Ginger. So please stop trying to get me to work with Ginger, or do anything with Ginger."

Mrs. Magnussen heaves a sigh, like Gage is being overly dramatic. His dad just keeps eating lasagna like nothing weird is happening.

"Fine," his mom says as she spears some lettuce on her fork. "Ginger is going to be so sad to miss out on the auction this year, though."

I can practically hear Gage grinding his teeth across the table.

"We can find something else for her, dear," Mr. Magnussen says.

I've only taken a few bites of my dinner, but my appetite has left me and I can't bear to eat more. I push the salad around my plate for a solid minute while Mr. Magnussen changes the topic to some story about his recent visit to the courthouse.

"We actually need to head out," Gage says, interrupting his father. "I forgot that the Debate Club was going to Lacey's tonight to celebrate our wins."

"Oh, of course!" Mrs. Magnussen cries out with a smile. "Please, go celebrate. You were so wonderful on that stage today."

"It's in his blood!" Mr. Magnussen says proudly.

"Thank you for having me over for dinner," I say.

"Anytime, honey," Mrs. Magnussen says. I push up from my seat and walk around the table, intending to follow Gage out of the dining room, but when I pass his mom's chair, she catches my arm and pulls me to a stop. "I'm sorry Gage is being so stubborn about Ginger," she says quietly. "If he would just let her help, he wouldn't have to rope you into this! You must be so busy working at the bakery and applying to colleges. If the auction ever becomes too much, just let me know."

Her tone is dripping with concern and understanding, but I can't tell how much is faked. Is she not listening to her son, or is she *that* convinced I'll ruin her event? I have no idea how to respond to her, so I just give her a tight-lipped smile and a nod of my head.

She returns the smile and lets go, her acrylic nails leaving a faint imprint on my forearm. I rush to follow Gage, who has made his way straight to the garage. Before I leave, though, I drop the binder on the kitchen counter, mostly because I'm sick of carrying it around, along with the reminder that his parents don't think I can handle it. I have all the information saved to my computer anyway.

Let them open it up and see everything I've done for their auction. I know for a fact I've secured a better roster of donations than they had last year, despite my recent setback with the bike shop.

In the garage, Gage is waiting for me by the passenger door.

"I'm so sorry," he says immediately, looking pained.

"Wasn't my favorite way to spend a Saturday night," I say honestly. "But I'm also sorry. Fake dating me was supposed to get the heat off you from your parents, and it seems like it's done the exact opposite."

He runs a hand through his hair, jostling the already messy locks.

"As hard as this may be to believe, that was less heat than usual. So much less it was almost no heat at all."

"Really?" I ask in surprise. I'd hate to see what a normal dinner looks like for him.

"So you don't have to feel bad, okay?" Gage says. "Our arrangement has actually been the one fun thing to happen to me this year. I'm glad you suggested it."

My belly does a swoop thing at the sound of those words, and for a moment I'm worried the one bite of lasagna I had gave me food poisoning.

"You know, I was hoping a visit to your house would include a tour of your bedroom," I say flippantly, attempting to distract myself from that concerning swoop.

"Oh yeah?" Gage says with a smile, eyebrows raised.

"Not like that!" I practically screech. "I just wanted to see if it matches up to my imagination. Trophies on the walls and giant posters of crabs and, like, a butler robot or something."

"You've really been thinking a lot about my bedroom, huh?" he asks, that same playful grin still on his face. I've seen glimpses of this Gage before—funny and teasing and a little mischievous—but it's still always so unexpected.

"Don't go getting a big head, or there will be no room left in your bed for your many marine stuffed animals," I tell him with a hefty eye roll.

Gage laughs. "If I wasn't so desperate to get away from my house, I would take you upstairs to prove how regular and boring my room is," he says over the car between us.

"That's exactly what someone trying to hide their collection of hermit crab shells would say."

"Well, I can't offer you a tour of my bedroom, but why don't we go celebrate both of our wins? You with the exam and me with defending zoos?" He pulls open the passenger door for me, and I climb in. While I buckle my belt, he jogs around the car and jumps into the driver's seat.

"Celebration at Lacey's?" I ask once he's settled.

"The thing about Lacey's was a lie," Gage says as he opens the garage door and backs out. "Devin is throwing a party tonight, and most of the crew is heading there. I figure after a week of hitting the books hard, you deserve to celebrate. And also to get over what I just put you through at my family dinner."

"A party?" I say in surprise. "Shouldn't you spend tonight,

I don't know, studying? Making diagrams? Perhaps a diorama? Dusting your collection of sea creature skeletons? Or are you just dropping me off at the party and going back home?"

"What? No!" Gage says in surprise. "I'm not abandoning you at a party. I also don't have any skeleton collections. I'm going with you. I think we probably both need a night off."

"I'm shocked to hear you say that," I say. I think about how upset his friends were this semester because he wasn't hanging out with them the way he used to. Gage has been so committed to school and studying, never showing up at parties or football games—but tonight he wants to celebrate. With me.

Gage shoots me a crooked grin as the car coasts to a stop at a red light. He looks a little rebellious now, his mysterious grin glowing in the red light. Something about it makes my stomach flip again, in a nervous way but also in a way I kind of like. "I think we both deserve to have some fun, don't you?"

Devin's house looks the same as it always does: big, a little dated, and full of drunk teenagers. Her parents must be on vacation without her, or on a business trip, or God knows where, and she's taken advantage by throwing one of her ragers. A friend of a cousin of a friend gets her decent booze, and her parents' pantry is always full of food. That's all you really need to get most of Port Murphy High—and any other nearby school—to show up.

Gage parks down the street, where lines of cars are already parked along the side of the road, halfway into a ditch. A couple of the houses on this street are vacation homes that rarely have anyone staying in them, so it's not often that Devin's parties get busted.

As I get out of the car, I decide to take off the cardigan and leave it on my seat. Devin's house doesn't have AC, and even with the cool night air, once that house is packed full of teenagers, it tends to get warm.

Gage meets me on my side of the car, and when I turn to face him, I watch in surprise and mild delight as his eyes jump down to my newly exposed chest. He's so fair-skinned that even by the dim light of the streetlamp behind me, I can see how quickly the blush spreads across his face, turning the tips of his ears pink in an instant. After settling on my cleavage for just a second, his eyes roam around nervously, landing anywhere but on me, as though worried I might continue to expose myself to him on the street one article of clothing at a time.

"This dress was the nicest thing I had in my closet, and I didn't want to come to dinner underdressed. But it's a little old and doesn't quite fit right," I explain. This only manages to make him look more distressed, and I can't pass up the opportunity to tease him a little. "Or does it fit just right?" I ask with an exaggerated wink.

"Oh, uh," he says, his Adam's apple bobbing as he swallows.

"Oh my God! You'd think I flashed you with the way you're acting," I say on a laugh. "I'm sorry I released my cleavage from the prison of that cardigan."

"No, no!" Gage says quickly, finally making eye contact with me. "I just don't want to be weird here. I'm your *fake* boyfriend, so I wasn't sure if it's okay for me to comment on how nice you look tonight, both before and after the cardigan removal. I don't want to overstep or make you uncomfortable or whatever."

"We're friends now, right, Gage?" I ask, and he nods immediately. "I don't think it's overstepping to compliment each other."

"Okay, good to know," he says with a nod. "You look really good tonight, Valeria." His voice is soft and gravelly, sincere and quiet in a way that feels distinctly intimate. I don't expect the flush of warmth that hits me at his words.

"Yeah, yeah," I say with a playful swat at his arm, trying to brush off the sudden dizzy feeling. "Let's get inside before this rain picks back up."

As we walk up the driveway, I can already see that the party is in full swing despite the relatively early hour. The weather has been miserable all day, a constant spit of rain and bracing wind, so it's no surprise everyone's decided to head over to Devin's before eleven.

We pass the smokers on the porch, laughing so hard at something it sounds like one of them is about to throw up, and push through the front door. As usual, Devin has a sound system going, string lights and snacks, and Mario Kart set up in the living room. Inside, the house is cramped, full of people leaning against walls and perched on everything but chairs.

As we push through the crowd, someone running past bumps my shoulder and I slam into the wall.

"Jesus," Gage mutters just before another guy, chasing after the first, comes barreling down the hallway. Gage moves quickly, folding himself over me and protecting me from any more jostling arms. My back is up against the cold wall, his chest pressed against my shoulder and his arm on the wall above us forming a cocoon of protection around me.

I'm tall, just shy of six feet, and I don't often find myself feeling delicate or small. I like it that way, just like how I like wearing baggy clothes and sneakers. I never liked the dresses my mom put me in, with the delicate lace and frilly trim, because I felt like I was more of an object than a person in those things. But it seemed like that's the way smaller girls get treated regularly, particularly by guys. Perhaps boys think they're more biddable, more subservient, because they can hold their size over them.

But most guys at our school can't do that with me. Either because my twin scares the shit out of them or because I do, no one tries to make me feel small and delicate. But the way Gage curls in around me, protective but not pushy, doesn't feel like a threat or intimidation like it might with someone else.

When the last of the rushing boys brushes past, Gage leans off the wall and reaches for my hand. He pulls me through the hallway, using himself as a shield for any more rambunctious teens, and leads us into the kitchen.

It's roomier in here, the breakfast nook table folded away and stored somewhere else to make room for the giant keg and cooler full of drinks. I've only ever been in this room at night, so I've never been able to see out the windows that line the hexagonal shape of the room, but I'm sure the view is stunning. The massive skylights over the kitchen would have a spectacular view of the night sky and nearly full moon if not for all the clouds.

"No way," someone cries out. "Our boy is back!" Noah

bursts from a group of people leaning against the kitchen counter and flings himself at Gage. Noah hugs his friend so tight Gage has to let go of my hand to pull him off.

"It's good to see you, too," Gage says, righting a wobbly Noah as he loses his footing backing away from Gage.

"Mr. President came to celebrate with us!" Avery cries out, lifting her red solo cup in the air in salute. Others in the group join the cry, celebrating the appearance of Gage Magnussen.

I know that Gage is well liked by his friends, I know that they've missed him during lunch, and I know that he is a guy worth missing. But knowing it and seeing it are two different things.

Colby surprises Gage with an arm around the neck and an honest-to-goodness noogie. Gage slaps away his friend's hands, embarrassed but enjoying the attention, at least a little bit. He didn't curl up and hide from them because he wanted to, not like I did. He did it because he felt like he had to, because for whatever reason, getting valedictorian matters more to him than this.

And here I am, with no friends of my own who would greet me with this kind of enthusiasm and no class rank to brag about for consolation. How did I end up here, after three years of high school with nothing to show for it?

"Okay, I get it, you missed me!" Gage cries out, finally pushing his friends off him. And then he surprises me by leaning back to pull me over into their circle. His hand goes from holding mine to draping itself across my shoulders. "You have this one to thank for getting me out of my shell. At least for tonight."

Someone, I don't see who, lets out a wolf whistle, and I flush with embarrassment. This is not the Gage I thought I knew before, the one who was quiet and private about his relationship with Ginger. Is he doing this because it's all fake? Or is this how he was with Ginger? Or is this how he is *because* of Ginger, because he wants to use me to make her jealous?

The topic moves quickly away from us and back to the tournament they were at today. Avery gets roasted for mixing up the words "divisive" and "derisive" while onstage, and even though she's not here tonight, everyone recalls the way Rose took down her opponent. I stand there and smile, not entirely getting what's going on but at least appreciating everyone's enthusiasm for the subject.

But then something out of the corner of my eye catches my attention. It's not really anything I see or smell or even hear, but something I sense. A shift in energy. The volume of the party stays the same, no one is running around, but all the same I suddenly know my twin is walking down the hallway toward the kitchen.

Before, at parties, I was never far from Adrian or his group. I know the way they move through a room like they own it, Adrian's best friend, Lane Sanders, stomping around in knockoff Timberlands and whichever girl my brother was talking to at the moment fawning over him at every opportunity. And me, stuck in his orbit with nothing to really do other than spin around in circles, ready to be eclipsed.

This is the first party I've been to since this summer, and suddenly the idea of Adrian seeing me here, without him, is scary. Further proof that our relationship really is broken, that my brother, my *twin*, could care so little for me that he would drop me like it was nothing.

Gage must feel me tense up, because he looks to where my eyes have wandered. Then, just like I had been expecting, someone moves aside and my brother waltzes into the kitchen with his groupies. It's the usual suspects: Lane, a couple of seniors from the football team, and . . . *Ginger?*

She's tucked into the crook of Adrian's arm, looking small and delicate and precious. Painted-on freckles pop out against her pale skin, and her blond hair is half pulled up with a pretty white bow. All her attention is on Adrian, like whatever he's saying is the most fascinating thing she's ever heard, so she doesn't notice the faint hush that falls over the room when Gage and my brother finally make eye contact.

I watch Adrian's eyes travel from Gage down to his arms, around to my shoulder, but never up to my eyes.

I tense up, waiting for him to say something sideways at us, something rude about Gage that will send this whole kitchen into a flurry of chaos. But Adrian turns away from us and heads over to the cooler. He scoops out a Rainier beer and pops it open. I know he can tell our eyes are on him, but he studiously ignores us, leans against the bank of windows, and watches as Ginger does a little curtsy to squat down to the cooler and pull out a hard seltzer.

Now that my eyes are on her, I can tell that she's aware of our gazes, but she's not as good at hiding it as my brother. She pops open the tab of her drink and brings it to her lips for a sip, her eyes slipping up to Gage and me for a moment before flitting back to Adrian.

"What does he think he's doing?" I say softly, just so Gage

can hear. I expect him to say something witty back, some clever retort that will break up the knot of anxiety forming in my belly. But Gage doesn't say anything, so I look over at his face.

His mouth is pinched, like he doesn't like what he's seeing, and his eyes are clouded. For the third time tonight, my stomach churns, but it's not pleasant like before.

"You know what, I think we both need a drink," I tell him, grabbing hold of his hand on my shoulder.

"I can't drink, I'm the driver," he says, but he doesn't resist my pull to the cooler.

"I didn't say an alcoholic drink, did I? I'm going to make you my signature drink."

This finally gets Gage's attention fully back on me.

"A signature drink?" he repeats.

"I grew up in a restaurant, Gage, and I was easily bored as a child. Of course I came up with my own signature drink. I'm no Ana Maria, but I thought it was good. I called it Salty Lemonade. I was so proud when I showed it to my dad, but he didn't add it to the menu."

"How old were you?"

"Seven," I say as we reach the cooler. "Excuse me," I say, giving Lane a hip check to get him out of my way. He grunts and looks down to see who bothered him, but his face contorts when he sees it's me. "You were in the way," I tell him, popping up the lid of the cooler and pulling out two plain seltzers.

Adrian and Ginger are in the corner of the room now, her leaning up toward him like a sunflower and my brother soaking up the attention like the sun. At least one part of my fake dating plan has gone off without a hitch: Ginger is no longer harassing Gage. But I'm not sure this alternative is better. When I see my brother's hand dip down to her waist, I avert my eyes and head toward the kitchen island.

I gather the rest of my tools, two cups, a bunch of ice, the containers of sugar and salt, and quickly get to work. Gage leans against the kitchen island and watches me work in silence as I make a quick simple syrup in the microwave. I rummage around the drawers for a zester but realize I hadn't grabbed the main ingredient for my drink yet.

"Gage, could you grab me some lemons from that bowl over there?" I say, jerking my chin at the counter behind him. I pull my syrup from the microwave, and when I turn around, Gage has placed three fat limes on the counter in front of me.

"Oh wow," Lane says in that irritating voice of his, "too distracted by your ex making out with Adrian to even listen to your girlfriend?"

I look down to the counter, confused by what Lane just said. I have three limes in front of me, just what I asked Gage for. And then I realize what must have happened. A bark of laughter escapes me, and I look up at Lane with a satisfied grin.

"Oh my God." I turn to Gage, that same goofy grin still on my face. "Did I say 'lemon' again?"

"You did, but I knew what you meant," Gage says, my smile mirrored on his face. Then he looks over his shoulder at Lane. "She always says 'lemons' when she means 'limes.'"

Gage turns back to look at me, and an overwhelming rush of gratitude hits me. I've known of Gage for pretty much my whole life, a smart kid in the smart classes with his smart friends. Maybe we'd end up in an elective together or be in the same group on a field trip. But I never really *knew* Gage. Not until this week.

And in so little time he's been able to fit so easily into my life. I thought before that I had been making a friend, sitting next to each other in the library day after day. But now, I *know* I've made a friend.

"You know me so well," I say in a sickeningly sweet tone, a little for show to piss off the onlookers but a little bit real, too. I decide to play it up more, to really seal the deal, and I lift up onto my tiptoes, just a bit, just so I can press a hand to his shoulder and lean in close to brush my lips against his cheek in a chaste kiss.

I fall back on my heels, satisfied, and return to my drink. I don't look up at Gage or my brother or Ginger as I pick up the limes and give them a rinse in the sink before zesting. As I'm wiping the limes dry, I can see Ginger out of the corner of my eye stomp out of the kitchen.

CHAPTER SEVENTEEN

Everything is uncomfortable in the kitchen after Ginger's departure.

"Damn," Lane mutters, and my brother socks him in the shoulder.

"Yo, Adrian!" someone shouts from down the hallway, and that call is enough to get Adrian and his cronies out of the kitchen.

The rest of the night is just weird after that.

I finish making the drink in silence, Gage by my side, quiet and still. I saw the look on his face when Ginger ran from the kitchen. A pinch of regret, a touch of concern, proof that not everything between them is over for him. Was my brother's performance successful? Did he make Gage jealous?

When I'm done, I hand him his glass of my salty lemonade—born from a childhood mistake of mixing up the salt and sugar—and he politely takes a sip from it.

"Do you like it?" I ask him over the rim of my drink.

"It's zesty," he replies, but doesn't offer up anything beyond that.

The earlier ease between us seems to have vanished. Something shifted in those moments with my brother and Ginger in the kitchen, and the worst thing is I'm not quite sure why.

Gage gets pulled back into Debate Club conversation, and I'm left floating with my drink, a hurricane of emotions and thoughts swirling inside me.

For a moment there, between talk of lemons and limes, this thing between Gage and me felt kind of real. Real enough for me to press my lips to his face and plant a kiss right there, in front of everyone. Real enough to enjoy the feeling of his body close to mine, either against the wall when he protected me from the crowds or when his arm was casually draped over my shoulder while chatting with friends.

Gage never returned his arm to my shoulder, never found the opportunity to tuck in close and touch me again. We spend the rest of the party with a bubble of space between us, and I can't tell who put it there.

We don't stay at the party very late. At some point, the Debate kids start to lose steam after being up so early for their tournament. Gage and I climb back into his car in silence, and he drives me home without asking for directions.

I don't know what to say when he pulls up to my house. *Thanks, I had fun*? Maybe, in between the terrible dinner with his parents and the awkward moment with Ginger, I had fun, but I think calling the night "fun" would be a stretch. *It was nice hanging out with you tonight?* Closer to the truth, but it feels too vulnerable to say out loud.

"I'll see you at lunch on Tuesday," is what I finally land on as he pulls to a stop. We have Monday off for the Fall Festival, giving me an extra day to stew in the misery of tonight before returning to school.

"Thanks for coming out tonight," Gage says, grabbing my hand to stop me from launching myself out of the car. "I know I put you through a lot with my parents. I'm sorry."

"It's all part of the deal, right?" I say with false cheer, trying to alleviate his guilt. "I suffer a mild inconvenience so that you can get them off your back."

I pull my hand from his with a shake, keeping the smile on my face so he won't think I'm trying to run away. Which I am.

"Good night, Gage."

I lie awake in my bed, tossing and turning, throwing the covers off and flipping around so my head is where my feet usually go, trying to shake loose some sleepiness from my mind. All week my restless thoughts were about Algebra II and the retake.

I would cycle through different scenarios, all of them bad, as I tried desperately to fall asleep. I imagined passing the retake only to go on to fail the class. I imagined falling down the stairs on my way to the final, and the pain would be so bad I wouldn't be able to focus and I'd end up failing. I imagined someone hacking into the school system and fixing my grade, only for the school to find out and snatch my diploma from my hands on the graduation stage in front of everyone.

Not very likely scenarios at all. But they could happen. Maybe. And then what would I do?

But I passed the retake. I'm now less concerned about Algebra II, my anxieties over that fading to distant whispers in the back of my mind.

Tonight as I fail to sleep, front and center is Gage Magnussen.

Gage, who is probably still in love with Ginger.

Gage, who agreed to fake date me but would never date me for real.

So I shouldn't explore what the fluttering in my stomach means when I'm around him. I shouldn't think about the way his hair is always a floppy mess that I want to run my hands through. I shouldn't think about the fact that if I wear platform shoes, we would likely stand nose to nose and I could take those glasses off and look him straight in those blue-gray eyes.

I toss and turn all night, dozing off sometime before sunrise and waking up only a few hours later.

I think I'm beyond talking myself out of whatever it is I'm feeling for Gage. In moments like this, I might turn to my brother for help or advice. But with him no longer being an option, I only have one choice left.

Still in my pajamas, I tear downstairs, straight through the empty kitchen and down more stairs to the basement. It's a daylight basement that was remodeled in the early 2000s, full of honey oak and lots of beige. The walls are painted a dark red, the sectional is upholstered in a suede fabric the color of aged puke, and the kitchenette was designed to be more of a miniature bar and less of a real kitchen. This space has kind of been a wasteland my whole life, the space Mom was eventually planning to get to in her slow progress to decorate the whole house. But since she left, it's been stuck in limbo.

Tia Isa's door is wide open, bed made and sun streaming through the blinds, meaning she's out running Sunday morning errands and Miguel is the only one down here. Which is good, because if Isa overheard what I was about to say and tried to insert herself into the conversation, I would combust.

"Miguel!" I cry out, desperate, despondent, as I make my way to his bedroom door. "Miguel! I need your help!" I give his bedroom door one loud knock, following by a groan of despair before crying out again. "I'm coming in!"

"Valeria, wai—" he says, but he's cut off as I slam his door open and wail. "Jesus!" He cries in surprise, standing at the foot of his bed like a weirdo.

"I don't know what to do," I whine, and swan dive onto his haphazardly made bed. The landing is less cushioned than I imagined, more lumpy and hard than any mattress should be, and then his comforter lets out a startled cry when I try to roll over. "What the—"

"Jesus Christ, Valeria—"

"I can't breathe!" someone cries from under the comforter, their voice muffled through the fabric.

"Oh my God!" I shout, leaping off the bed in surprise and pulling the comforter off with me.

Lying in the middle of Miguel's Christmas gnome–themed sheets—unfortunately, all our guest sheets are holiday-themed—is one Ana Maria Ybarra, flattened like a pancake in the shape of a homicide tape body. Able to breathe, with both me and the comforter now off her, she sputters and sits up with a perhaps overdramatic gasp of breath.

"Ana Maria Ybarra!" I screech, pointing an accusatory finger at her—fully clothed, thank God—unexpected body.

"Be quiet!" Miguel hisses, flinging a pillow at my head. "Are you trying to get me caught?"

"I cannot believe goody-two-shoes Ana Maria *slept over at her boyfriend's house*!" I exclaim in a much more subdued whisper. "Miguel," I say, slapping a hand down on his shoulder. "I really think you turned our world on its axis when you came to Port Murphy. Some cosmic power is at play here. I feel like I'm living in an alternate universe."

Miguel swats my hand off him and sits down on the edge of his bed. Ana Maria scoots up and drops her legs over the side of the bed, a blush creeping up her neck and consuming her face.

"Please explain why you decided to ruin our morning," Miguel says evenly. And then I'm reminded why I'm here, and the full-body frustration hits me again so hard I fling myself onto the floor this time and scream straight into the carpet, my mouth filling with dog hair.

"Oh, I know what this is," Ana Maria says sagely. "I used to do that all the time."

I flip around on my back and stare up at Ana Maria.

"I don't think you know what this is. In fact, I guarantee you don't," I say.

"Well, I know it's about Gage," Ana Maria says. "Am I right?" she prods.

"Yes," I say with a pout.

"How did you know that?" Miguel asks her, perplexed. Ana

Maria rolls her eyes at him and scoots down to the floor, resting her back against the bed.

"What's going on?" she asks me, ignoring Miguel.

I take a deep breath before admitting, "I'm not really dating him."

"What?" Miguel snaps to attention.

"We have a mutually beneficial deal," I explain, bracing myself for the reveal, "that involves fake dating. Don't tell anyone, though."

"It— What—?" Miguel is flummoxed. Ana Maria turns her face up to him and places a gentle hand on his leg.

"Listen, I don't think Valeria has had anything to eat for breakfast yet. Why don't you make us some coffee and bring us something to eat? I can handle this."

"But— " Miguel protests, looking frustrated and confused.

"No." Ana Maria says firmly. "I'm telling you right now you will be no help in this conversation. Right, Valeria?"

I mean, when I ran down here I had thought that it would be helpful talking to him about this. But seeing him now, confused and a little lost, next to Ana Maria's confidence and poise, she's the one I want to talk to.

"Right," I agree.

Miguel plays up a look of pain at my rejection, but he's a wise man, and he knows when to listen.

"Fine," he says, throwing his hands up in defeat. "But once this is settled, you'll tell me what the hell is going on?"

"Only if you make me that breakfast sandwich you told me about," Ana Maria tells him.

"I might as well take your order, too, Valeria," Miguel says as he walks to his door.

"If it's good enough for Ana Maria, it's good enough for me," I tell him. "But can you make a café con leche with evaporated milk instead of regular milk? With a double shot of coffee?"

"Your wish is my command," Miguel says with an over-the-top bow before leaving his room and closing the door.

Ana Maria and I sit in silence for a minute, her patiently sitting on the floor and me star-fished on the carpet, staring up at the ceiling in the hopes that a black hole might open up and suck me out of here.

"I don't even know where to start," I say, finally sick of Ana Maria's understanding silence. Do I tell her the whole truth? Or just enough of the truth to help me with my newfound feelings?

"Well," Ana Maria says slowly. "Why don't we start with the deal you two made?"

"I might not graduate this year," I say, surprising myself by opening with the worst of it. Then the rest quickly spills out. The desperate need for a tutor for the retake, a reluctant Gage besieged by people who want more from him than he can reasonably give, and the unexpected friendship that has formed between us.

Me placing a daring kiss on his cheek in front of everyone in that kitchen last night.

"Miguel wasn't kidding when he said your family has a flair for the dramatic," Ana Maria finally says when I finish. "And I don't mean that in a bad way," she assures me. "Honestly, I'm impressed. I could never call any of you boring."

"That doesn't help me, Ana," I complain.

"It had to be said, though," she insists. "I think because all of you are so dramatic you make things harder for yourselves than they need to be."

"I'm not making anything hard," I argue, sitting up to glare at her. "I'm just an idiot who is . . ." I struggle to come up with the right word. "I don't know, *falling* for someone who still has feelings for his ex-girlfriend. That's the problem here."

"I know this is a pretty radical thought, but have you considered . . ." She lets her words hang there for a moment before continuing, "Just telling him how you feel?" I let out a pained groan at this suggestion. "You're complicating things by driving yourself crazy over assumptions you don't know are even true—"

"You didn't see him last night," I argue. "When Adrian was flirting with Ginger, and then after I kissed his cheek, when Ginger ran off . . . he got so closed off. What if I tell him how I feel and he doesn't feel the same, and then he wants to end the fake dating, which also means ending the tutoring, and then I end up both getting rejected and failing high school?"

"Okay, that's fair," Ana says carefully. "Valeria, I don't know Gage very well, but I at least know he's not vindictive or the kind of person who would go back on his word. And he still needs your help with the gala. So no matter what, I don't think he's going to stop helping you. As for how he feels about you, I can't say—"

At that moment, Miguel kicks open the door, bearing a tray full of food and drinks.

"I *can* say," he says as he sets the tray down on his desk. The smell of butter and chorizo and freshly brewed coffee wafts over me, reminding me that I haven't really eaten since lunch yesterday.

"Were you eavesdropping?" Ana accuses.

"No, you have an unusually loud voice that manages to travel," Miguel says. "And also I did stand outside the door and listen, but only for the last bit." Ana rolls her eyes and stands up to inspect the food. Miguel turns his attention to me. "I can say," he repeats, "how he feels about you. Gage has been single-minded about getting his grades back up since school started. No one could convince him to take a break or loosen his own leash. But, somehow, you did."

"I don't know—" I start, but Miguel cuts me off.

"People don't change their ways for no reason," he continues, "so you should just talk to him. I have a feeling it might go over well."

I pick up my coffee from the tray and take a sip to avoid saying anything. Because for anyone else, I'm sure this is perfectly practical advice. But for me?

The thought of telling Gage how I feel, of baring myself to him, is too scary. To give that much of myself up to a person with no guarantee that they will accept it?

It's a risk too high for me.

CHAPTER EIGHTEEN

I don't take Ana Maria and Miguel's advice.

I spend the rest of the day avoiding the subject and trying to convince myself I haven't actually developed feelings, while simultaneously hoping Gage will text me.

Come Monday, I almost wish we didn't have the day off for the Fall Festival so I'd have school to distract me. But it's become tradition that the opening day of the fest is for students to enjoy. The Port Murphy Fall Festival goes all out, from haunted hayrides and apple picking to pumpkin patches, and so much fresh seafood. Morales Bakery usually has a booth, selling camarones enchilados and frituras de bacalao to the masses drunk on hard cider and live music. The festival also hosts our local beauty pageant, where poised women vie for the title of Miss Gala Apple and toddling kids throw around batons to compete for Miss Crab Apple.

On students' day at the festival, local bands play on the stage and vendors are careful to keep the alcoholic ciders well hidden.

One year, a junior managed to sneak into the back of someone's tent and steal ten cases of hard cider. That night ended in total chaos.

Now vendors usually avoid storing cases out in the open.

I should know, because I'm working the Morales booth today and spent all morning unloading boxes into our tent: cartons full of napkins and paper plates, and the hard cider hidden in a cooler under a table. I take watchdog duty while my dad serves plates of Cuban seafood dishes, with Eddie Ybarra—whom my dad hired after the Ybarras' shop closed—manning the cash register.

I watch in envy as my peers run around the grounds, going to the petting zoo tent to play with baby goats and taking pictures at the autumn leaf exhibit. People pass by with the giant pumpkins they'll take home to carve and big cups of warm apple cider to stave off the slight chill in the air.

We're lucky, at least, that today has been relatively dry, with only a light drizzle falling while I was unloading the truck.

"Oye, Pedro, we're running low on lime slices," Eddie calls out to my dad after ringing up a customer.

"Vale," my dad calls out to me over his shoulder from the deep fryer, where he's just dropped in two filets of beer-battered cod. During this festival he serves his own spin on the local classic of fish and chips, mojo-marinated cod that gets battered and fried and then served with yuca fries and an addictive sour, tangy, garlicky sauce that customers can't get enough of. "Check the cooler in the car, there should be more in there."

"But I'm guarding the cider," I say, a little petulantly. I initially agreed to help Dad on student festival day because I thought it would be less excruciating to have an excuse, to have a reason not to participate in the fun besides the truth: I have no one to enjoy it with. But instead I'm just watching my peers from the other side, probably reeking of fried fish, and I still feel awful.

Usually, Adrian and I would go to the Fall Festival together, and he would play some of the games like darts or whack-a-mole, and I would hang back with the rest of his friends, shooting the shit and eating cotton candy and fried Oreos. But he hasn't even stopped by the booth today.

"No one is going to come and steal the cider while I'm in here," Papi says authoritatively, and he's not wrong. Adrian and I got our size from our dad, who is six foot three even, and he looks like the kind of guy you wouldn't want to mess with: sleeves rolled up to reveal a tattoo of mysterious origin that he refuses to explain to either Adrian or me, and a thick brow that gives him a mean look like a rottweiler. But under that tough exterior, Papi is a teddy bear, and he's no real threat to anyone. Probably.

"Fine," I say, abandoning my watch on the hard cider and heading toward the truck.

Our van is parked just a few feet behind our booth. It's the same truck we use for deliveries, with the dessert burrito mascot painted on the back doors. Ana Maria is trying to bribe my father to switch the burrito for the cartoon I made of her doughnut because she insists the dessert burrito causes her psychic damage, but my dad hasn't relented yet.

Unlocking the van, I pop open the back doors and climb inside. There's a cooler packed with extra ingredients, deli cups full of our coveted mojo dipping sauce, and dozens upon dozens of limes. I pick up an empty box to haul them in and begin moving over the limes. I'm so engrossed in my work that I don't hear someone approach the open doors of the van.

"Valeria?"

I scream in surprise, drop the limes I'm holding, and stand up so fast I hit my head on the roof of the van.

"Shit!" Gage cries out when my skull thuds against the solid metal, a sound that echoes through the entire van. "Sorry, I didn't mean to scare you. That looks like it hurt."

"It sure did," I groan, pressing my hand to the spot on my head where I'm certain I'll have a goose egg tomorrow. "Good thing I'm next to a cooler with ice."

I pick up an empty plastic bag and scoop up some of the melting ice into it. I press it to the back of my head, the cold a relief against the throbbing in my skull.

"I'm so sorry," Gage says again as he climbs into the van. "I stopped by the stand, and your dad said you were back here."

"It's fine." I wave off his concern, but he closes in and peers into my eyes.

"Do you feel dizzy or nauseous?" he asks, his gaze wholly focused on me, blue eyes dark with concern. We haven't spoken since the party Saturday night, and if he's texted me today, I wouldn't know, because I left my phone at home before heading to the festival.

During my sleepless nights, I had tried to convince myself that I wasn't developing feelings for him. I was just making a friend, and since I'd never really done that before, I didn't know the difference between friendship-like and . . . like-like. But now, in close quarters, surrounded by the pine-needle-and-grass scent of his soap, I'm not sure. The world around him seems to dim, making him glow around the edges with golden light. I do feel a little dizzy looking at him, overwhelmed by his presence and the feelings it draws up in me.

"I'm not sure," I admit.

"Count backward from fifteen," he instructs, and I comply, not missing a single number along the way. He nods in a kind of approving way, but his intensity doesn't dial down.

"Follow my finger with your eyes," he says next, in full doctor mode. He makes an X in the air between us with his finger, and I follow it with my eyes. "Doesn't seem like you're concussed," he says, but he's still hunched in close to me and gazing worriedly into my eyes.

"I'm fine," I insist, placing a hand on his shoulder and giving him a gentle push back, because having him this close to me is a little overwhelming. "I just need to take a second."

"What were you doing? I can help," he offers. With the way we go through limes at the booth, I know Papi will be expecting my delivery soon.

"Yeah, actually," I say, pushing my box full of limes closer to him. "Could you take these limes to the booth? We were about to run out."

"Wait," Gage says, pausing a little dramatically. "Now I'm not sure, I think you might actually be concussed. Do you know your name? What day is it?"

"What?" I say, laughing a little bit at his serious tone. "You just confirmed that I was not, in fact, concussed. Just a little dazed."

"That was before you called these," he says, shaking the box in his hands so that the limes jostle around a little bit, "*limes.*"

"I don't always confuse lemons and limes!" I argue. "Just most of the time. I promise I'm not concussed. No nausea, no double vision, my name is Valeria Middle-Name-Redacted Morales, and it's festival day."

"Okay, fine," Gage relents. "I'll run these over to the stall and let your dad know what happened."

Gage hops off the van with the limes, and I take a seat against some boxes, my now-wet bag of ice still pressed to the back of my head. The initial sting of pain has faded into a dull thrum that will likely stick with me for the rest of my shift at the booth.

I close my eyes and try to take a moment to rest, but the lingering scent of grassy soap still fills the van, and the look in Gage's eyes as he examined me is playing on a loop behind my lids. We had no plans to meet up today. So why did he come to look for me?

My mind starts going through the worst-case scenarios without my asking, a film reel of my worst disappointments one after the other. *He wants to end this. He's getting back together with Ginger. He can't tutor me anymore. All of the donations for the gala are gone.* Thankfully, Gage returns quickly and I don't fall too deep into my spiral of despair.

"Done," he says as he hops into the van. "And I got you the rest of the day off," he announces proudly.

"What?" I say in surprise. The festival is starting to fill up, and soon my dad and Eddie will need another pair of hands.

"I told him you hit your head and asked if you could take the night off. I promised to drive you home. Then he asked who I was—"

"Oh God, did you tell him you were my boyfriend?" I ask,

mildly panicked. Papi didn't blink twice when Adrian brought his first girlfriend around back in eighth grade, but I've always expected my experience with bringing a partner home might be a little different.

"Yes?" Gage says, a little confused by my panic. "I thought that was fine? Since this"—he points a finger between the two of us—"is fairly public? I'd imagine Adrian would have already told him if you hadn't."

It's a fair point and something I hadn't considered. Adrian could have brought up my "boyfriend" to Papi as a move to get us to break up or at least to irritate me. But he hasn't mentioned it to anyone at home. Did he keep it to himself as a courtesy to me?

"It's fine as long as my dad didn't threaten you in any way or start cursing in Spanish," I tell him.

"Well, he was in the middle of plating up some food when I told him, so maybe he didn't entirely register what I said?" Gage suggests. "Either way, you have the night off, and I am morally obligated to keep an eye on you for the next couple hours to make extra sure you don't have a concussion," Gage says magnanimously.

"Who knew this fake relationship deal would come with health care? What a boon," I say, lifting the bag of ice off my head. "What do you have in mind, Doc? It's not algebra, is it?"

Gage takes a step closer to me and offers me his hand with a warm smile.

"Let's go have some fun."

CHAPTER NINETEEN

I take hold of Gage's hand, his grip firm and comforting as he pulls me up and out of the van. I lock up and pocket my spare keys, my right hand still in Gage's. We walk toward the festival like that, hand in hand, like it's nothing, like it's everything, like it's the best thing in the world.

I make sure to avoid our booth, in case Papi is having a bit of a late reaction to the boyfriend news, and head straight toward the corn maze. Plenty of farms in the area have their own for fall travelers, full of wimpy stalks that barely reach your shoulders. But the farmers behind this maze must have the secret to growing massive cornstalks, because as soon as you step inside, the world disappears.

"Should we split up?" I ask as we take our first turn, which ends up looping us back around to the start.

"Absolutely not," Gage says. "Remember?" He taps the side of my head once with his finger. "I'm on watch. I can't let you out of my sight. But I think I also can't let you lead us through this maze, because we'll never get out."

"I made *one* wrong turn!" I argue. "That hardly disqualifies me."

"Fine, fine," Gage relents. "Lead away."

Gage was right not to trust my guidance. I take us wrong turn after wrong turn, seemingly finding every dead end in the maze. One dead end leads us straight to James Locicero making out with some girl against the cornstalks.

"Oh!" I cry when we nearly collide with them, but James and his partner are too . . . engaged to notice our sudden arrival. Gage and I trip over each other's feet in our rush to get away from the couple.

I giggle nervously through our escape, unable to stop stumbling over dried corn husks and roots until Gage lets go of my hand and wraps his arm around my waist to keep me stable. I'm trying to suppress my laughs as we trip our way down some other narrow path, but we just end up at another dead end. The sight of it causes another peal of laughter to explode from me.

"At least this one is empty," Gage says, slipping his arm from my waist and taking a turn around our latest dead end. "This has to be the biggest corn maze on the planet. How have we found so many dead ends but no way out?"

"I'm going to blame my navigational skills on my recent head injury," I say, trying to peek through the wall of cornstalks. I push aside a couple of stalks, but everything is a little too dense to see through. "I think we're close to the edge."

"At this point, I'm not going to trust any assessment you

make in regards to our location," Gage says, but he still comes up behind me and peeks through the corn. "It's so quiet over here."

The distant shouts and music of the festival have faded, swallowed up by all the stalks deep in the maze. The only sounds here are the rustle of leaves in the wind and my heart pounding in my ears.

"What if we just . . . cut through?" I suggest.

"But we don't know what's on the other side," Gage points out.

"That's half the fun, though, isn't it?" I ask, glancing over my shoulder at him. I'm surprised to find that he's closer than I expected, his face mere inches from mine. His breath skates across my skin, and my stomach plummets when his blue eyes catch mine. He looks more awake than he used to. The deep bags under his eyes are gone, and his eyes don't look as heavy. A little bit of the liveliness he lost has been injected back into him somehow, and I wonder if the sleep I've lost has gone to him.

"After you, then," he finally agrees, slipping past me to pull aside the cornstalks. I go in first, getting swallowed by the dry leaves, my feet sinking into the damp soil as I venture through the confines of the maze. Gage keeps close behind me, using his long arms to push stalks away as we cut through.

By some miracle, I was right, and not much farther through the corn, we find ourselves on the outside of the maze where the farmland butts up against the woods. There are some hay bales stacked near the edge of the maze, some abandoned milk crates, and an unopened case of hard cider that someone likely stole and stashed for later.

"As good a spot as any for a break, wouldn't you say?" I tell him as I flop down on the hay bale, which is harder than I expected, but still a welcome rest after the maze. Gage sits down on the ground against the bale, and we both gaze out into the woods, far from all the Fall Festival chaos.

"You never did say what brought you here," I say after a moment of comfortable silence. "You don't seem like the type to eat candy apples and watch the battle of the bands."

"The caramel just gets stuck in your teeth!" Gage complains. "They're a waste of a perfectly good apple." Gage heaves a huge sigh, and the simple act of breathing seems to loosen him up, relieving him of some weight he had been carrying until now. "I was actually here for the pageant," he admits.

I gasp in surprise at the admission.

"Am I looking at this year's Miss Gala Apple?" I cry out in delight. "What is your talent? An instrument? Do you even play an instrument? Oboe? Trombone? Bass clarinet?"

"Cello, first chair," he says. "I also play on the Seattle Youth Symphony."

"Lord, what *don't* you do?" I ask, feeling a little tired just thinking about his schedule.

"What *I* want to do," Gage answers honestly, and I think he's a little surprised he admitted it out loud. He licks his lips and sighs, looking like he wishes he could take all the words back. I slide off the hay bale and sit next to him on the damp soil. "And pageants. I don't do pageants. My mom is judging for Miss Crab Apple this year."

I can tell he wants to gloss over what he said, pretend he never admitted it to me. And as much as I want to know more, want to take him apart bit by bit so I can learn everything there is to know about him, I can tell it's not what he wants right now.

But I hope, maybe, someday it will be.

"Well," I say, resting my head against the hay bale and glancing up at the clear blue sky. I'm not ready to tell Gage about my feelings. I'm still afraid of what could happen, of him rejecting me and of me losing this friendship, but also of what it could mean if he felt the same. But Gage just gave me a piece of himself, unbidden, and I want to give him a piece of myself in return. "Did you know I was in the Miss Crab Apple pageant in kindergarten?" I tell him.

He looks over at me in surprise, eyebrows nearly to his hairline, and his sudden disbelief makes me sputter with laughter.

"This is a bit," he insists. "There is no way."

"Oh, there was a way," I laugh, remembering the taffeta and tulle and dance lessons. At that age, I had still been a fun doll for my mom to play dress-up with. Sparkles and sequins and tiaras! Oh, the outfits I was wrangled into that year. "My mom," I tell him, his face turning serious as I start this story. "She isn't from here."

No one at school talks about it, but everyone knows my mom hasn't been home in years. I've heard people speculate about the Morales family and their missing mother, her temporary departure that became a permanent absence. But everyone has the good sense not to talk about it to our face, or worse, ask us about her. Adrian gets angry at anyone who asks, Papi plays dumb, and I get closed off. But I'm willing to open up now, just a little bit.

"She grew up in Miami and did the pageant scene in high

school. She won Miss Teen Miami in a fire-red ball gown with a dance routine and all the charisma her five-foot-three body could hold. She had plans to compete for Miss Miami and, after, Miss Florida. I was never clear on why she was so invested in the pageant scene. It's not really a part of Cuban American culture, and it wasn't something her parents pushed her to do. She was just hungry for those crowns," I say. "But either way, she never got to do it. Because when her eldest cousin was getting married in New York, she drunkenly hooked up with some guy from the groom's side at the wedding and . . ." I trail off.

Gage reaches a hand to my lap and takes hold of mine, gripping it tight in a show of support.

"I think you know what came next," I say, letting loose a deep sigh. "Needless to say, I was not pageant material. I tore the bows out of my hair, I hated the feeling of tulle on my skin, and I had no passable talent. I think that's when she gave up," I say. I'm surprised to find tears pooling in my eyes and my face going hot with shame. "I'm normally fine about it, the pageant and the festival, but thinking about it this year is really doing a number on me for some reason. Sorry."

A moment of silence stretches between us, but it's that same comfortable quiet I always feel with Gage. A silence that feels like he's listening, he's considering, he's giving me space to feel whatever I need to feel without stepping on it or rushing me through it. In a family where it's like I have to scream to be heard, to jump before I'm ready, it's nice to have someone who lets me take my time.

"It's okay to not be fine about it," he finally says, his voice soft and careful. "I don't know a lot about . . ." He trails off for a moment, stuck on what to say. ". . . your mom, but I can imagine none of it is easy to deal with."

A bark of bitter laughter escapes me. What a way to sum up my mom.

"It's hard," I say hesitantly, afraid to say the words, words I've whispered in the back of my mind but have never breathed aloud. "Your mom is supposed to love you unconditionally, right? You watch those true crime documentaries where a child has committed a terrible crime but their mom still loves them, but the only crime I ever committed was not conforming to the idea of what her daughter should be. And that was enough to make her turn her back on me."

I take in a deep, wobbly breath, trying to calm my sudden rapid heartbeat. Gage's thumb rubs soothing strokes across my skin and holds on tighter to my hand, a small gesture that serves to quell the rising panic that comes with talking about my mom.

"My parents are like that, too," Gage says softly. "Trying to mold me into their image. It's not a good feeling, especially when they try to trim off the parts that don't fit. Like Math Club. I needed something off my schedule to focus on getting my rank back, and they don't see the point in Math Club, since 'it won't do anything for me in pre-law.' I don't even know if that's what I want to do."

"Wait, you *don't* want to go into law?" I ask, glad to have the subject off me for a moment. "I thought that's why you took Latin and were on the Debate Team."

"Oh, how naive of you to think I make any of my own academic decisions. Or life decisions, honestly. *Everything* goes through them. I swear, even Ginger felt orchestrated by them."

"What do you mean?" I glance down at our intertwined hands, nearly the same in size, but his fingers are thin and knobbly around the knuckles, and mine are narrow with brightly painted nails. They fit together well, neither overpowering the other, just holding each other in a warm embrace.

"We've been paired up since childhood because our parents are friends," he tells me. "Weekends were always spent on the Davis boat or all together at my grandparents' cabin or at a barbecue at the Davises'. When Ginger told me she liked me, I just followed the script."

"But you guys were together for so long," I argue. "You must have felt *something*."

"Of course," Gage agrees. "I don't think I'm the kind of person who could be that close to someone for years and not feel something." He trails off, struggling to find the right word. "I thought I loved her, and when everything happened, I was hurt and confused and struggling to understand why. But more than anything, I was just worried about her."

"Worried?" I repeat, remembering the Gage from the end of last year, tired and tortured-looking. Of all the rumors that were swirling around campus back then, none of them were about how *worried* he was about Ginger.

"Of course I was worried," he says firmly. "Some gross college creep was putting the moves on her, and I was worried she was getting in over her head with him. And I felt like it was my fault, because I couldn't be the boyfriend she wanted, or needed, or whatever." He waves his hand in front of his face, like he's brushing off the thought, but I can tell the memory of this still hurts him. "But I never really felt upset that the relationship was over. I felt—" He pauses, pursing his lips, and I see him testing whether he wants to continue that thought. His gaze flits over to me for a moment, just a glance, but it must be enough to reassure him, because he continues.

"I was relieved when it was over."

Relieved? That's certainly what I'm feeling right now. I was never entirely sure whether he was over Ginger, whether the lingering feelings of first love still burned or if he was ready to move on. Especially after the party this weekend, when he started to act closed off after the "Adrian and Ginger Show."

"I think that's fair," I say softly, squeezing his hand in reassurance. At my words, Gage puffs out a sigh of relief and glances over at me with a small smile. "But I also think you're wrong," I tell him firmly.

The smile drops and his brows furrow as he tries to figure out what I mean.

"What Ginger did is not your fault," I tell him. "You have to know that."

"I certainly played a part in it," he argues. "I tried so hard to be the boyfriend she wanted, but I could never measure up."

"Gage, are you even listening to yourself?" I ask, a little outraged. I let go of his hand and turn to face him, making sure I have his eye contact to really drive my point home. He looks confused by my outburst, his mouth open and eyes watching me warily. "I'm sorry," I say, reaching across and squeezing his arm. "I don't mean to yell at you, but it's frustrating to hear you talk about failing someone because you couldn't change for them. That's not how a relationship works. It sounds like Ginger wanted you to be someone you weren't, but that doesn't mean *you* failed her. I think that just means you aren't the person *she* needs. You can't make yourself into what someone wants, believe me," I say, thinking of tulle and sparkles and tiaras.

"I had no idea you were such a relationship expert," Gage says, his tone light, trying to lighten the dour mood that has fallen on both of us. I roll my eyes playfully at him, glad to have some of the tension between us relieved.

"I've just seen a lot of bad relationships," I tell him.

"But you've never dated anyone," he says, his voice going up at the end in question.

"Nope," I say, popping the "p" and resting back against the hay bale again.

"No one's ever caught your interest?" he asks. "Or has Adrian just scared off every romantic prospect?"

"He didn't scare you off," I point out, my heart racing as we circle close to a subject I'm not ready to delve into.

"Oh, I didn't tell you about the parking lot rumble?" he asks. My eyes go wide, and for a second I believe him, especially considering how mad Adrian was. But when I turn and look at Gage, he has a goofy smile on his face.

"Gage!" I cry out on a laugh, leaning over to slap his shoulder. "Don't joke about that!"

He catches my hand before I'm able to slap him, and he's smiling that big, bright smile that I've really grown to like.

"I'm not lying!" he says on a laugh. "We met in the Wendy's parking lot, and Adrian pulled off an amazing pirouette in your defense."

"Please tell me the entire football team was behind him doing coordinated snaps to his dance," I say, playing along.

"*Valeria!*" he sings out suddenly. "*I've just met a girl named Valeria!*" He clutches my hand to his chest as he bellows out—terribly off-tune—this butchered rendition of "Maria."

"You're so brave for facing down my brother, with a voice like that," I say. "Your keening must have scared him away."

"*Valeria*," he sings again, his voice soft and crooning this time, and wonderfully in tune. His eyes bore into mine, serious and focused. "*The most beautiful sound I've ever heard.*"

My heart stutters to a stop. What started as a playful joke has turned serious in a blink, and I'm not sure how to play this. Gage is watching me with a playful smile, my hand still pressed to his chest and his lips slightly parted after singing to me. And I'm just staring at him, a little surprised and a little terrified.

"You know," I blurt suddenly, "we don't have to fake date anymore."

"What?" he says, thrown off by my sudden change in course.

"You fulfilled your end of the deal, I passed my exam."

"What about the gala?" he asks.

"Oh," I say, looking down at my hand on his chest. "Of course I'll still help you with the gala. We just don't need to . . ." I trail off, my mind going a little fuzzy and jumbled because I've just noticed that I can feel the pulse of his heart under my hand.

"Pretend?" he finishes for me.

"Yeah," I breathe, looking up through my lashes at him. His eyes look more green in this light, hooded and sparkling with something I'm afraid to name.

Buzz, buzzzz, buzz, buzz, buzzzzz.

I'm leaning toward Gage, caught in this sudden gravity that is pulling me toward him bit by bit.

Buzz, buzzzz, buzz, buzz, buzzzzz.

His eyes jump down to his pocket, attention finally drawn away by the persistent phone call that is trying to break this moment between us.

Buzz, buzzzz, buzz, buzz, buzzzzz.

Gage drops my hand and reaches into his pocket. I fall back against the hay bale, sucking in air and trying to get my racing heart to settle down. Gage's brows furrow when he sees who's calling, and he glances at me quickly before answering.

"Hello?" he says, his voice cracking a bit at the end. He clears his throat once and then glances at me again. "Uh, yeah." Pause. "Sure." Then he passes his phone to me. "It's your brother."

I stare at the phone like it's a bomb, and I flinch when he tries to hand it to me. *Adrian called Gage??*

"It sounds serious," Gage whispers.

Concerned, I reach for the phone and put it up to my ear.

"Adrian?" I say nervously.

"Valeria," he says, and it's the first time since this summer that he's said my name without disdain or attitude. He sounds happy and excited. "Come home now," he says.

"I don't—" I start, but Adrian is quick to cut me off, bursting at the seams with energy.

"Mom's back."

CHAPTER TWENTY

I have to go."

I drop Gage's phone on his lap and leave him there, hidden away at the back of the corn maze. I run through the festival, past little kids in face paint and parents carrying giant pumpkins, straight to the parking lot and into my car.

My hand fumbles as I try to stick my key in the ignition, my heart still racing and my head pounding. It takes four tries before the key catches and I can turn on the car. My mind is reeling, my thoughts blurring by too fast to catch.

Mom's back? What just happened with Gage? Mom is in Port Murphy. Adrian is happy to see Mom. Was Gage trying to tell me something? Was I trying to tell Gage something? Am I happy that Mom is back? Is she back *back?*

Without my phone, I have no idea what's going on. After Adrian's announcement, I hung up before I could ask any questions. Now I have the thirty-minute drive home with the setting sun blinding me as I speed down an empty country road. I turn up my music, the loud blur of guitar and bass enough to drown out my thoughts.

Because as my mind repeats Adrian's statement over and over again, my hand is still warm from Gage's touch and I can't forget that look in his eyes, the intense focus that he turned on me as he sang my name.

No, I have other things to worry about right now.

Because my mom is back.

The drive feels like it takes hours, even though I hit every green light on my way home. When I pull up to our cul-de-sac, I see everyone's cars lined up in their spots on the driveway, but there is an unfamiliar convertible, cherry red and parked in my spot.

Mom.

I pull in next to the car, noticing the license plate from Nevada and a sticker from a car rental company on the bumper. I try not to think about what a rental car means, of how temporary they are, here and gone by a contracted date.

My gut twists as I turn the car off, nervous and scared to go inside. Why can't I drum up the same excitement my twin had? Why am I always the dark mirror to my brother? Why can't I just be happy she's finally home after so long? Maybe once I'm in the house, once I see my mom and my family back together and whole, it will feel right.

Taking a deep breath, I get out and head up the stairs to the front door. I can already hear excited voices spilling outside, the familiar timbre of my twin's voice and a tinkling laugh I haven't heard in years.

Pushing open the front door, I step into the house and into a dream I've had a thousand times.

Mom is perched on the end of the couch, framed perfectly by a window glowing with the warm colors of sunset behind her. She looks radiant, tan and glowing with the Florida sun still clinging to her skin. Her hair is expertly highlighted and blown out, teeth bright white and dark lashes long and wispy. She looks ten years younger than when she left, but she still looks achingly familiar.

"Mom?" I say, my voice hesitant, like I may wake up at any moment.

Maite Morales looks over her shoulder with a big smile at my voice. This is my mom, the woman who taught me how to make Cuban coffee and who rubbed Vivaporú on my chest when I was sick. In the summer she braided my hair and rubbed sunscreen on my face, and in the winter she bundled me up in scarves and made snow angels with me. Of course I missed her, of course it feels like the missing puzzle piece in my life has been found and placed right back where it belongs.

"Ay, mi niña!" she cries out happily, holding her arms out for me. I cross the room in seconds, Leo bounding excitedly behind me as I launch myself at my mom. Her spindly arms reach around me and press into my back as I bury my nose in her hair. She smells the same, a powdery violet smell that follows every memory I have of her. She leans away to look at my face, pulling back to wipe something off my cheek. "You're covered in dirt," she remarks.

"Oh," I say in surprise, pulling back and wiping away at the same spot. "I was just at the Fall Festival. I must have gotten it from the corn maze?"

"The festival!" she says brightly. "Remember when we did Miss Crab Apple?"

I sit down on the ottoman in front of her and smile, trying to mirror her joy.

"Remember how precious she looked in that dress, Pedro?" Mom looks over at Papi, who is sitting across from us in his usual armchair. Tia Isa is next to him, lips pursed and legs crossed.

"She looked like a little wedding cake with all those frills you put on her," Papi says with a laugh.

"And you wouldn't stop tearing out the bows I put in your hair," Mom adds affectionately. "Now look at you, covered in dirt and so big!"

"I'm going to make some coffee for everyone," Tia Isa says suddenly, jumping up from her seat and heading to the kitchen. I look around quickly for Miguel, but he's probably still at the festival.

"What have I missed? When did you get here?" I ask.

"Mom was just telling us she finally sold Abuela's place and put some of the money in our college fund," Adrian tells me.

"It's what she would have wanted," Mom says with a smile. "And I just flew in this afternoon! I was so excited to see all of you, and I wanted it to be a total surprise, but let me tell you, it was so hard keeping it to myself!" She sighs loudly and waves her hand in the air. "But, Lord, what a long flight. And then the drive from the airport—it feels like I've been traveling for days at this point."

"Do you want to go rest?" Adrian says, his voice pinched with concern.

"Oh, no," Mom waves the suggestion away. "I'm sure the coffee Isabel is making is just what I need."

Leo comes snuffling up to Mom now, his tail wagging frantically against the couch as he tries to sniff her feet. Mom twitches at the dog's approach and tries to fend him off with a wave of her hand.

"Don't worry," I assure her. "He's really friendly."

"I'm sure he is," Mom says, still trying to get Leo to back away. "But I don't do well around dogs. I was bitten by one as a little girl, and those memories stick around."

Papi does one short, piercing whistle, and Leo immediately retreats to his side.

"Coffee's ready!" Tia Isa announces, walking back into the living room with a tray full of coffee and treats. She places it down on the coffee table, and Mom is quick to serve herself a shot.

"So, what have you been up to, Maite?" Tia Isa asks as she settles back down in her chair, legs crossed and coffee in hand. I'm a little irritated that she's forcing her way into this family reunion. This should just be me and my brother with our dad enjoying our time with Mom for the first time in years, but Tia Isa is here, in the way, like always.

"Well, I finally got my mother's things in order," Mom says with a pained sigh. "You wouldn't believe the mess that woman left behind," she continues, like she's sharing fun gossip with us. "That house was in shambles, she couldn't throw anything away.

I found a Cartier watch from the eighties at the bottom of a box in her spare bathroom, can you believe it?" She throws her head back in a laugh, baring her neck and the smooth skin there.

"Oh man, that sounds cool, though," Adrian says. "Find any Rolexes in there for me?"

"I doubt you'd like any of the things your grandparents hoarded," Mom says. "But I did bring gifts for you two," she adds with a winning smile. "Adrian, will you grab that brown duffel bag? They're all in there."

Adrian bounces up from the couch and jumps over to the mountain of luggage Mom brought with her. He sets the duffel down next to her and she unzips it.

"I didn't know you were still going to be here, Isabel, so I didn't bring anything for you and Miguel," she explains as she pulls out the gifts. They are meticulously wrapped, just like I remember, with perfectly flat sides and neatly tied bows on top.

"Oh, we don't need any gifts from you," Tia Isa says. "It's just so great to see your family back together. I haven't seen Adrian smile like this in a long time."

"Well, he has to be careful with those smiles!" Mom says with that same tinkling laugh. "He's so handsome, that thing is like a weapon, I'm sure." She hands him a small rectangular box, wrapped in blue-striped paper with a gold ribbon.

Adrian tears into the gift like he always does, one good rip down the middle to extract whatever the goods are. He pulls out a white box with a familiar Apple logo and looks up at our mom with a big grin.

"No way!" he says before turning his attention back to the box and opening it to reveal a brand-new Apple Watch.

"I also got you some nicer bands to go with it," Mom says, pulling out a couple of small gifts from her bag and handing them to Adrian.

"Thanks, Mom," Adrian says, taking the boxes from Mom's hands and folding her into a hug.

"Oh, you're so big!" Mom cries out as my brother's arms crush her. "Valeria, here." She pulls away from Adrian and picks up a present in bright gold wrapping paper with a white floral pattern and pink ribbon. It's a huge box, way bigger than Adrian's, and takes two hands to pick up from my mom.

"You're going to love it," Mom insists as I pull up one of the corner flaps and carefully pull back the wrapping paper. Inside is a huge white box with the logo Dyson printed on it. For a second I think mom bought some kind of hand vacuum, which would be a weird gift but fairly useful, I suppose, but when I pull back more of the wrapping paper, I realize it's actually a worse gift than that.

"A hair dryer," I say, trying to affect some excitement in my voice but falling short. I never blow-dry my hair, and not from lack of access to a blow-dryer. I have a shitty one I got at the drugstore for those winter mornings when I'm running late with wet hair, but it's never been used as a tool for styling.

This is a tool for styling. It has all the gadgets and gizmos and bells and whistles for shampoo-commercial-worthy hair.

"Now that your hair is so long," Mom says, reaching to pull on a strand of my bright auburn hair, "I figure you could use a nice styling tool! Your hair looks so much better at this length," she adds, reminding me of the day freshman year she came home to find me with the bob haircut I had given myself in the bathroom that afternoon. She had yelled at me like I was a wayward toddler and took me to the salon to "fix" what I had done, but I was just left with an even worse pixie cut.

After that, I had gotten a little addicted to the power of changing my hair. It drove my mom crazy to see the things I would do, micro bangs and shaved undercuts, and finally the red hair dye. Only one of those things stuck around once she was no longer here to give an outraged reaction.

"I can show you how to use it," Mom offers. "I have one, and I *swear* by it. Fastest blowout ever."

I touch my hair gingerly, the air-dried waves falling messily around my face, sad and limp compared to Mom's shiny, bouncy hair.

Mom lets out a loud, dramatic yawn then, patting her chest in surprise.

"Two shots of coffee and I can hardly feel it," she says after another yawn.

"Why don't you go up to the room and rest, Maite?" Dad suggests. "Adrian can help you take your bags up."

"I'm sorry I can't be better company," Mom says, "but travel days really do take it out of me!"

Mom gets up from the couch and leaves the half-full duffel bag for Adrian to pick up. He grabs her suitcase, purse, and travel neck pillow all in one hand and follows her up the stairs.

I watch them go, surprised by how familiar the sight of my mom walking up the stairs in her heels still is. Once she's out of earshot and settled upstairs, Tia Isa gets up from her chair and starts to clean up the coffee mess.

"Did the blow-dryer come with a receipt?" she asks me as she stacks up Mom's empty cup with mine.

"What?" I ask, my head still a flurry of thoughts and feelings.

"I can ask her where she got it and see what the exchange policy is," Tia Isa continues. "So you can get something you'll actually use."

"I could use the hair dryer," I argue, pulling the box in close to my chest. "I bet it works better than the cheap one I have."

Tia Isa purses her lips in response and heads to the kitchen, where she begins to loudly clean up. Papi is still sitting in his chair, his eyes on the staircase in contemplation. Adrian comes bounding down, barreling toward me on the couch.

"She's back!" he whispers in my ear as he pulls me into one of his bear hugs, shaking me around like a rag doll. "She's finally back!"

"Did she say how long she was staying?" I ask, still feeling a little tentative about the whole thing.

"What do you mean?" Adrian says, pulling back with drawn brows. "You saw the pile of stuff she brought—she's come back home. Right, Papi?"

"I don't know what her plans are," Papi says, "but it's nice to see everyone together."

"She can come to homecoming and see me play," Adrian continues. Adrian didn't get on the football team until after Mom left, so she's never been to any of his games. "You have an extra ticket for her, right?"

"I'll make sure she has a ticket," Papi agrees. His phone rings, and he glances down at it with apprehension. "That's Eddie. I left him alone at the festival." He picks up the phone, and I can hear Eddie through the phone asking Papi a million questions a second. "Hold it, hold it," Papi says, standing up and heading toward the garage. "What do you mean you can't find it? It should be— No, that's not the right one. It's over on the bottom left— Okay, llámame por video y te lo mostraré." The rest of the conversation gets cut out with the slam of the garage door.

"I can't believe she's finally back," Adrian says, his voice still full of wonder and hope. I wrap my arm around him and hug him tight to me, hoping I can absorb a little of what he's feeling. Part of me is happy. I feel like I have my brother back, the Adrian who is vibrant and happy and so full of life. This is the first time in months that he's been like this with me, like we used to be, and that alone feels like this could be worth it.

CHAPTER TWENTY-ONE

Tuesday morning feels like I've woken up in a dream.

Mom is back. My family is whole again.

I would think it was all some dream if not for the unopened Dyson box sitting on the floor next to my door. I roll over in bed and pick up my phone, scrolling through my notifications and stopping when I see the texts that Gage sent last night. After Mom went to her room, I had grabbed some leftovers from the fridge and barricaded myself to process my emotions.

Seeing her fawn over us, all smiles and hugs, makes me doubt my memories. Did I make her out to be worse than she really was? Instead of absence making the heart grow fonder, for me it had soured. Does that mean that *I* have to be a better daughter? Do good daughters turn against their mothers so quickly?

Seeing my family together, *whole*, did feel good. And even if she didn't get me a gift I liked, she hasn't been here in a while, so of course she wouldn't know what I like.

What's important is that she's back.

Right?

I open the text thread with Gage and go through the unread texts.

Are you okay? I'm here if you need to talk or get away or anything.

I have Latin homework if you just want to hear me drone in Latin.

Also I tried to find my way back through the corn maze and got lost, so neither of us can be trusted with directions.

Then, this morning, another text.

If you need to take the week off from gala work, I can take over for you.

I smile down at my phone like an idiot and type back a quick response.

Thanks for checking in. Just some family stuff happening, you know how it goes.

The smell of cinnamon and butter and the sound of early-aughts pop waft up from downstairs. Without seeing who is in the kitchen or what's cooking, I know exactly what is going on from the smell alone.

Tia Isa is firmly a savory breakfast kind of person, making tortillas and sausage and toast, with the only sugar present being in whatever fresh fruit she serves and the café con leche.

Mom, on the other hand, has always been a fan of sweet breakfast. Pancakes and waffles and French toast, and maybe some sausage and eggs once Adrian became concerned with his protein intake. But always something sweet and lavish as the centerpiece.

And I know right now Mom is whipping up her classic

cinnamon brûlée brioche French toast, which she always serves with warm maple syrup and some kind of caramelized fruit. I can also tell from all the sounds coming from downstairs that most of the house is already awake.

Any other morning, I would just splash some water on my face and put on some clean clothes before going downstairs. I hardly ever pay too much attention to my appearance, my only vanity being sunscreen on my face.

This morning, I jump out of bed and go straight to the bathroom. I run a brush through my messy bed hair, which only serves to make it fluffy and more unkempt than before, so I braid it back in the best French braid I can muster before washing my face. I grab the tinted sunscreen instead of my usual one, and it has just enough coverage to even out my skin tone and blur my freckles. Before leaving the bathroom, I inspect every inch of my face, making note of the red spot that's emerging on my chin and the chapped state of my lips that seemingly no lip balm can cure.

Adrian and I don't look much alike. Part of that is by design, with me dyeing my hair red month after month while Adrian maintains our natural light-brown hair that mellows out to a chocolate brown in the winter. We have the same face shape, long and a little angular, but the details are all different.

He has thick, intense brows over dark, heavy-lashed eyes. His nose is long and straight, his skin clear and tan. The best description for my features is mousy. My eyes are dark and unremarkable, lacking the inky-black eyelashes of my twin. My skin is prone to redness and acne in addition to the freckles, and everything else is just . . . fine. And usually, I don't care. I don't *want* people to look at me the way they look at my brother, like they want to own a piece of him. Or the way I remember people looking at my mom, an open hungriness that felt uncomfortable to witness.

"You're fine," I tell my reflection, hoping that I can get myself to believe my words. I brush my teeth without making any further eye contact and slather some Vaseline on my lips before heading down the stairs.

Leo isn't there to greet me like usual when I make it to the living room, tennis ball in his mouth in hopes of an unlikely morning game of fetch. Then I hear his sad yowl from the backyard, and I see that his doggy door has been closed.

"Oh, little dude," I coo as I walk up to the back door. As soon as he sets his big, limpid eyes on me, his tail goes wagging madly, shaking so hard his whole lower body is part of the movement. "I've got you," I tell him, reaching for the doggy door and pulling up the cover. Leo sticks his nose through as soon as there is enough space to lodge it in there, and then he has his whole face pressed against my leg, giving me excited licks over my jeans.

Once he slithers his way through the doggy door, he bounds around the living room excitedly before barreling into the kitchen.

"NO!" I hear someone shriek, followed by the sound of clattering plates. I jog over to the kitchen to check up on what chaos Leo has wrought and find Adrian pulling Leo away from an upturned plate of French toast that has fallen on the floor.

"Did you let him in?" Adrian accuses me, trying to prevent an eager Leo from inhaling the still-hot French toast from the floor. Mom is pressed up against the counter, not wanting to get near Leo.

Oh yes, Mom's fear of dogs.

"Yeah, he was locked out," I argue, bending down to help clean up the mess. "I'm sorry, Mom," I apologize, plopping the delicious-looking pieces of toast into one hand so I can throw them in the compost.

"I'll take him back out," Adrian says on a sigh, dragging poor Leo outside again.

"What's all the commotion this morning?" Miguel says, appearing from the basement door with his usual floppy bed-head. "Oh, Tia," he says in surprise when he catches sight of Mom. "Good morning."

"Miguelito!" Mom cries out at the sight of my still bed-rumpled cousin. "¡Qué grande estás! ¡Ven pa' ca, dame un besito!"

Miguel steps over me and gives my mom a kiss on the cheek.

"Looks like something happened to breakfast," Miguel notes as he steps away and swoops down with some paper towels to help me wipe the butter and maple syrup smears from the tile.

"That crazy dog of Pedro's tried to jump on the counter," Mom explains. "Adrian had a few pieces before the disaster, but I'm afraid you two missed out on today's breakfast."

"No worries, Tia, we usually grab something small to eat," Miguel says.

"A big, growing boy like you?" Mom says on a laugh. "No, you need to have a full spread or you'll go hungry!"

"Okay, Leo's back outside," Adrian says as he walks into the kitchen. He pulls out his lunch from the fridge and turns back to face Mom. "We have practice until six, so I'll see you at dinner."

"Te voy a hacer tu favorito esta noche," she promises. "¡Rabo encendido!" Mom gives Adrian a parting kiss on the cheek and waves him off. Miguel digs into the pantry for something to eat, and I follow him.

"Costco muffin?" he offers, holding up the carton full of large blueberry muffins.

"Why not," I agree, grabbing a granola bar for later as well.

"Rose is having trouble getting her car to start this morning, so we're going to pick her up, which means we have to leave, like, now," Miguel says, taking a bite of his muffin mid-sentence. "I'll meet you outside. Bye, Tia!" He waves to Mom before backing out of the kitchen and into the garage.

I pull out the lunch box I packed for myself last night and stuff it into my backpack.

"Sorry about Leo," I say again, and Mom waves this off with a smile. "I'll see you after school?"

"Of course," Mom says. I turn to leave the kitchen, but Mom calls out for me when I'm just a couple steps out. "You aren't going to say goodbye? Come give me a kiss before you go."

I jog back to my mom in a hurry and press a kiss to her cheek, the smell of violets closing in on me.

I can't focus at school. My mind is still too caught up on the fact that Mom is home, that Adrian seems happy for the first time in months, but I still feel like the rug can be pulled out from under me at any moment.

It doesn't help that it's Spirit Day and most kids are dressed up as orcas, our school mascot. Some wore full-on whale costumes that immediately got confiscated by the dean, some have black-and-white face paint mimicking the face markings of orcas, and some guys have styled their hair into mohawks that look like a whale's fin.

Things get even weirder when the bell rings for lunch and Adrian intercepts me at my locker.

"Eat lunch with us today," he says, and it feels more like a command than a question.

"I have"—I was about to say "tutoring" but catch myself just in time—"plans," I say instead, but it feels weak. "I eat lunch with Gage."

"Yeah, in the *library*," Adrian says, rolling his eyes. "Come on, come to our table. We miss you."

I wanted this at one point, for Adrian to let go of what happened this summer and let me back into his orbit. I wanted my spot back at his side, safe in his shadow. But I'm not sure I want that exact scenario anymore.

I want Adrian to talk to me again, to let me back in like he used to, but I want there to be room for me this time. I've found things that *I* like doing now, people *I* like spending time with, and I want to see what else I can find for myself. But I'm not sure I can do that from Adrian's shadow.

"Do it for homecoming," Adrian says. "The cheerleaders made us all those orca black-and-white cookies that I know you like."

"Those *are* the best part of homecoming week," I admit. I love the cakey cookie with vanilla and chocolate frosting. Adrian smiles, knowing he's got me, and I push aside my concerns for now.

"Let me just text Gage," I tell him as I pull out my phone.

"To be clear, he's not invited," Adrian says, and I look up at him sharply.

"You're going to have to get over that," I tell him as I open my conversation with Gage.

I haven't told Gage my mom is back, but I'm sure he'll hear it from Miguel soon enough, assuming my cousin hasn't blabbed already. And it feels like a weird thing to tell him over text anyway. *Sorry, I can't have lunch with you today. My mom is back and her return has somehow righted the universe and it's back on its normal axis, which means I have to eat lunch with my twin because he's speaking to me like he's not mad at me for the first time in* months. *Chat later!*

Yeah, no. I'll go with something simpler.

I have to skip out on lunch today, sorry!

"The guy is boring, I don't even know what you see in him," Adrian scoffs.

My phone buzzes with a quick response from Gage.

No problem, I have work to catch up on anyway.

I pocket my phone and aim a retort at Adrian. "Excuse me, you've dated airheads, meatheads, that one girl who was *so* racist—"

"Okay, as soon as she said that thing about—"

"AND," I continue, raising my voice to speak over him, "I never said anything against them, because for whatever reason and for however long, *you* liked them. And I respected that."

"This is different," Adrian insists, like a dog with a bone. "I don't trust him not to hurt you."

"Oh my God!" I shout, spooking the group of freshmen passing us in the hallway.

"Look, Mami's back home, and I really just want us all to be a family again. Can you please just come to lunch with me?" Adrian says, not quite understanding how upset he's made me. And maybe that's my fault. Maybe I mask my feelings too much, hide away my truth from the people around me to protect myself.

But I would think my brother, my twin, my *better half*, would be able to see through my bullshit.

As always, Adrian can only ever see what he wants to see.

"Okay, fine," I say, trying to keep my voice level.

"Okay," Adrian says, his mouth kicking up in the corner. "Good. Thank you, Valeria. I missed you."

"I missed you, too," I tell him, lips tight.

He throws his arm around my shoulder, and we walk into the cafeteria side by side. We fall into our old, familiar rhythm, Adrian taking control and me falling back, falling further into myself to make more room for him.

At the table, his usual crowd awaits us, but I nearly trip over my own feet when I catch sight of Ginger there. She's nibbling on the end of a carrot stick and looking wistfully out the window at the gray weather, so she doesn't notice our approach. Adrian smoothly takes the seat next to her and points me to the seat across from him.

"Oh, shit," Lane says in surprise as I elbow him to make more room for me. "She's returned."

This catches everyone's attention at the table, and conversation stops as all eyes lock on me. Ginger's gaze feels particularly pointed, but I do my best to avoid making eye contact with *anyone* and pull out my sandwich.

"I'm just here for the black-and-white cookies," I say, quickly nabbing Lane's from in front of him and throwing it in my bag. "Don't make a big deal out of it."

Lane pouts but doesn't fight me on the cookie, and slowly, everyone's attention slips away from me. After that moment, it's like no time has passed. I'm back in my old spot, safe from people's attention in my brother's shadow, enjoying lunch from the best table in the cafeteria. My sandwich tastes better here, with no smell of ammonia to stifle my appetite or sharp, cold wind to freeze my fingers.

But better isn't best.

Because the best lunch I had was in a library, next to a boy, eating a lunch he had packed just for me.

I don't speak the entire lunch period, focusing on my food and listening to everyone else talk about homecoming and the game and the prank that they're planning to pull on our rival school. Adrian doesn't comment on my silence; in fact, he doesn't even seem to notice it.

It's the same at home that night. I end up playing the same role, quiet witness at dinner while Adrian waxes poetic about football and homecoming and college applications and Mom listens on with adoring eyes.

Adrian invites me to lunch again the next day, and the next. I try to convince myself that it's nice, being a family again like he said. That is all I've wanted this year, after all, for Adrian to bring me back into the fold, for things to go back to the way they were. But anytime I try to say something, someone talks over me, so I end up saying nothing at all. After three days, it doesn't just feel like I'm living in Adrian's shadow, but that I *am* a shadow. Silent, my existence entirely dependent on another person. And that's not what I want anymore.

What's worse is that I start to backslide in Algebra. Without Gage's daily tutoring and with *MOM'S BACK MOM'S BACK MOM'S BACK* running through my head at all hours, I start to fall behind again. Ms. Metsker's brows are furrowed when she passes back my homework—a solid C—and I know I'm not out of the woods yet.

Gage must hear from someone about my mom, but he doesn't push me to talk about it. Instead he texts me pictures of the feral colony of cats living in his neighborhood that he feeds, along with voice notes of him reading Latin "just in case you need something to fall asleep to." He never brings up the weird place we left things at the festival, and he never touches on the subject of my mom.

I think he might be waiting for me to bring those things up, but I can't even fathom how to do that right now.

At the end of lunch on Friday, I already know this will be my last time at this lunch table. Adrian runs off as soon as the bell rings, leaving me behind as I pack up the algebra homework I was working on.

"So," someone says as I shove my notebook into my bag, "does this mean Gage broke up with you?"

My head snaps up to find Ginger standing over me, head cocked to the side and arms crossed over her chest. She has Adrian's number painted on her cheek and a teal bow in her hair.

"What?" I say, caught off guard by her question.

"You guys aren't hanging out anymore," she points out. "And I saw that he hasn't bought homecoming tickets for you two."

"You're keeping tabs on us?" I ask, eyebrows raising in surprise.

"I don't have to keep tabs, it's obvious."

Two months ago, I would have brushed off this interaction. I would have rolled my eyes and walked away unbothered. Granted, two months ago I wouldn't have put myself into an absurd situation like this, but still.

These last couple months have changed me, or maybe they've given the cramped-up parts of me room to grow, space to form into the person I'm truly meant to be. She's still messy, she's still confused, but she can stand on her own. Ginger doesn't know that yet, but she's about to learn.

"I don't know why you're so interested," I say, gesturing to the number painted on her cheeks. "Or did you paint that on your face to make Gage jealous?" I stand up, pull my bag over my shoulder, and get closer to Ginger, making sure to step into her space so I can really tower over her. "You're going to have to start working a little harder, Ginger. You may have convinced the bike shop not to donate anything to the auction, but I've bagged every other business in town." Ginger frowns, and I flash my teeth at her in a feral grin. "Anyway, why go dance and be sweaty with the entire student body when I can go and be sweaty with just Gage?"

Ginger's face flushes scarlet, and before she can form a response, I walk away, but not before bumping into Lane, who is standing there, mouth agape and staring at me in total horror.

Oh God. I had an audience for my grand statement about *getting sweaty with Gage*, a guy I haven't seen in nearly a week after a very charged moment next to a hay bale, who I might very well no longer be in a fake relationship with, for all I know at this point.

"I really wish I hadn't heard that," Lane says, still looking horrified, as though I were actually his sister.

I can't get out of this cafeteria fast enough.

CHAPTER TWENTY-TWO

There is no doubt in my mind that Lane is going to tell my brother about what I said at the first opportunity. And I'm sure Adrian will have something to say about it, but I certainly don't want to hear it.

I manage to avoid him for the rest of the school day and rush to Rose's locker for safety after the last bell. Adrian was never really scared of Ana Maria or her sister Sofía, but he always kept well away from Rose, who we considered to be the Ybarra family guard dog. If I'm hanging out near her, he will steer clear.

"I think you need a new eye cream," Rose says to me without preamble, looking me up and down before returning to the contents of her locker. She has a voodoo doll of questionable origin sitting on the top shelf of her locker and a bedazzled mirror on the inside door, along with dozens of photos of her and Ana Maria, photos of Rose in school plays, and a picture of her and her mom when she was little.

"I don't use eye cream," I tell Rose. It's not worth commenting on the fact that what Rose is saying is a non sequitur, because Rose is always saying non sequiturs.

"Okay, well, you should probably start," she says, throwing her last textbook into her locker before closing it. "Need some recommendations?"

"I think I just need sleep," I tell her honestly.

"Gage keeping you up at night?" she says with a salacious waggle of her brows. Did Lane tell *her* about what I said? I can feel a flush start to climb up from the back of my neck.

"How does Ana Maria put up with you?"

"She puts up with me because I am a *delight*," Rose says haughtily. "And she secretly loves my teasing."

"Well, what I love about you is the fact that my brother is terrified of you. And since I don't want to talk to him right now, you are the perfect shield," I tell her.

"He's scared of little old me?" Rose says, batting her lashes innocently, but I can see the vicious beast underneath. She wouldn't be so kick-ass at speech and debate if she wasn't so scary under that cute veneer. "I'm happy to be of service."

I link arms with Rose and we head out to the parking lot toward Miguel's car, keeping an eye out for my brother just in case.

When Miguel and I get home, Tia Isa tells me Mom is out doing some shopping, so I head up to my room to work on the fundraiser stuff I've admittedly been neglecting this week. I update my spreadsheet and send it off to Gage to check in. My face flushes when I type his name into the email, remembering the confidence I'd had when I insinuated that Gage and I were going to be *getting sweaty* tomorrow night. I send off the email and try to dispel that memory by focusing on homework.

I'm staring down some formulas when Mom bursts into my room in a flurry of energy.

"Valeria!" she cries out in surprise when she sees me curled up in my bed with a notebook and math textbook open at my feet. "What are you doing?"

"Homework?" I respond, a little confused by her concern.

"You need to start getting ready! We leave for the game soon!"

"I know," I tell her. "I'm ready."

Mom looks physically wounded by my response. Her mouth pops open in a pout of disappointment and a hand reaches out to clutch at her chest like she's at risk of a sudden heart attack over my dowdy appearance.

"You can't go looking like that," she says, sounding a little horrified.

I look like I usually do, in a pair of green slouchy corduroy pants and an oversized sweatshirt with a cartoon version of our orca mascot, Neptune, named after one of the transient orcas that occasionally make their way up to Puget Sound. "Go Orcas!" is written across the top of the sweater in bubbly serifed letters. This is arguably the best thing I could wear to the homecoming game. It's spirited, comfortable, and warm.

"I'm in spirit-wear," I argue, pointing at the comically cheerful whale.

"Please dress up," Mom begs. "This is your brother's last homecoming game. I want the family to look nice."

I bite my tongue and smile, not mentioning it may be Adrian's last but it's her first in two years.

"Here, while I was out shopping, I saw this and thought of you," Mom says, dropping a large paper bag from Nordstrom by my door. She must have gone all the way to Seattle to get that kind of shopping done. "Wear this, okay? And put on some lip gloss?"

My family is back together, and they are happy, I tell myself. *I cannot be the one to ruin this for everyone.*

"Sure thing," I say, my cheeks hurting under the strain of my fake smile. Once she leaves, I approach the bag. It's full of tissue paper, disguising the articles within, so I dump it all out on my bed. A pair of jeans and something black come tumbling out.

I can already tell I'll hate both items just by looking at their crumpled heaps on my bed. The jeans are *bedazzled on the butt*, and the top is one of those corset-like crop tops with actual boning. This is the furthest from anything I would actually wear, especially considering it's going to get down to forty-two degrees tonight.

I pick up the jeans warily and inspect the tag, nearly choking when I catch sight of the price. I drop them like they're on fire and immediately check the black top. *Also* an astronomical price for something with so little fabric.

Then I remember what Tia Isa asked about the hair dryer and sift through the tissue paper for a receipt. But there is none. I'm stuck with this.

Frustrated, I pull off my comfortable pants and sweater and switch it out for the outfit Mom got me, better suited for a night on the town than a small-town homecoming game. But if this is what it takes to have peace in the family, it's not so big a sacrificc.

That's what I think, anyway, until I try zipping up the jeans. These pants are tight on my hips, the denim having nearly no stretch to it. They end up fitting, but at what cost? One loaded chili dog from the concessions stand, and I'm going to pop out of these. The top fits slightly better, not nearly as constricting as the pants, but still tight enough to make me uncomfortable. I root through my closet for a jacket to wear over the outfit, something big enough to disguise how uncomfortable the clothes make me.

"Oh, mijita!" Mom cries out from my bedroom door. "You look so good!"

I'm still uncovered, having not settled on which puffy jacket would conceal me the most, when she catches sight of me.

"Turn around, I want to see the pants sparkle!" she cries out excitedly.

"I think the pants are actually a little tight," I tell her, pulling out one of my longer raincoats from the closet. "I think you might need to return them."

"What? No, they look like they fit you perfectly," she argues, walking over to physically turn me around for inspection. "They'll loosen up as you wear them anyway," she insists. Then she looks up at my face and frowns, not impressed with the lack of makeup. "Why don't you go put on some mascara and then meet us downstairs?"

"Sure," I say, backing away from her toward my desk, where the top drawer contains my limited selection of makeup. There's no mascara, but there is a reddish lip gloss that should appease her. I apply some and grab a purse from the back of my closet door before loping downstairs.

Everyone is settled in the living room, my dad with a big sign that says "Go 22!" in big fat sharpie with a crude drawing of a football, Tia Isa and Miguel with the number 22 painted on their left cheeks, and Mom in a short black denim minidress despite the cold weather outside.

"Come here," Mom says when I get to the landing. "I'll add Adrian's number to your cheek, too."

She pulls me to the dining room table, where her purse and makeup bag are open. As she pulls out her liquid eyeliner, I notice Tia Isa's attention slide our way.

"Are you bringing your boyfriend to the game, Valeria?" she asks suddenly. "Do you want to head over with him and your friends instead?"

"Hey, you didn't make me that offer," Miguel complains before letting out a startled yelp.

"Boyfriend?" Mom asks in surprise, stepping back from me to get a better look at my face. "No one mentioned a boyfriend."

"Oh, well, actually," I start, irritated that Tia Isa brought Gage up, but Mom cuts me off.

"You have to invite him to come sit with us," she insists. "I'd love to meet him."

"I'm sure Gage is busy with homework tonight. He's not really the kind of person to go to things like this," I say as Mom grips my chin to hold me still.

"Ay, but I want to meet him!" Mom says, pressing the felt tip of her eyeliner to my cheek. "Text him, tell him to come tonight."

Mom steps back and looks at me expectantly, and I know I'm not getting out of this.

"Fine," I say, trying to will a pleasant smile onto my face, but I know I fall short. I pull my phone out from my back pocket, angling the screen away from my mom, and type out a quick message.

I am being forced to ask you to go with my family to the homecoming game tonight. Please reject the offer for both our sanity.

"So, what is he like?" Mom asks, eyes wide and interested.

"Smart," I say, and Mom wrinkles her nose at that. "Kind," I add, my eyes dropping to my feet as I remember all the times his hand pressed gently to my back to guide me through crowded rooms and awkward situations.

"He's a really cool guy," Miguel says after I zone out for a second. "He's one of the first friends I made when we moved out here."

My phone buzzes in my hand, and I swipe to see Gage's response.

So I do have to reject the offer, but only because I'm already going with my parents. They're awarding a student with a scholarship and we have to do the whole song and dance with a giant check. So I'll see you there?

"So, he's coming?" Mom asks, trying to peer at my phone screen.

"He'll see us there," I say through my teeth, trying to keep hold of my false smile.

We all pile into Dad's car, which has also been painted with various phrases meant to cheer on Adrian and strike fear into the hearts of our rivals, the Vikings. I know Mom must have cooked this up because there is a drawing of a whale on one of the passenger windows with an eye drawn in her classic style.

Mom is the reason I got into art in the first place, starting with me copying her cartoon eyes on my schoolwork and then snowballing into an obsession with arts and crafts. She used to add drawings to our napkins in elementary school, anthropomorphic apples telling us that "an apple a day keeps the doctor away" and attempts at drawing whatever our favorite cartoon character was at the time.

Coming from sporadic texts and the rare phone call, it's weird to see Mom suddenly go all in on our lives. She's in the passenger seat, her denim dress at maximum *cinch* in a way that shows off her cleavage a borderline inappropriate amount for a high school football game, and talking a mile a minute about her trip into Seattle this morning.

When we pull up to the school, the parking lot is already packed, dozens of students and parents and community members rolling into Port Murphy High School for the game of the year. Everyone is dressed head-to-toe in our school colors—black, white, and teal, to represent orcas in the ocean—and someone is even wearing a disturbing orca mask that looks like something out of a horror movie.

"Unclench your jaw," Miguel whispers into my ear as we head toward the field. "You look like you're going to crack a molar with all that tension."

"Is it that obvious?" I ask, pulling the collar of my coat up to ward against the chill.

"It's hard not to notice you when you're glittering like a disco ball," Miguel jokes. I roll my eyes and punch him on the shoulder. "Oh look, your *boyfriend* is on the field," Miguel points out, and I give him a jab to the ribs for good measure. He laughs at my attack and waves at Gage. "Yo, Gage!"

Gage is standing on the small makeshift stage in center field, where a group of adults and students are gathered. He perks up when he sees us and gives a returning wave.

On a small pedestal are the Homecoming King and Queen crown and tiara, and the senior class president is standing next to it with a bouquet of flowers and sashes in her hands. Gage is behind them with his parents in another perfectly tailored suit made up of black tapered dress pants and a white jacket left open with black buttons. His parents are dressed similarly in mixed and matched black and white.

The homecoming court is standing just off the stage in all white, and I'm surprised to see a disgruntled-looking Sofía Ybarra standing with the elected court. Where Ana Maria is known to be the sweeter Ybarra sister, Sofía is savory with a *bite*. And she's clearly been elected against her will.

"That's him?" Mom asks curiously as we climb the bleachers to our seats. "He's cute."

I make a noncommittal sound and follow Tia Isa to an empty row of seats.

"Hello?" Dean Pera's voice booms from the speakers, followed by the screech of feedback. The audience cries out at the sound, and Dean Pera stares plaintively at the control deck until the sound is finally resolved. "Sorry about that! Welcome to this year's homecoming game—go Orcas!"

The crowd, still only half full, cheers and hollers and makes whale sounds in response.

"Before we announce this year's Homecoming King and Queen, we have Mr. and Mrs. Magnussen here tonight to award their community commitment scholarship to a very deserving student. Please come up here—wait—do we have a second mic?" Dean Pera looks frantically around the platform, where everyone just shrugs and shakes their heads. "No? Okay, here, take this, oh, your hands are full—" Dean Pera tries handing off the mic to Gage, whose hands are indeed full holding an honest-to-goodness giant check. "Oh, yes, here, take this—it's on, don't worry," the dean continues to sputter as she passes the mic on to Gage's dad.

"Oh, I remember them," Mom says as Mr. Magnussen begins his speech. "They're that lawyer couple with the office downtown, right, cariño?" she asks Dad, who hums in agreement. "Nice job, mi niña!" she whispers to me, giving me a sly nudge.

After a speech about the importance of community service, the Magnussens award the scholarship to Avery, who gladly takes the giant check from Gage and waddles off the field with it. King and Queen are announced with all the usual fanfare, and I try not to laugh as I watch Sofía force her way through the whole thing with a grim face. Unfortunately for my own amusement, she does not win Queen and practically runs off the field at the first opportunity.

"Let's go introduce ourselves to the Magnussens while they get the field ready," Mom says, tapping my leg before standing up and heading down the bleachers. I can't even argue with her before she's halfway down and making a beeline to where the Magnussens are chatting with Dean Pera on the track, racing ahead of me despite wearing three-inch stilettos.

I chase her down and catch up just as she's squeezing in next to the dean.

"I'm so sorry to interrupt," Mom says, not sounding nearly sorry enough, "but I just had to introduce myself! I'm Maite Morales, Adrian and Valeria's mom." She holds out her hand to the Magnussens.

"Hi, Mrs. and Mr. Magnussen," I say, a little out of breath, as I squeeze in next to Gage. He looks down at me and gives me a quick, reassuring smile. Then his eyes slide to my mom and his brows furrow, before returning to me.

"You look . . . shiny," he says, the corner of his mouth turning up.

"Don't start," I admonish him.

"I've heard wonderful things about your son from my kids," Mom is saying as she shakes their hands.

"Oh, really?" Mrs. Magnussen says in surprise, her forehead hardly moving.

"Well, there's nothing like a rival to make you strive for your best. My son wouldn't have worked nearly as hard in school if your son hadn't been there to keep challenging him." I'm surprised she knows that much about Adrian and Gage's rivalry. They didn't really become academic rivals until well after Mom left. "I'm really grateful to you both for raising such a wonderful young man," she continues, saccharine sweet.

"It's true, nothing makes you work as hard as competition

does," Mr. Magnussen says, eating up everything Mom is saying.

I bite my lip as I watch, unsure how to feel. Gage's parents, who looked a little prickly when we approached, have started to loosen under my mother's gilded tongue. And that's a good thing, right? If she can charm them enough to like me, hopefully they will ease up more on Gage.

Gage reaches down and grabs my hand, holding it firmly in his. I flinch at the sudden contact, but quickly hold on tight as Mom begins to compliment Mrs. Magnussen's necklace.

"Nicole?" Dean Pera calls from a few feet away. "Christopher? Could you come over here?"

"I'm so sorry, Maite," Mrs. Magnussen says, sounding genuinely sorry to be cutting the conversation short.

"No, please, go ahead." Mom waves them off with a smile. Gage's parents leave him behind, and once they're gone, Mom's attention turns to him.

"Oh, you two make such a precious couple," Mom coos, eyes dropping briefly to our clasped hands. "I'm surprised to not see you out on the field, though, Gage! You look so tall and athletic, I would have guessed you were on the team with Adrian."

"Oh, uh," Gage says, and when I look up at him, he's blushing a little under my mom's attention. "I'm not really all that athletic."

Mom lets out that tinkling laugh of hers, her hand playfully pushing at Gage's shoulder.

"Come on, you two, why don't we all go sit together? Gage, let your parents know you're going to sit with us, okay? I want to know everything about you if you're going to be dating my little girl." She doesn't give Gage or me a chance to argue, she just presses gently against his shoulder until he's heading back toward the bleachers.

"I'm sorry," I whisper to him as Mom climbs the bleachers in front of us.

"Hey, I threw a last-minute dinner with my parents at you, so it's only fair that you get to do something equal in return," he says, squeezing my hand.

"Miguel, scoot over," Mom commands as we get back to our row. "Gage is going to sit with us for the game. Pedro, Isabel, you've met Valeria's boyfriend?" Mom pulls Gage over to show him off to the family like a prized pig.

"Oh, yes, from the festival," Papi says, brows furrowing, and I worry that he might have some kind of protective outburst. But Papi manages to be the first guy in our family to not throw a fit upon hearing this news.

"It's good to see you again, Mr. Morales," Gage says politely as Mom pushes him to sit down in the middle. I squeeze myself in between him and my mom, and Miguel helpfully passes over a bag of buttery popcorn.

"Don't they make such a cute couple?" Mom whispers to Dad, loudly enough that we can clearly hear her. I shovel popcorn into my mouth. "She looks just like me at that age," she says wistfully.

"Gage, now, that's not a very common name," Dad says, leaning over to get a better look at Gage. "You must be the one Adrian is neck and neck with for valedictorian."

"Uh," Gage says, his lips twisting in discomfort. "Yeah, that's me. The only Gage in town."

"I don't know where our son got it from," Dad says, shaking his head with a rueful smile. "No one else in the family is good at school—"

"Hey!" Miguel cuts in. "I'm plenty good at school." He's made a grave mistake inserting himself into this conversation, but Miguel hasn't been around my mom long enough to know that.

"You're not at the top of your class like Adrian, though," Mom points out.

"Everyone in the family has their own special skill," Papi says magnanimously. "Miguelito is great with his cameras, Valeria is an amazing artist, and Adrian is—"

"A great test taker?" I cut in despite myself.

"*Student*," Mom corrects. "It's all for the best that it ended up that way," she says cheerfully. "If Valeria had been the one who was good at school, then her and Gage would be rivals instead of being this cute couple!" She laughs at her own little joke, and it gets swallowed up by the crowd cheering as the game starts.

Gage leans over, his mouth hovering next to my ear, breath warm and minty, and whispers so quiet only I can hear him over the roar of the crowd around us.

"Vivamus mea Lesbia, atque amemus, rumoresque senum severiorum," he starts, and a rush of relieved laughter escapes me. More Latin. I elbow him gently in the ribs.

"You trying to put me to sleep?" I ask in a whisper, trying to keep my mom's attention off us. She's gone on to waxing poetic about Adrian and what an amazing young man he is.

"It's a distraction technique," he explains. "To take your

mind off of . . ." He trails off for a second, and I watch his eyes as they slide over to my mom. "Stuff. Should I keep going?"

"We're Catholic, Gage, someone is going to think you're possessed if you keep whispering in Latin," I tell him. "Just keep holding my hand."

Gage's face breaks out into that giant, relaxed smile I've come to love. He wraps an arm around my shoulder and tucks me in close to him before taking hold of my hand again. I lean into him, greedily inhaling his crisp forest smell, feeling the most relaxed I have all week.

CHAPTER TWENTY-THREE

The game starts, and Mom's attention is taken up by Adrian. When he runs onto the field, she jumps up from her seat and cries out his name. Whatever calm I found tucked into Gage's side soon fades as I watch her.

I'm relieved to have her focus off me and Gage, but at the same time some part of me hurts to see her like this. What about my life can my mom jump up and celebrate? The fact that I managed to nab a rich boyfriend who isn't even really my boyfriend? That I was about to flunk out of high school but now I just might make it by the hairs on my chinny-chin-chin?

And where is this all coming from, anyway? How can she be like this here, with us, and then like a ghost and gone in an instant?

I feel wretched after the first quarter, while the rest of the crowd is screaming in excitement as the Orcas score another touchdown. No amount of whispered Latin is going to make me feel better right now.

"I'm going to run to the bathroom," I say as I stand up.

"I can come down with you," Gage offers, and I want to let him, I want to give him the chance to get away from my family for a second, too. But more than anything I just want to be alone for a moment. To gather my thoughts. To calm down.

"No need," I say quickly, trying to give him a placating smile that I'm not sure if he can see through or not.

I try not to run down the bleachers and out of the stadium. But I do run straight to my lucky stall, where I've eaten countless ham sandwiches and memorized the speckled patterns on the walls. No one is in the bathroom, and it's far enough away from the stadium that it's not likely anyone else will show up.

The run has me gasping for breath, swallowing big gulps of air through my mouth that aren't nearly enough to fill my lungs. I feel lightheaded and out of sorts, the tight clothes pressing so deep into my skin that I know they'll leave marks on my stomach and thighs long after I take them off. Even wearing this costume of Perfect Daughter, I end up falling short.

Being around your mother shouldn't hurt this much. Why does being around her make me feel this way? What am I doing wrong?

All I know is, I don't want to be at this fucking football game.

Since we all came together in Dad's car, I can't just drive away and climb in bed like I want to. But Port Murphy is small and I'm wearing sneakers, so I leave the bathroom and head straight to the parking lot. Some students are hanging out, sharing a cigarette for an illicit smoke break, and some people are already heading back to their cars and leaving (these all appear to be the few Vikings fans in the crowd, who must feel let down by their team not scoring a single point so far in the game).

The sun has already set, but thankfully the rain has let up, and I just have the cold to protect myself against as I walk out of the parking lot and onto the street. It's quiet, the distant noise from the football field fading little by little as I make my way down the tree-lined street.

I know I should tell someone that I've left, but if I do that now, Miguel or Dad or, worse, Gage will come get me, and I don't want to deal with any of them right now. I'll text them once I'm safely home and out of these godforsaken jeans.

I hear the rumble of an engine behind me, and I step to the side of the road to let them pass. But the car begins to slow down. I glance over my shoulder anxiously at the approaching headlights, trying to think if I have anything on my person to use as a weapon. My purse has a Swiss Army knife, mostly for on-the-go craft projects, and a can of Mace that is probably expired.

I stop and tuck myself deeper into the side of the road, hoping to escape their attention, but the car pulls to a stop just a few feet from where I'm standing. I squint, trying to get a better look at who's in the car after being blinded by the headlights.

"Valeria?" a familiar voice calls out, a little unsure. "Is that Valeria Morales, or am I talking to a walking disco ball?"

Oh God, my pants. Of course every driver is going to notice me walking down this street, I light up on the ass cheeks.

"Do you need a ride?" The back door of the sedan pops open, automatically turning on the interior lights of the car, and I finally get a good look at who spotted me.

And it is none other than Sofía Ybarra, in a white A-line minidress with bell sleeves and a Homecoming Court sash over her shoulder, a bouquet of teal-dyed flowers discarded next to her in the back seat, and the same old bored expression on her face.

Now that the hatchet has been buried between our families, I've hung out with Sofía once or twice. But I've never really gone out of my way to speak to her. She's always there as a by-product of Ana Maria being present, and as close as they seem to be as sisters, they don't really keep the same social circles. So I don't know Sofía all that well, and she certainly doesn't know me.

"You're going to blind some poor driver if you keep walking down this road in those pants," Jac, Sofía's best friend, quips from the driver's seat. "It's for the safety of Port Murphy that I must offer you a ride."

I have no good reason not to take them up on the offer. They won't bring up my mom or ask about Adrian or make some comment about my new boyfriend, Gage. Because they don't care. And I need that right now.

"Yeah, actually," I say, stepping up to the car. "That sounds great."

"Hop in!" Jac calls out, leaning over the center console to pop open the passenger door.

"Is there a reason Sofía isn't sitting in the front seat?" I ask as I climb into the car.

"Oh, no," Jac says, waving off Sofía and shifting the car into drive. "Sofía is throwing a temper tantrum and treating me like some Uber driver because she thinks I'm the one behind her Homecoming Court nomination."

"Who else would it be?" Sofía snaps from the back seat.

"My love language isn't *tormenting* people, unlike someone I know," Jac says primly. "Where do you live?" he says to me, and I give him a quick rundown of directions.

"I'm just glad it's over," Sofía huffs from the back seat.

"It's not, though. You have to go to the dance tomorrow," Jac reminds her with a Cheshire grin.

"Roberto Reyes Jacinto!" Sofía screeches from the back seat. "I'm going to throw all your left shoes into the sound and replace all of your crew socks with no-show Fruit of the Looms."

Jac gasps in horror at the threat and then breaks into maniacal laughter while Sofía continues to seethe from the back seat.

Even though Jac and Sofía are arguing with each other, I feel like I can finally fully relax. In front of my family I have to pretend like everything is fine and my future isn't facing a huge roadblock. And then in front of Gage, whom I *did* feel so comfortable with, I'm constantly worried about letting my feelings slip. What if I tell him how I feel and he doesn't feel the same? What if I mess up and ruin a perfectly good friendship?

So it's really no surprise that I prefer being in this car that smells vaguely like stale French fries. I lean my head back against the headrest and glance up through the window, marveling at the clear sky full of stars. I hadn't realized exactly how wound up I had been feeling this week until right now, in a car with two juniors yelling back and forth at each other over nonsense.

"Take a right here," I point out to Jac, who almost misses the turn because he was too busy singing to Sofía. Jac ends up taking the turn a little too fast, and Sofía, who isn't wearing a seat belt so she could drape herself despondently across the back seat, goes flying into the car door.

"You did that on purpose!" she cries out.

"That girl has a pair of lungs on her," Jac says to me as he slows down to listen to my street-by-street directions.

"If it's any consolation, Sofía, you did look really badass up on that platform."

"I will find out who did this to me and I *will* get back at them," Sofía promises, and I wonder if both our families are now on the search for new feuds.

"Sofía, you are the real reason I never messed with the Ybarras," I tell her appreciatively. "Your enemy has no idea what's coming for them."

Sofía looks at me through the rearview mirror with a feral smile.

"This is my street," I tell Jac, pointing toward my cozy cul-de-sac. We left the front porch light on, and it now feels like a beacon illuminating the stairs up to the front door and to my solitude. "Thanks for picking me up," I tell them both.

"From one football game escapee to another," Sofía intones from the back seat, "you're welcome. And get rid of those pants."

On a laugh, I step out of the car and give the two a parting wave before bounding up the stairs and unlocking the front door. Leo isn't there to greet me like usual, locked away in the backyard by my mother's fear of dogs again. I open his doggy door as soon as I get inside, and he comes rushing in, covering me in excited licks as I try to wipe down his paws.

"You're coming with me, buddy," I tell him as I lead him upstairs to my room. The first thing I do is shuck off the bedazzled jeans, which never loosened up over time and somehow managed to only feel tighter, and then unzip myself from the containment of the corset top. I toss both articles of clothing back in the Nordstrom bag and leave them by my door in hopes of never seeing them again. I pull on a giant oversized shirt and sweatpants, and I feel my mood improve by a fraction.

Leo has made himself comfortable on the dog bed I keep at the foot of my bed, curled up with his turtle stuffed animal. I shoot off a text to Miguel to let him know I'm home and leave him with the responsibility of relaying that information to the family. I tell him a lie about feeling sick and catching a ride with a friend, which he might not buy.

Then I pull up my text thread with Gage, the guilt of leaving him alone with my family almost too strong.

ME: I'm sorry I just left without notice. Started to feel sick and got a ride home.

GAGE: Do you need anything? Meds? Gatorade? One of those eye mask head massage things?

ME: That last one is tempting, but I'm fine. Just need to lie down in the dark. Please tell me you were able to get away from my family.

GAGE: Miguel pulled a fast one and got us out of there not long after you left, don't worry.

ME: Good

Part of me wants to keep texting Gage, to fall into a familiar rhythm of conversation, but a larger part of me is still too scared. He was so nice and supportive tonight, but Gage is universally known to be a good guy. I'm sure he would do that for any of his friends. If I text him, I'm worried I'll just black out and start typing out how much I like him, how many times I've imagined him turning to me in the library to explain some confusing math lesson but instead of speaking his eyes catch mine and the words get trapped in his throat and he leans forward and—

I put the phone down. *Don't think sweaty thoughts.*

I crawl across my bedroom floor and lie down next to Leo, who's immediately fallen asleep and has started to snore softly. I pull a pillow down from my bed, grab my TV remote, and turn on the most mind-numbing TV I can find and settle in. Somewhere in the house, the furnace kicks on, and dry heat begins to blow through the vent in my floor. I doze off, escaping from all my worldly troubles.

The thing about escaping worldly troubles, however, is that they usually find their way back to you.

"Valeria!"

I bolt upright, the sound of my name being screamed startling both Leo and me awake. I look around, confused for a moment, the low murmur of my TV playing a *Friends* rerun and the darkness of my room befuddling my senses.

"VALERIA!"

I don't get any time to orient myself before my bedroom door bursts open, the bright light from the hallway immediately blinding me.

"How could you?!" my mother cries out from the threshold of my door. She's featureless and hidden in shadow, just the shape of a memory of a mother. But then she clicks on the light to my bedroom, and she is fully illuminated, seething in anger, her chest heaving in a period-romance kind of way.

"Maite, please," Papi is calling out from the top of the stairs.

"No, Pedro, she can't do this," Mom argues, stomping into

my room. "We went to the game together *as a family*, and you left without telling us!"

"Your mother is right," Papi says gently, trying to settle Mom's anger a little. "Something could have happened to you."

"Do you know what happened tonight?" Mom continues. "They won, and when we ran out to the field to celebrate, your brother was looking for *you*."

That's a punch in the gut I didn't expect. I had the old Adrian back this week, the Adrian who looked me in the eyes when he spoke to me, the brother who cared about me. And I wasn't there for him.

"You are his other half, Valeria," Mom says. "And you left him behind because you decided to be selfish instead— "

"It's selfish to get *sick*?" I cry out. But Mom rolls her eyes at this, like I'm the one who's out of line, or like she can see through my lie.

"Cariño," Papi says, laying a gentle hand on Mom's shoulder. "I know Adrian was upset that Valeria wasn't there, but I think that's something they should handle between themselves."

For a second I appreciate Papi trying to get Mom to back off, but his tactic of letting Adrian and me handle things between ourselves hasn't exactly worked out this year.

Mom purses her lips, clearly not wanting to let this go, but Papi's words have managed to convince her. She turns on her heel and leaves without another word. Papi watches her departure for a moment, brows furrowed, before turning back to me.

"Who did you get a ride home with?" he asks me.

"Jac, Sofía Ybarra's friend," I tell him. "He's a very good

driver," I hurry to add, thinking of the too-fast turn and Sofía's small crash against the door. Other than that, he kept to the speed limit and didn't blow any red lights.

"Don't do that again," Papi warns me.

I just nod, because I know if I speak again, I'll probably end up lying. And I've done enough of that today.

CHAPTER TWENTY-FOUR

I toss and turn in bed all night, my mother's words ringing in my head. *Selfish.* And maybe she's right. Running away from my family because of the strange cocktail of emotions I feel being around them was selfish of me. But that doesn't mean it was wrong.

I give up on my bed around three in the morning and climb back down to the little nest I made earlier in the night. Around hour two of not being able to fall asleep, I start googling tips for sleeping, and at the top of every list is NO SCREENS, so I have to switch to analog methods of slowing my mind down. I don't keep many books in my room, and the closest one to my bed is my Algebra II textbook, which probably has the best chance out of everything at making me fall asleep.

When it inevitably fails to do so, I return to playing a rerun of my least favorite memories in my head. I don't *mean* to do it, but for some reason these are the only thoughts my mind can provide me with. It is what my mind turns to when I can't distract it with anything else.

Remember when you bled through your pants in middle school without realizing it and an eighth grader ended up having to pull you aside to break the news? Who knew how long you were walking around like that with people noticing and not telling you? And remember when you came home and your mom was horrified to see you had stained the new jeans she had just gotten you?

Or what about the time you went to a family reunion for your great-aunt's wedding anniversary in North Bergen, New Jersey, and it happened to coincide with your tenth birthday? And Adrian was just showing his early promise at being not only an excellent student, but also a promising athlete? And you . . . got really good at drawing horses? So when your family went out to dinner to celebrate your birthday at some fancy restaurant in the city, the waitress misunderstood that you were twins and only had one small chocolate lava cake with a candle to present to the table? And when Dad pointed it out, Mom brushed it off and said we could blow out the candle together but I was getting too chubby to be eating a chocolate lava cake anyway, and Adrian ate our birthday cake all by himself because he was a promising young athlete who burned off the calories he ate?

"Oh God, please stop," I mutter to myself.

It feels like no thought is safe this late at night. So I start trying to envision future art projects I have in my mind. I've been so caught up with school and the gala and all the other drama in my life, I've had no time to create anything recently. Like the mural I'd like to paint somewhere in town. There are a couple buildings with empty side walls just waiting to be covered in art.

I map out the composition in my mind, imagining all the different elements I'd want to include. It would be something with lots of florals and greenery, big fat leaves and huge blooming flowers. Rhododendrons in bright and muted pinks, wisteria dripping purple petals, bright green palm fronds, and dozens of orchids in pinks and whites and purples. Ana Maria likes to create fusion food, taking classic Cuban dishes and flavors and applying local produce. I'm the same, but my medium is my art, and I like to pull inspiration from the beautiful foliage of both the home I might never know, Cuba, and the home that might never fit just right, Port Murphy.

I must fall asleep somewhere between the thoughts of color palettes and composition and flowers, because morning light wakes me up. I'm curled up in some kind of pretzel position, my head twisted to the side and my legs resting up on the foot of my bed. I'm sore all over from sleeping on the floor, and it's a struggle to pull myself up.

I wonder if I can hide out in my room for the rest of the day, but a growl from the pit of my stomach convinces me to risk it all and go downstairs.

Leo is trapped outside again, his plaintive dark eyes watching me descend the stairs from the back door. No one else seems to be awake yet, so I scour through the kitchen in the dark for something to take up to my room with me. I'm crouched over, halfway in the pantry, trying to see if my favorite flavor of instant oatmeal is hiding somewhere back there, when someone taps my shoulder.

"Valeria?"

I screech in response, caught in full gremlin mode, doubled over in a stained oversized T-shirt with bedhead, but I relax once I see it's Tia Isa.

"Sorry!" she says immediately, backing away and letting me collect myself.

"It's okay, you just startled me," I tell her, trying to smooth down my hair.

"Your mom is out with Adrian," Tia Isa tells me. "She wanted to take him for breakfast and a haircut for the homecoming dance."

"Where's Dad?" I ask.

"Where else?" she says with an eye roll. "At that new location. He wants to pick out the tile and paint colors for the bathrooms, but his contractor doesn't like the kind of tile he picked out because it's a pain in the ass to install, so your father has decided to learn how to install tile himself."

"Of course he has," I say, joining her in her eye roll.

I hear a scratching at the back door, and both Isa and I turn to see Leo pawing at it.

"Do you mind if we keep Leo downstairs with us?" she asks. "I just feel so bad for him, trapped outside all the time, and it's starting to get cold at night."

"Of course," I say. "I wouldn't mind that at all. I hate that he's been outside so much."

"Okay, good," she says with a smile. "Can I make you some breakfast?" she offers, and my stomach grumbles loudly before I can even respond. Tia Isa laughs and turns to the fridge. "I'll take that as my answer. What are you feeling up for? Tortilla? Pancakes? Waffles? A sandwich?"

"You know what?" I say, the memory of not getting to eat a sweet, delicious treat on my birthday still echoing in my head from last night. "I'm kind of craving a batido de trigo."

"Oh," she says, raising her eyebrows in surprise. Tia Isa, unlike me, is dressed and perfectly groomed this morning. She's wearing khaki slacks and a white-and-tan-striped shirt tucked in, with gold bracelets on her wrist and dark hair messily blown out. The Pacific Northwest hasn't infected her yet with trail gear, and she keeps dressing up like she still has people to impress in Los Angeles. I'm expecting this "oh" from her to be judgment, disapproval over my choice for breakfast, since it lacks pretty much any beneficial nutrients and is full of sugar.

I'm ready for her to say something, I can feel my body tensing up, I can feel myself ready to spit and shout and blow up over whatever response she has to my craving.

"I haven't had one of those in forever!" she says instead, laughing suddenly, her eyes crinkling at the corners. "My grandmother used to make those for us all the time in the summers to help keep us cool, since they didn't have any AC." Tia Isa turns toward the fridge to start gathering her ingredients. "Will you grab the cereal from the pantry?"

I'm frozen for a second, my pent-up anticipatory aggression having nowhere to go. I might expect it to blow up anyway, but it deflates just as quickly as it came.

"Yeah, sure," I say, reaching into the pantry for the sealed container of puffed wheat cereal.

"You have me craving one now, too," Tia Isa says as she pops open a can of condensed milk. "I think drinking one of these on a day as gray as today will help me remember what sunshine felt like."

"Do you miss LA?" I ask her as I settle into one of the chairs on the peninsula.

"Oh, I don't know," Tia Isa says, pulling out the blender and plugging it in. "I miss the sunshine, I miss the food, I miss the energy of the city. But while I was there, some parts of me missed Port Murphy, too," she muses. "I missed the quiet, I missed how green it was, and as much as I hated it while I was living here, I kind of missed how close-knit the community is."

"So you're not planning on going back?" I realize I've never asked. I don't often talk to Tia one-on-one. Honestly, I've avoided it.

"As if I could afford to," Tia Isa says on a laugh. "Do you think I would still be living in my brother's basement with my son if I had any chance of going back to LA?"

"I didn't realize it was that bad," I tell her, feeling a little guilty for how snappy I've been the last few months.

Tia Isa just sighs and kicks on the blender. It doesn't take long at all for the drink to come together, a delicious and sweet treat that Tia Isa pours into two glasses. She hands me mine and gives me a little tap with hers in a "cheers" motion before taking a sip.

"Oh my God, I forgot how good this is," I say after my first sip. It's sweet and nutty from the cereal, with just a hint of cinnamon and vanilla.

Tia Isa smiles at me over the rim of her glass. Her mouth

purses up for a moment, and it looks like she's considering saying something, maybe something about Los Angeles or her divorce, but she just sighs again and takes another sip of her drink.

I take my milkshake upstairs with a granola bar and settle into my bed with my sketchbook. I map out the mural I envisioned last night, adding in birds in flight and leaves in the empty spots of my composition. I've mapped out a dozen different designs, mimicking the motif of classic Cuban cement tiles, but using flowers and nature as the individual elements that make up the design.

A blooming guava flower with dozens of white stamens radiating around in an almost starlike pattern. Wisteria boughs fanning out in a circle around a bundle of cherries. Limes cut in half to reveal their beautiful pattern of seeds and segments, arranged in a circle to make the negative space between the limes look like a star.

With my sketch done, I move to the floor and pull out the oil pastels from under my bed. I start on a color version of my same compositions, landing on a style that isn't as graphic in nature as Cuban styles but isn't too focused on capturing realism. I change up the color palette between each tile design, going from dusky pinks and sage greens and white to lavender and deep cherry red and bright green.

My phone pings with a text from Gage, reminding me of how I left him to the wolves last night.

GAGE: How are you feeling today? Should I go through and finish that exorcism I started last night?

ME: I'm fine. Spending today working on an art project to take my mind off things. And this Latin thing of yours is getting out of control.

I send him a picture of some of my sketches.

GAGE: These are amazing! Also, is that the corner of a stuffed animal I see? Are you the one with the creepy collection of stuffed animals and skeletons and whatever else you accused me of?

ME: No comment.

I throw a blanket on top of my giant alligator stuffed animal and get back to work, ignoring Gage's teasing text.

Hours later, dozens of finished tile patterns are spread around me on the floor, some loud and bold and others more subdued and delicate. I'm so focused on my project, headphones on and in the zone, that I don't notice when Adrian and my mom get back home until my bedroom door pops open. The draft of cool air from the hallway catches my attention before anything else, and I glance over my shoulder to see Mom standing in my doorway, just like she was last night.

She looks less threatening now, not cast in shadow and looming over me like some avenging angel. But she still manages to look a little threatening anyway, just by being so put-together and sharp. She's wearing a pair of tight white jeans that look like they could be painted on and a loose striped button-up that has enough buttons undone at the top to show off her décolletage. Her highlighted hair is pulled up tight in a sleek ponytail, and she's perfectly accessorized from head to toe.

"You're not getting ready for the dance?" Mom asks, her eyes flitting only briefly to the chaos of paper around me.

"Not really my scene," I tell her as I sit up and try to look a little less slouchy.

"Your boyfriend didn't ask you?"

"Not really his scene, either," I say through my teeth.

"But it's your senior year," she prods, arms crossed over her chest.

"It sure is," I say, not really knowing how else to respond to this strange investigation.

"Well, your brother has to go pick up his date and take pictures at her house, so we're getting together downstairs now before he leaves," she tells me. "You should come down and see him. It's the least you owe him."

With that pronouncement, she turns on her heel and clomps downstairs. Her appearance in my doorway has shamed me enough to want to get out of my grubby clothes, so I step into my bathroom and splash water over my face and brush my hair so I can braid it. I wash the pigment from my fingers and rub some Vaseline on my lips before going to my closet and pulling out something comfortable but less shabby. I take out a pair of loose plaid pants and a black turtleneck, an outfit that I think my mom wouldn't have too many negative things to say about, and head downstairs.

No one could ever accuse Adrian Morales of not being fashionable. Where I hated back-to-school shopping in the summers with Mom, Adrian *loved* it. He takes a lot of pride in how he looks, always keeping himself well groomed, his clothes neat and trendy and never too loud, but just loud enough for me to hide behind.

Tonight is no exception. He's wearing a stylish ivory knit

polo, a set of ivory dress pants and coat, and the short Cuban link necklace we each got for our sixteenth birthday. It was the gift Mom sent us from Miami that first year she was gone, and it's so expensive that I'm honestly afraid to wear it out.

I let out a wolf whistle from the landing on the stairs when I catch sight of my twin, and he immediately looks up at me with his big smile. Whatever feelings he had about me not staying for the game last night seem to be resolved, because he's giving me that goofy grin he only gives when he's *really* happy.

"You're looking sharp!" I call out as I continue down the stairs. "Who's the lucky lady that earned the honor of your hand at tonight's dance?"

"Vivi," Adrian says with that same proud smile, and I'm relieved to learn that Ginger didn't get picked. Vivi is one of five Olivias in our graduating class, not to be confused with last year's prom date, Liv, also short for Olivia. "Lane is coming over soon and we're heading over to her dad's place."

"¡Mira a mi hijo!" Mom cries out. "Tan grande y guapo." She gives his cheek a little squeeze for good measure. Adrian brushes it off good-naturedly.

"He cleans up well," Papi says, his voice a little gruff.

I want to ask after Miguel, but since Tia Isa isn't here watching the Adrian Morales show, I assume Miguel is somewhere else getting ready or already at the Ybarras' house. I would have thought that the homecoming dance wouldn't interest either Ana Maria or my cousin, but Miguel insisted that he wanted to experience the small-town charm of homecoming in Port Murphy, though I fear he's in for disappointment.

Our homecoming dance happens in the gym every year,

despite the basketball coach's pleas to spare the expensive floor. Each year the student government tries their best to transform our circa 1972 gym into a teen movie dream, but every year they fall short, especially given how protective Coach Miller is of his precious court. It doesn't have quite the same allure as what Miguel is used to. He told me his last homecoming dance in Los Angeles happened on a rooftop at some fancy hotel.

"Quiero tomar unas fotos afuera," Mom insists, starting to push Adrian out the door. "The light is just right." She turns back to Papi briefly and hands him her phone. "¡Toma!"

It seems like my transgression from last night has been forgotten, replaced by the spectacle of Adrian going out to homecoming. I'm just a fly on the wall, watching my family coo over my twin as I fall deeper and deeper into shadow.

CHAPTER TWENTY-FIVE

The fanfare around Adrian's final homecoming dance fades as soon as Lane comes over. Both boys climb into Adrian's car and set off into the sunset to make some girls' dreams come true. I'm sure dating my brother is on plenty of people's vision board.

While my parents are still outside, distracted with teary goodbyes like Adrian was leaving for war, I run to the kitchen for a quick meal. The stove is empty, no delicious concoction by Tia Isa waiting to be eaten, and there are no leftovers to reheat in the fridge.

Not wanting to spend too much time downstairs, I throw a random assortment of things on a plate for myself. Cold cuts, two different types of cheese, a spoonful of olives, a smattering of cornichons, a sleeve of crackers, five cherry tomatoes, and one of the hard-boiled eggs that Adrian likes to keep stocked in the fridge. Then I sneak one of the fancy bars of chocolate that Dad thinks he's hidden in the pantry, except that I'm nosy enough to look into a box of Grape-Nuts to see what's inside.

I try to make my escape with my plate, but Papi comes in through the front door as I take my first step up the stairs. I slip the contraband chocolate bar into my pocket and out of sight.

"No plans for tonight?" he says, closing the door behind him and eyeing my plate of food.

"I'm actually going to start putting together the presentation for the auction I'm helping Gage with," I tell him, feeling a little proud of my accomplishment. The list of auction items for this gala is *stacked*. And even though Gage's parents haven't said anything about it one way or another, I'm going to take their silence as a good thing. Because I'm sure if I had done anything wrong up to this point, they would have let me know. *Loudly*.

"You put together quite the pitch for that auction," Papi says proudly, because of course Morales Bakery is participating. "It's all very impressive."

"I'm glad you think so," I say with a smile.

"That doesn't look much like dinner, though," he notes, glancing down at my plate. I thought I had done a good job putting this plate together. I'm pretty sure all major food groups are accounted for. "We can go out for dinner with your mom if you want? Locicero's might be packed with pre-homecoming chaos, but we can drive out a little farther for something?"

I would normally be happy to take my dad up on this offer. On the nights when Adrian had away games, Papi and I would go out for dinner at different spots near Port Murphy. The fish-and-chips shack by the water, a no-frills Hawaiian spot half an hour east with killer loco moco and fried chicken, the '50s-style drive-through with buttery burgers and perfect fries. But that was a tradition that started After Mom Left, and it's not really one I want to do *with* her.

"I really need to work on this presentation," I lie, because no one actually asked me to do this. No one is waiting for it or expecting it. I just thought it would be a handy visual to have for the auction. "And I think this plate looks plenty like dinner," I argue. Papi is a meat-and-potatoes kind of man, or rather, meat and rice. And sometimes also potatoes.

"Okay, mijita," he relents. "Enjoy your rabbit food."

I rush upstairs, worried that if I linger any longer on the landing, my mom will catch me. I turn on some random TV show and sit on the floor with my plate, enjoying every bite.

There is a DIY art drying rack I made in my bedroom, built out of dowels and one-by-twos, that I carefully place my tile drawings on. I'm not finished with all the pieces, but putting them on the rack will at least protect the pastels from smudging while I do other things.

I start building out the template for my presentation, hoping that if I keep myself as busy as possible, my mind won't have time to wander and, when it's time to go to bed, I can keep my brain quiet enough to fall asleep.

But despite the hours I spend on the presentation and googling how to legally paint a mural on a wall, when midnight hits, I still can't fall asleep. Adrian isn't home, likely at some after-party, and the house is silent.

I toss and turn for a good while before sitting up in frustration.

I cannot take another night in my bedroom unable to fall asleep. I will lose my mind.

Picking up my phone, I open my messages and stare at my thread with Gage. Even though I offered him boring stories to help him fall asleep, he's never taken me up on the offer, instead just sending me dozens of voice notes in Latin that I can't understand.

Me: *Are you up?*

I wait anxiously for the typing dots bubble to appear on my screen. When a minute passes, I want to throw my phone across the room in embarrassment. Did I really just send my fake boyfriend a "u up?" text??

But my phone buzzes in my hand before I can go any further down that spiral.

GAGE: Unfortunately. I have a big project due next week that I decided to restart at the eleventh hour.

ME: I would ask if I could help you with it, but I think my skills aren't really applicable to anything you do.

GAGE: Actually, you're wrong. I think I could use your help on this.

ME: Gage, I already told you, I speak Spanish, not Latin. I can't do your homework for you.

GAGE: It's not Latin, which I do think you would be good at because you know Spanish. It's for my Marine Robotics class.

ME: HA!

GAGE: I'm not joking. I need your help. Desperately. Please.

ME: Gage, I don't know how to tell you this, but I'm technically still failing Algebra II. Have you recently hit your head? What is going on?

GAGE: Come pick me up. I just took three shots of espresso and feel like I am going to bounce off the walls, so I don't feel comfortable driving. We can go to Lacey's. I promise I'm so serious when I say I need your help.

ME: At this point I'm just too curious, I have to know what about MARINE ROBOTICS you think I can help with. I'll pick you up, you caffeine wimp.

I check myself in my mirror once, just to make sure I don't have chocolate smeared all around my mouth—I ate half of Papi's cannoli-flavored dark chocolate bar, full of chunky pistachio cream and crispy cannoli shell in a white chocolate truffle filling that had just the smallest hint of mascarpone flavor—and shove my computer into a tote bag before creeping downstairs.

I would normally have to be careful about Leo's attention when sneaking out, since he can't help but excitedly greet any human he sees, but now that he's safely in the basement, I'm in the clear. The last obstacle in my way is the alarm system, which has already been turned on. If I turn it off, all the beeps will be more than enough to catch my parents' attention, so I have to go the more humiliating route: the doggy door.

Thankfully Leo is a large dog, so when my dad got this thing installed, he went for the bigger size, which also happens to fit wayward teenagers. Climbing through the doggy door is easy enough, and while walking through the backyard does trip the automatic lights, I know how to stay out of the eye line of any window with curious adults.

The worst part of this escape route is the back fence, which Papi keeps padlocked, leaving me to climb. Thankfully my height is an advantage here. The decorative trellis at the top of the fence is covered with overgrown blackberry vines that Papi has let grow out of control, so I just have to be careful where I put my hands.

I haul myself up a little before swinging my leg over the fence and make sure I'm balanced and secure before throwing my other leg over. I usually hop off from here, but a rogue blackberry vine catches on my right sleeve and rips through the fabric. I stumble from the sudden yanking and fall awkwardly the rest of the way down, landing directly on my ass.

Not my most graceful exit.

I do a quick assessment of my arm in the dark—it's still attached, so we're safe in my books—and jog over to my car. With Miguel and Adrian out doing homecoming things, my car is free and clear for an escape.

I back out of the driveway without turning my headlights on and check the house one more time to make sure no lights have turned on. Pleased to see all the windows still dark, I turn right at the stop sign and head out.

The streets are empty this late at night, the streetlamps doing little to illuminate the road. I roll down my windows to let the crisp fall air blow through my car, bringing with it the damp smell of leaves and smoke. Some people might say that summer is the best season in the Pacific Northwest, when everything is bright green and in bloom, with blue skies and warm days. But I love the cooler fall days, when the sunshine gets trapped behind moody clouds and the gradient of fall colors overwhelms the evergreen trees. The tourists leave for sunnier spots and the locals turn indoors.

It's even better at night, when the threat of winter looms

closer and closer, and you can feel its chill breath down your neck. People turn on their fireplaces at home, and the air fills with the warm smell of woodsmoke. And if you know where to go, you can catch glimpses of the aurora borealis at night.

When I reach Gage's, I make sure to stop a little down the street from his house and shoot him a text. He's bounding down the driveway in seconds, wearing a pair of sweats and carrying a large tote bag. I pop the trunk for him and he places his bag in the back before climbing into the passenger seat.

"Hey," he says with a grin as he settles into the seat. With the door open, the lights in the car are on, and I get a good look at late-night Gage Magnussen. He's more mussed than I've ever seen him, his hair going every which way, and wearing a well-worn quarter zip with a graphic T-shirt peeking through the top. But he has a sleepy smile on his face as he looks at me, before his eyes dip down to my arm and widen with concern. "You're bleeding!"

I look down at my arm in surprise, expecting to have a gash with a bone sticking out, considering his reaction. I pull down the ripped sleeve and try to inspect the cut, but it's on the outside of my arm and hard to see.

"It's just a scratch," I assure him. "I cut myself on some blackberry bushes."

"Where's your first aid kit?" he asks.

"Um, it doesn't exist?" I'm not even sure if we have one at home beyond the one bathroom drawer full of mismatched Band-Aids and expired Neosporin.

Gage rolls his eyes dramatically.

"Hold on," he tells me, hopping out of his car and running

back up to his driveway. He disappears into his house for a couple of minutes before returning to my car with an honest-to-goodness first aid kit in his hands.

"Where did you get that?" I ask as he sets to work, opening the kit and pulling out his tools like an ER doctor.

"The downstairs bathroom," he tells me, lining up everything he needs on a piece of paper towel on the dashboard. Cotton swabs, an antiseptic wipe, a Band-Aid, and a cute, tiny tub of Vaseline. "And now it's going to be your car first aid kit, because I can't believe you're driving around without one."

"I can get my own, really—"

"No arguments, this is your first aid kit now. Give me your arm," he says briskly. I give him my arm, and he quickly gets to work, cleaning the area around my cut with the antiseptic wipe. His grip is firm but careful, one hand gently holding on to my wrist while he works. "I didn't realize you were so accident-prone," he says, picking up the Vaseline.

"Oh, I am," I assure him. "Adrian got all the coordination in the womb."

"That's not true," he argues, not looking up from my arm. "Art takes plenty of coordination, and you're really good at that. Those sketches you sent me today are amazing."

My cheeks heat suddenly, not sure what to do with this compliment from Gage while he's cradling my wrist in his hands and endearingly looking after a silly little scrape. I'm so flustered I can't think of anything to say in response.

"Also, if I'm remembering correctly, you won the seventh-grade juggling competition and won your class a pizza party," he adds.

"What?" I say, pulling my arm out of his grasp. He looks up at me, startled. "How can you possibly remember that?"

I had totally forgotten about it. What I do recall is Jake Griffith saying something about girls not being able to juggle because our hands were too small, and I remember becoming infuriated. I spent an entire month teaching myself to juggle, not only for the promised pizza party if I won, but to prove Jake wrong.

The competition was simple: the last person still juggling wins. And I managed to be the last one standing on the stage in the cafeteria, three beanbags flying in perfect arc after perfect arc. It was by no means a *popular* thing to win, but the social capital of earning your class a pizza party was enough to make up for how goofy it felt juggling in front of everyone.

"I remember," Gage says, pulling my arm back into his grasp, "because I was juggling against you that day."

I gasp out loud at that, like Gage has just told me his deepest, darkest secret. He grins at my reaction and turns his attention back to my arm so he can apply my Band-Aid. I don't remember Gage being on that stage with me. I just remember Adrian in the crowd cheering me on and Rose somewhere booing loudly.

"We were the last two of the seventh-grade class left standing. It was neck and neck until my finger got stuck around a beanbag and my whole rhythm was thrown off. Anyway, the point of bringing this up was to say you may be accident-prone, but that doesn't mean you lack coordination. Or gumption, honestly. You put your mind to something, and you see it through."

"I don't know, that sounds more like stubbornness to me," I tell him.

"Well, you have plenty of that, too," he says with a smile,

dropping my arm gently on the center console and cleaning up his nursing station.

"Thanks for that," I tell him, trying to get a look at his handiwork. All I can really see is a carefully applied Band-Aid. The cut stings a little, but I'm sure once I stop thinking about it, I'll stop noticing it.

"Dr. Gage, am I cleared to drive now?" I ask.

"Good to go," he says, tucking my new first aid kit in the back seat before buckling up.

CHAPTER TWENTY-SIX

Lacey's Diner is engulfed in a layer of fog when we approach, its golden light glowing ethereally through the mist. I'm surprised to find the parking lot nearly empty when we roll in, and it almost feels like we have the diner to ourselves as we step inside.

This place is usually a hot spot in Port Murphy no matter what time of day it is. In the mornings, elderly couples sit at the Formica tables with the newspaper and endless cups of coffee. In the evenings, young families and loud teenagers can be found eating burgers and milkshakes for dinner.

But after midnight? All the usual charm is there, but there's something special about a nearly empty diner at night. It feels like a liminal space, with the angled light from the open blinds casting strange shadows over the aged wood paneling and shiny chrome.

My favorite waitress, Robin, is behind the counter wiping some milkshake glasses dry, and she doesn't even glance up at us when the bell rings above the door, announcing our entrance.

An elderly white man is sitting in the corner booth, half-illuminated by the pendant hanging over his table, his focus entirely absorbed by the crossword puzzle he has laid out in front of him. There's a sleepy couple in mussed-up dress clothes sitting at the counter sharing a milkshake, but other than that, the place is empty.

Gage has his mystery tote over his shoulder as he picks out a booth in the middle of the diner. I go to set my bag down on the opposite side, but Gage stops me with a hand across the table.

"No, you should sit next to me," he insists. "Remember? I need your help."

"Ah, yes, your Marine Robotics project, which I wasn't even aware was an elective we could take," I say as I slide in next to him. "So, what is it? Do you need help with the marine part or the robotics part? I do know that the blue whale is the largest mammal on Earth. Does that help you?"

"No, that's not quite the help I was looking for," he says. Then he reaches into his bag and pulls out . . . a Tupperware full of wires with a GoPro and two fans attached. Not what I expected.

"What're you ordering?" Robin barks, appearing suddenly and bringing with her the stale smell of cigarette smoke and patchouli. She has been working at Lacey's since I was a kid, and I've never seen her warm up to *anyone*. She has bleach-blond hair, a raspy voice from smoking, and surprisingly leathery skin for someone who lives in the part of the country that gets the least amount of sun. I like to imagine she spends her vacations in Aruba soaking in the rays and slurping on daiquiris.

That or she has a tanning bed problem, like a lot of other white women in this town.

"Mozzarella sticks?" Gage says, caught off guard by Robin's approach.

"What pies do you have left?" I ask.

Robin glances over her shoulder and with what I presume is X-ray vision inspects the pie fridge behind the counter.

"Pistachio plum, Dutch apple, banoffee, hazelnut chess, and corn pudding." She turns back to me with her expressionless eyes. "Though I wouldn't get the banoffee."

"Thanks for the tip, Robin," I say, considering my options. "I'll have the pistachio plum." Robin nods and walks off before we can ask for anything else. I turn back to Gage and his mystery box, ducking down to inspect all the wires encased in the clear box. "Do you want me to paint this Tupperware to make it look like some kind of sea creature? Or rock, I guess?"

"Not what I was thinking," Gage says, "But it is a good idea. Do you know what this is?"

"Absolutely not," I tell him. "I can't even come up with a joke answer, I'm so confused by this."

"It's a robot," he says, sounding surprised that I didn't guess that.

"What?" I say, looking back down at the bundle of wires in the plastic box. "No way. Shouldn't it have a creepy humanoid face, or limbs at the very least?"

"It's not that kind of robot," he says patiently. "It's a remotely operated vehicle for underwater exploration, and it's my midterm project. This thing is worth around a third of my grade in that class."

"And you're trusting me to help you with it?" I ask him in alarm.

"Look," he says, scooting in close to me, the smell of his green soap washing over me suddenly. He leans over to the side, shoulder pressing against mine, as he pulls his phone from his back pocket. His touch is there and gone in a second, but it's enough to set my heart racing. *Homework! We're here for homework!*

"We've spent most of the semester building the robot," he explains, unlocking his phone and navigating to an app with an unfamiliar icon. "But the last leg of the project is building the user interface for the remote. Everything on the robot works, it's totally functioning, but the app looks terrible."

The app in question does look awful. He's pulled what appears to be clip art images for his buttons, and everything is butting up against each other, with no margin or space for things to breathe.

"Oh wow," I say, taking hold of his phone and pulling the screen toward me. "That is bad. I can see why you wanted my help."

Gage's leg starts to bounce up and down anxiously, and I press a hand down on it to reassure him. The touch of my hand on his leg is enough to get him to stop fidgeting, but then I realize what I've done and exactly where my hand is and I snatch it back like it's on fire. I can feel the blush rising up my neck, and I flip my hair over my shoulder in an attempt to hide it.

"Don't worry, we can fix this," I assure him. "Let's start with this layout." I take out my computer and open Photoshop—the subscription is generously provided by my school, but I've mostly used it to take pictures of Adrian and subtly change his features before posting to my Instagram to drive him crazy—and start out on a new layout for Gage.

He watches over my shoulder as I lay out the basic blocks with rectangles. He points out what works and doesn't work from my design based on how the app will be used, and we work together to build a streamlined wireframe for him to reference.

"Hot plates," Robin hollers before throwing down our food. Gage quickly moves his robot out of the way, and we tuck our computers back into their bags for a break.

"So, Marine Robotics?" I ask, picking up my fork and pulling my slice of pie close. I break off a piece and inspect the layers: a flaky, buttery crust, a thick layer of pistachio frangipane, and slices of shiny plums nestled into the filling.

"Marine Robotics," Gage repeats, dipping his mozzarella stick into the marinara cup until half the sauce is sitting on the stick. "The fact that Port Murphy High offers that class is the reason I begged my parents to let me go here instead of that magnet school half an hour away."

"Is that what you really want to do? Explore the deep, mysterious depths of the ocean?" I ask him before taking a bite of my pie. It's *perfection*.

"More than anything," Gage admits. "My parents have been hoping since middle school that my interest would fade into some forgotten hobby, but I've only gotten more interested in the field." That would explain the inordinate amount of crab and marine-themed bumper stickers on his car.

"But they're still pushing you to go into law?" I ask, my

voice gentle. Gage has circled around this subject with me many times at this point, but he's never been so up front with it before.

"They won't let it go," he says, dropping his mozzarella stick and leaning back in the booth. "At one point I thought I could suck it up because I kind of idolized them. They were this amazing power couple in a world where all my friends' parents were getting divorced or struggling to make ends meet. My parents were the blueprint of what I wanted for my life for the longest time. But after last year, I've started to see the cracks, and I'm . . ." He sighs, throwing his head back to look at the ceiling. "I don't want to be like them."

I don't know what to say, what I can do to take that despondent look off his face. I don't really know what it's like to have a dream crumble before your eyes, because I never let myself wish for things like that. Hope and desperation are too close for comfort to me.

"Well, if that's the case," I say, sneaking my hand into his to give him a comforting squeeze, "then we have to make sure you kill it with this project, right?" Gage looks over at me, eyes bright from caffeine and emotions that I can't quite read. "So let's finish this food and get back to it, okay?"

Gage and I clear our plates in record time, our conversation turning toward more mundane topics. When Robin clears our table, we pull our computers back up and get to work. I send Gage the wireframe for him to reference as he rebuilds the user interface, and I open the auction presentation back up.

"I wanted to ask . . ." Gage says suddenly, after a few minutes of working in silence. I look up from my screen to his face, which looks hesitant and unsure. "What happened last night? I know you said you were feeling sick, but you left without saying anything."

"Oh," I say, my turn to feel uncomfortable. And even though Gage was just vulnerable with me, I can't bring myself to go there. Not here, under the florescent lights of Lacey's Diner while the old man doing crosswords clears his throat and the couple giggles in the corner. "I just didn't feel well. I got a ride home with Sofía's friend, Jac."

"And your mom was there," he adds. "I was not expecting that."

"None of us were," I say, and I can't help but laugh. "She surprised us all. Adrian is over the moon about it."

"And you?" Gage prods.

"Well, it was quite the shock," I admit. "But my family is back together. I can't complain."

"But you can if you want to, you know," Gage says softly, like he's scared I might run away now that he's prodding this open wound I've been trying to hide. Could I tell him those dark, twisting feelings swirling around inside me? Show him the feelings of resentment and frustration and rage toward my family, the ugliest side of myself? If I want him to like me, I can't let him see that part of me.

"Thanks," I say, trying to swallow down the panic.

I'm not sure if Gage senses how uncomfortable I am about this subject or if he just wants to get back to work, but he leaves the conversation there. And I'm grateful.

We work for another hour, Robin dropping by to refill our waters while the diner slowly empties out. Gage, who was all anxious energy from the surplus of coffee, has started to mellow out, and my eyes have started to feel a little heavy. At one point, I can't hold back my yawn.

"We should get going," Gage says, shutting his laptop. I follow suit and stick my computer back in my bag. Gage carefully tucks his robotics project back in its tote and packs up his laptop. "You still good to drive? You look like you could fall asleep right here."

"I just look like that," I tell him. "I've had more than one teacher tell me they don't like my 'listening face' because I look like I'm falling asleep. But that's just what I look like when I'm focused."

"You never look like that when I'm tutoring you," Gage points out.

"Well, maybe you need to step up your tutoring game," I tease. "Your tutoring isn't interesting enough to warrant *all* of my focus. Did you catch that last Wednesday there was a kid in the stacks planting booby traps in the nonfiction F shelf? No one caught him, but then on Thursday I passed down that aisle, and there was glitter *everywhere*."

"That *happened*?" Gage asks in surprise as we step outside, and I shiver a little at the sudden gust of cold wind that hits me. "Why didn't you tell me? I would have loved to have seen that, or at least known about it."

"I don't know, you were so focused on explaining something about exponents to me, and I didn't have the heart to interrupt you," I tell him. "The next time I see someone lollygagging in the library, I will tell you. Promise." We put our bags in my trunk and quickly get inside.

We coast down the empty streets of Port Murphy, the radio tuned to some station that plays Japanese city pop in the middle of the night. We ride in pleasant silence together, Gage tapping his fingers along to the music on his thigh and me humming to the songs that I know.

When we get to his street, I make sure to roll to a stop two houses down from his, like earlier. Gage unbuckles his seat belt but doesn't move to open the door.

"You know," Gage says, shifting uncomfortably in his seat, his focus firmly somewhere around his feet, "I don't think it's fair that I don't take up all of your focus when I'm tutoring you."

"I'm telling you, people get up to shenanigans in that library—"

"I don't think it's *fair*," he says again, firmly this time, but with an edge of nerves, "because I have to work so hard to make sure you don't take up all of my attention."

The confession burbles out of him, and it takes me a moment to process what he's said. Maybe I did fall asleep on my laptop tonight. Maybe none of this is real and I'm just dreaming that Gage is watching me with the most earnest expression I have ever seen.

But the beating of my heart feels very, very real when he continues, "I am entranced by you, Valeria. It drives me crazy, because even when I'm not around you, I find myself thinking about you, wanting to be wherever you are. But then when I am with you, it's only worse, because we're fake dating and none of these feelings are supposed to be real, and I think maybe you tried to fake break up with me last week, but I'm not sure, and I don't want to cross a line with you or hurt you in any way—"

"Okay, okay," I say, reaching out and grabbing his hands. "Hold on, slow down."

"I really like you," he says, unable to help himself. His gaze finally drags up to meet mine, defenseless and vulnerable. He's waiting for me to say something, his eyes shadowed and dark but still burning with intensity.

I've dreamt of this moment, of Gage telling me he feels the same way I do, that what started out pretend has evolved into something new, and delicate, and sweet. I've dreamt that I wouldn't have to be the first one to come forward, that he would put me out of my misery by admitting to his feelings first. It *should* feel like a dream come true right now, to be holding his hands in mine as he confesses his feelings to me.

But my hands are growing clammy, and I can feel my pulse begin to climb, the *ba-dum ba-dum* too loud in my ears in the quiet car. I'm sure he can feel my racing heartbeat where his thumb is carefully stroking the base of my wrist, drawing tiny circles to soothe either him or me. And as much as I want to believe that my heart is getting ready to beat out of my chest out of happiness or excitement, I know that's not the truth.

I hate this. I hate how vulnerable I feel right now. I hate that even though he's telling me everything I could have ever wanted to hear, all I can think of doing is pushing him out of my car and driving away. All I feel is panic.

But I don't want to do that to Gage. I don't *want* to run away, even though my body is screaming at me to do it *now*, before he can break my heart or leave me or something worse.

Gage is the first thing I've ever really, truly wanted. I'd never let myself dream before, but I dreamt of him. And if the bravest thing I ever do is fight through my fears in this moment, push past the panic to make that dream real, then I will have to be brave. At least for a moment.

"The reason why I can't give you all my focus," I tell him, my voice soft, "is because if I do, I'm afraid I'll lose myself to you. I want this, I do. It's just . . . a little scary." I can feel my face burn, embarrassment over admitting how fragile I really am, feeling like I'm ruining what should be the most romantic moment of my life by being honest. I've lost myself to people before—my mother, my brother—and when they left, I was destroyed, while they went on living their lives. I'm scared to let myself get that close to someone again. To risk being lost and left again.

"I don't need all of your focus, not really," he says, voice just as soft. "I'll be happy with whatever you want to give me. If it's just lunch in the libraries and afternoons at Lacey's Diner, I'll take it. I just want to be with you for real, to know that you're holding my hand because you like me, to make you smile and call you in the middle of the night to read Latin." He lets out a long breath before continuing. "I know you're going through a lot right now, and I really don't want to push you, I just— " He cuts himself off and sighs. "I want to be here for you, Valeria. Just tell me we can make this real, because I've been losing my mind playing this fake dating game."

My eyes have drifted down to the center console as I take in his words, as I let the warmth of them wash over me. He lets go of my hand and reaches across to touch my jaw gently, his index finger tipping under to turn my face back up to his. When our eyes meet, he smiles cautiously, like he's trying to tame a wild animal.

"I've been dreaming of kissing you since you kissed my cheek at that party," he whispers, drawing me in closer with the power of his focus alone. "I imagined you would taste like limes." His thumb sweeps across my cheek, his fingers curling around my jaw, his touch confident and sure. Inch by inch, I hover closer, tempted by his sweet words. "Please, Valeria," he says, my name a prayer on his tongue.

I've never been kissed. I've never been drawn to a dark corner at a party, or awkwardly smooched in the middle of a seventh-grade dance, and I've never felt like I'm missing out on something because of it. This would be my first, in the dark of my car, the windows fogged from the heater, with a boy who's looking at me like I could destroy him.

His breath is warm against my skin, his eyes focused entirely on my lips now, waiting for me to give him an answer. I reach up gingerly and press my fingers to his neck, where I can feel his heartbeat wildly out of control *for me*. He hisses softly at the contact, like my touch has electrified him, but he manages to keep still, his fingers curling under my jaw.

My nose skims along the skin of his cheek in the moment before my grip tightens on his neck and I drag his lips to mine.

Gage groans at the sudden contact, his lips opening as they touch mine, and the colors behind my eyes go kaleidoscopic. My other hand reaches for his neck, digging into the hair that curls up at his nape.

For ten seconds, it's all just new sensations washing over me, the soft touch of his tongue on mine and the gentle glide of his fingers on my face.

But then my thoughts start to creep in on this perfect

moment, breaking through the longing and desire that fogged my brain.

What if he's thinking about Ginger right now? What if she kissed better than you? Did he have sex with Ginger? I'm sure he did. What if you don't want to have sex? What if he leaves you because of that? What if he doesn't want to be with you because you're a terrible partner? What if he graduates and goes off to whatever prestigious college is begging him to attend and you flunk out because you're an absolute failure? Why would a guy like Gage ever want to be with a failure like you?

I pull back from Gage abruptly, a gasp escaping the both of us as I shoot myself back into my seat, as far away as I can get from him.

"I don't— " I gasp, out of breath, overwhelmed by my thoughts, overwhelmed by the ghost of the feeling of his lips on mine, of his fingers digging into my hair. "I'm not— " I try again, struggling to get my thoughts into order.

"It's okay, it's okay," Gage says quickly, his hands up like he's back to calming the feral beast he's trapped in a car with.

"It's not— " Again, the words fail me. "It's late. I need to get home."

"Yeah, of course, of course," Gage says, fumbling to reach the door handle. He practically jumps out of the car, fleeing the awful awkwardness I just thrust us into. "Please, just— "

"Good night, Gage," I say, prompting him to frown and shut the door.

I throw the car into drive and race home, screaming until my voice gets hoarse, desperate to silence my racing thoughts.

CHAPTER TWENTY-SEVEN

I have enough sense to slow down and turn off my lights once I approach my house, silently pulling into my driveway and turning off the car.

My brain is cycling through a million things at once—the look on Gage's face when I sped away, the thoughts of him and Ginger, the memory of his lips on mine—and the only way to silence them is to scream or to press hard on the cut from the blackberry vine that Gage carefully bandaged for me.

Adrian beat me home, and there is no doubt he noticed my car missing from the driveway when he got back. Would he tell on me? Or has Mom's return to our life resolved the fight between us?

My phone buzzes twice just as I turn my car off. Nervous, I turn it to see who's texting. My stomach flips at the sight of Gage's name, a mix of terror and embarrassment roiling through me.

We don't have to talk about tonight if you don't want to.

But I did leave my project in your trunk. It's due on Monday, so if you could just bring it to school that would be fine.

I quickly type out a reply to him as I open my trunk, catching sight of the project in question.

You sure you don't need it back before that?

I have to wait only a couple seconds before his reply comes in.

It's all wrapped up, you can just bring it in Monday.

I don't know how to read the tone in his text, whether he's angry or upset or hurt by what just happened between us. I throw my phone in my tote and lock my car.

I go to sneak back into the house the same way I left, though more clumsily now that my mind is running a million miles a minute. I jump up once, trying to get my fingers on the lip of the fence, but they slip, a fat splinter lodging itself into my index finger.

"Fuck!" I hiss, half irritated at the injury, half grateful for the sharp jolt of pain that is enough to slice through my thoughts like a lightning bolt. I pluck out the chunk of cedar from my finger, a bead of blood pooling that I immediately press to my mouth. After a moment to collect myself, I try the jump again, my fingers finding purchase on the edge of the fence.

I pull myself up, arms shaking under the effort, careful not to let my feet bounce against the fence to avoid making too much noise. I continue to climb, arms over the decorative trellis, far from any thorny vines, and slowly haul myself over the fence.

One deep breath, and then I'm jumping off and into the soft soil on the other side, an abandoned vegetable patch that fell to ruin after Mom left. Will she take the time to clean it up and plant new things now that she's back?

I hope not, because it would make sneaking out much more annoying.

Creeping along the side of the house, I keep next to the exterior wall, passing the dark basement windows and heading toward the deck. The wind is rustling the leaves, serving as a nice backdrop to hide the sounds of my approach, and for a second, I almost miss the other sound bleeding out into the night.

The backyard, which should be dark, is illuminated by the faint glow of the sconces on the wall along the deck. For a second I think I'm about to be caught, that someone noticed I snuck out and is waiting for me, but then I hear whispers.

"Why can't—" The words are snatched away by the wind as a gust shakes the bough of the pine and maple trees above me. I inch closer to the deck and catch sight of two pairs of feet near the sliding glass door.

Curiosity gets the best of me, and I decide to brave the wilds underneath the deck, a swath of rocks, dirt, and weeds; an aging collection of logs for the fireplace; and dozens upon dozens of spiders and their webs. There's not quite enough space under the deck to stand comfortably at full height, so I have to hunch a little bit as I make way under, moving as carefully and silently as possible.

Once I'm directly under the two sets of feet—one barefoot and the other in a pair of slides—I can make out what they're saying much better.

"—to work things out," Papi is saying, his voice hushed and frustrated.

From down here I can make out the flaming orange tip of a cigarette, blooming bright as Mom takes a drag before speaking.

"I came back because you were being obstinate," Mom says, using none of the honey she usually laces in her voice. "You've been making things very difficult for me."

I watch Papi's feet through the grooves of the deck as he takes a step back and turns around. He lets out a frustrated sigh before turning back to Mom.

"Maite, you can be selfish sometimes, but this is something else—"

"*Selfish?*" Mom hisses, and I flinch at the venom in her voice. "Tú me robaste *la vida*, robaste la juventud, Pedro. And you're calling me selfish? I was finally brave enough to do what was right for me, and you want me to feel bad about that?"

"Yes!" Papi almost yells the word, his emotions getting the better of him.

The anxious thoughts swirling in me since I was in the car with Gage have fallen away, my focus wholly taken in by this argument. If my parents ever fought when I was growing up, they hid it well. Mom was always sunshine smiles, and Papi was always laughing, doting on Mom at every turn.

But the way they're fighting now, I can tell, I can *feel* how natural this is to them, like they're caught in a cycle following the same path as before. This argument doesn't feel new, it feels tired and worn and ready to give out.

"Sí, lo espero, because you've made the kids miserable with this adventure of yours," Papi says, voice calmer now. It feels strange to hear my dad talk about me and Adrian as a fly on the wall, and I'm not sure I like it.

"Estoy cansada de esto, Pedro," Mom says, dragging on her cigarette, bored and indifferent to Papi's turmoil of emotions. "Por favor, firme los papeles. You've dragged this out long enough."

Papers? What papers would Dad need to sign?

"¿Y los niños qué?" Papi asks, voice desperate, and I find myself holding my breath, waiting for an answer to that, too. What *about* me and Adrian? Do I even want her to stay? To go? If she stays, will I ever get the mother I want her to be, the mother she is to Adrian? If she leaves, what will it do to Adrian?

"You and my family *made* me have those kids," Mom says, and the small part of me that was hopeful, that was waiting, cracks. "And then there ended up being two of them. My body was never the same. My *life* was never the same. And I had no choice in it. They turned eighteen in August, they're grown, I can go now."

"Now?" Papi says, a spiteful laugh escaping him. "You left two years ago, Maite. I hoped that you would come back, that you would change your mind and come back because of the kids. How you could ever leave them like that in the first place—"

"Don't make me out to be the villain in this, Pedro. *You* dragged this out. I sent you those papers months ago. You made me come here."

"I'll sign the fucking papers, Maite," Dad says, resigned. "You can be free to go live your new life in Miami. But please don't turn your back on them. They still need you."

"If they need me, they can book a ticket to Miami," Mom says blithely, like a cross-country flight is a drop in the bucket. "But I'm never coming back here, Pedro, te lo juro."

A heavy silence stretches between them, a final standoff. I watch the cigarette glow bright and fade and glow bright again, a sprinkle of ash falling through the cracks of the deck and fluttering to the ground next to me.

"At least give them a proper goodbye this time," Papi begs. "Don't just up and leave and tell them you'll be back. At least be fucking honest with them."

"Honest?" Mom laughs. "Sure, Pedro, I'll be honest. Just like you've been, right?"

I wish I could see Papi's face, to see whether he's heartbroken or angry or something else. But I can see the shadow of his feet taking one step back, two, three, before turning around and whipping open the sliding glass door. He shuts it behind him quietly, leaving Mom alone on the deck.

She sighs, like the whole ordeal was a waste of her time, and moves toward the steps. She walks down halfway, and I tuck myself deeper into shadow, worried she might spot me, but she sits on the step in the middle to finish her cigarette.

The satin of her pajama set glows in the moonlight, and I watch, riveted, as she finishes her cigarette in silence. One last long drag, the end burning bright, before a final exhale of wispy smoke. She flicks the cigarette down the stairs and it bounces off a step and under the deck. Mom doesn't bother to put the cigarette out before going up the stairs and back through the sliding glass door.

I watch, entranced, as the last of the glowing embers fade into ash.

CHAPTER TWENTY-EIGHT

After witnessing that argument, I assume one of my parents is probably going to be sleeping on the couch. So I creep out from under the deck and around to the other side of the house, where the daylight basement has a small patio and sliding glass door.

I'm hoping no one bothered to reset the alarm as I slide the perennially unlocked door to the basement living room open. No blaring alarms go off as I slip inside on light feet.

Leo is fast asleep, small snores escaping him as I creep into the room. I close the door as quietly as possible before sliding onto the couch. Grabbing the throw blanket that is always draped over the back, I settle into the old, worn cushions.

Since Tia Isa and Miguel moved in, the old smell of violets and musk has been replaced by Tia Isa's bright citrus scent, a smell that has managed to permeate every surface in this basement. I wrap myself in the blanket, surrounding myself in that clean scent, and shut my eyes tight.

Some mix of exhaustion, heightened emotions, and anxiety

has my mind fading to black instantly. It feels like only minutes pass before I feel a gentle prodding at my shoulder.

"Valeria?" Miguel says, voice still soft and sleepy. "Valeria?"

My eyes blink open, and I immediately wince at the bright sun leaking in through the sliding glass door, filling the living room with the buttery light of early morning. Miguel is hovering above me, hair mussed from sleep, looking down at me in confusion. And there's an unexpected weight on my legs that makes it impossible to move.

At some point in the night, Leo must have climbed up from his doggy bed and onto the couch with me.

"Good morning," I tell Miguel, bleary-eyed, as I plop back down on the couch and cover my eyes with my arm. I'm not ready for light that bright just yet.

"Any reason you slept on the couch? You weren't here when I got back from homecoming at, like, one in the morning."

Flashes of last night play against my eyelids, chrome and fluorescent lights, foggy windows and soft touches, a bright orange glow and the sprinkle of ashes. My eyes snap open against the bright light, willing it to wash away those memories.

"I had trouble sleeping," I tell him, giving him a small piece of the truth. "And I missed Leo." The big dope is curled up on my legs like he's a puppy, head resting on my hip.

"I feel bad for the guy," Miguel laments. "I had no idea your mom was scared of dogs."

"I don't think she's really scared of them," I tell him. "I think she just thinks they're dirty."

"What? This guy lives like a prince, he goes to the groomer every other month and always smells like roses."

"I assume he hasn't gone outside this morning?" I ask, and at the sound of the "o" word, Leo perks up, his focus entirely on me. "I take that as a no. Come on, Leo."

Leo bounds off the couch and goes excitedly to the sliding glass door. I push it open, and he goes rushing out, making sure to smell the bag of mulch and old basketball on the patio before running off into the grass.

"So, are you going to tell me why you really slept down here?" Miguel prods again, probably noticing I climbed out of bed fully dressed. Dead giveaway.

"How was homecoming?" I ask, trying to get him off the topic. But instead of answering, Miguel frowns at me before shaking his head and sighing.

"I'm going to take a shower."

Glad to be free from his interrogation, I step outside and go back to the bottom of the deck, where the cigarette from last night lies discarded. I pick it up, not wanting Leo to find it and try to eat it, and walk around the side of the house to the trash. I throw Leo's ball a couple of times for him, letting him get some energy out, before dropping him back off in the basement.

No one seems to be around, and when I look outside to the driveway, I see that Papi's car is gone. I go upstairs, intending to go to my room and flop on my bed to stare at the ceiling listlessly for a few hours, but then my eyes catch on Adrian's door.

I don't know what's going on between us, but right now, I need him. And soon, I think he's going to need me. I knock once on his door, then twice fast, then once, then twice fast again. Our knock.

I can hear the creaks and groans from his bed frame as he gets up, his footfalls muffled by the carpet as he walks up to his door. He opens it a crack, peering down at me with tired eyes.

"Vale?" he croaks.

"Can I come in?" I ask, voice quiet, the door to my parents' room only a few feet behind me and burning a hole in my back.

"What's up?" he asks, confused, but it's enough permission for me, and I push through and let myself into his room. His suit from last night is discarded on the floor, a giant poster of *Scarface* hangs above his bed, and the TV is on mute playing the pregame show for today's Seahawks game.

"I have to talk to you," I say, my voice barely above a whisper. "Close the door."

Adrian rolls his eyes at my dramatics and closes his door before flopping back onto his bed, phone in hand as he scrolls through Instagram.

"Put down your phone, this is serious," I tell him, sitting down on his bed across from him. I pull on the comforter, trying to get him to look up at me, and he finally drops his phone with a frustrated sigh and looks up.

"What?" he prompts.

"We . . ." I stumble now with my twin's focus on me, the realization of what I'm about to say making me stutter. Looking at Adrian has always been like looking at a funhouse mirror of myself. We don't share much in common from the outside, him with his bubbly personality and me with the dark cloud over my head. But in Adrian I see everything I could be if I wasn't afraid. I could be happy that Mom is home, hopeful that things could be different this time. I could be outgoing and friendly if the crushing fear of losing that friendship because I wasn't funny enough or cool enough or whatever enough didn't hang over me. "We haven't really talked," I say finally. "About Mom."

"What about Mom?" he asks, his eyes narrow and hesitant.

"Her miraculous return," I say, frustrated that he's making this difficult. "She's just picked up where she left off like she wasn't gone for two years."

"What do you want her to do?" Adrian says. "Act like we're strangers?"

"It's not— " I heave a sigh. "That's not what I mean. It just feels so sudden, and it makes me nervous. What if she leaves again?" I can't bring myself to say the full truth I heard last night: that she's practically already gone.

"Why do you go there?" Adrian finally snaps. "Why do you always go to the worst thing?"

"Because she's done it before! She left and basically didn't speak to us for two years out of nowhere."

"That's not true," Adrian says.

"Oh, sorry, do birthday cards and gift cards in the mail count as communication?"

"It was always *your* choice not to talk to her, Valeria," Adrian points out. "When she left, *I* called her. *I* texted her. I kept in contact with her that whole time, while you, what? Just moped around and waited? She was busy, Abuela was dying, and then she was having to take care of all the shit that came after, and you weren't there for her. *I* was."

"I shouldn't have to beg for the scraps of my mom's attention!" I hiss at him, trying not to yell, trying not to be overheard. And even if I begged, if I got down on my knees in front of her and cried, would it make a difference? After what I heard last night, could I ever believe that she would give up an ounce of her own comfort to take care of me?

"You say you want attention, Valeria, but you've spent your whole life hiding. You think I can't tell that you've always used me as your shield? And now you're upset that someone doesn't see you?"

"I'm sorry," I say, standing up from the bed, anger rising in me like a tide. "I'm sorry I don't feel like busting my ass to be the best at everything just to get the attention of someone who will only acknowledge me if I give them something to brag about. That's not love, Adrian!"

"Get out," Adrian says, tone bored, his eyes back on the TV. He picks up the remote and unmutes, the room filling with the booming sound of a sports correspondent.

"I'll be here, Adrian," I say over the noise of the TV. "When everything goes to shit, when you fall from grace, whatever it may be. I'll be here."

I leave it at that, turning my back toward him and leaving his room.

I take a shower, letting the hot water beat against me until my skin gets pruny. When I step out of the bathroom, wrapped in a robe and towel-drying my hair as I walk to my bedroom, I hear the front door open. The sound of a dozen bags jangling gets me curious enough to step up to the banister and peer down toward the front door.

Papi is trying to wrangle all the tote bags he's carrying in both hands while also pulling the key from the door. He fumbles, one of the bags slipping from his hands and crashing to the floor.

"*¡Comemierda!*" Dad hisses under his breath, still struggling to pull the key from the lock.

"I've got it!" I tell him from the top of the stairs. Papi looks up at me in relief.

"Gracias, mijita," he says, sighing deeply before picking up the lost bag. I race down the stairs to help him, pulling the key from the lock and relieving him of some of his bags.

"What's all this?" I ask, looking into one of the bags I took. A giant jug of orange juice, cans of coconut cream and condensed milk, and butter.

"I'm making breakfast!" Papi announces excitedly, like he didn't have that devastating conversation with Mom on the deck last night, like our lives aren't about to change forever. "Want to help out?"

"Sure," I tell him with a smile, like I didn't overhear that conversation, like a part of me didn't burn away to ash last night, too. "Let me go upstairs and change, and then I'll be back to help."

I drop the bags off in the kitchen and run up to my bedroom. I put on my usual Sunday best: a pair of sweatpants and an oversized knit sweater I stole from Papi, all brown and stripes and dripping with retro charm. I throw my damp hair in a claw clip before running back downstairs.

Papi already has everything put away, and he's started to set up his workstation. The cutting board is out, along with his favorite knife, and he's gathering all his ingredients.

"What's on the menu?" I ask, grabbing an apron from the back of the pantry door. I'm no ace in the kitchen, but I'm a pretty good helper.

"The usual Sunday special," he says, turning from the counter to face me. "My *famous* Cuban eggs Benedict, coquito French toast, and nonalcoholic sangria. How does that sound?"

"Festive," I say. This is the kind of spread Papi would prepare for the holidays or for a celebration. His Cuban eggs Benedict are a breakfast staple for the holidays: English muffin, citrusy-garlic lechón, Canadian bacon, Swiss cheese that he always hits with the blow torch for just the right melt, a perfectly poached egg, diced cornichon, and a mustardy hollandaise sauce. But the coquito French toast is my favorite, a buttery brioche bread sliced and soaked in a spiced coconut cream custard and then baked until crisp on the outside and gooey on the inside.

I wonder if this meal is an olive branch, a final attempt to make Mom want to stay or something. Or maybe it's an apology to Adrian and me, in the language my dad feels most comfortable with.

"Where do you need me?"

I spend the morning slicing fruit for sangria, mixing the custard for the French toast, and making coffee for us both. Papi prattles on about the new location for the shop, how he expects to be ready to open by the new year, Ana Maria's plans for a grand opening menu, and the giant rat he fought in the alley behind the bakery.

He doesn't bring up Mom, or homecoming, or any topic of substance. It feels like we're playing pretend, living in a world where there is nothing outside waiting to take us down.

"Damn, that smells good," Miguel says as he appears at the top of the stairs, his mom trailing behind him. "Is there any coffee?"

"Sí, cómo no, sírvete," Papi says, nodding to the coffee pitcher sitting on the peninsula. It probably has just shy of a shot of coffee left in it, so I pour that out for Miguel and get started on making another batch.

"What's the occasion?" Miguel asks, plopping down on a stool and drinking his coffee straight.

"Does there need to be one?" Tia Isa asks, stepping around me to pick up an orange wedge from my sangria station. "Our dad used to always make a big breakfast on Sundays when we were kids. Pancakes and sausage and tortillas and muffins of all kinds. That man loved being in the kitchen."

"Food is how our family shows love," Papi says, voice a little tender. "It's always been that way."

Papi pulls out the French toast from the oven, the kitchen filling with the sweet smell of coconut and the rich aroma of cinnamon and nutmeg. He has all the components for his eggs ready to assemble, and the sangria has been chilling in the fridge.

Miguel and I set the table for six, using one of the nicer tablecloths for the occasion. Tia Isa helps Papi plate the meal in the kitchen, Isa slicing into the French toast and Papi building his eggs Benedict.

"Can you go upstairs and get my mom and Adrian down?" I ask Miguel after we set out all the flatware. Miguel watches me curiously but follows my request without question. He goes halfway up the stairs and hollers straight up to their rooms.

"BREAKFAST IS READY!" He waits a second for a response. "COME DOWNSTAIRS."

Some door clicks open, and Miguel lopes back down to the dining room.

Behind him, Mom sweeps down the stairs, elegantly made up for a casual breakfast with the family. Her hair is perfectly blown out, same as usual, sleek and shiny. She's wearing a brightly printed dress that feels garish against the gray light of the day and a stunning stack of layered necklaces with little baubles hanging from them.

"Are you going to say good morning to me?" she asks me from the other end of the dining room as I fold napkins.

"Um," I say, flustered. I didn't think how strange and confusing it would be to see her after everything I heard.

"Morning, Tia," Miguel cuts in, thankfully, leaning in to kiss Mom on the cheek.

"Ay, Miguelito, how was your homecoming? Nestor Ybarra didn't threaten you with a machete or anything?"

"No, Tia," Miguel says. "We've cleared the air between our families, the rivalry is over, and now I get just the normal amount of threats from her dad."

Mom laughs, that charming tinkle that's supposed to make you feel smart and funny.

There's a clamor of sound coming down the stairs, and then Adrian is joining us in the dining room, throwing an arm around Mom's shoulder and giving her a kiss on the cheek.

"Morning, Mami," he says brightly, like we didn't fight in his room earlier. "I'm starving, where's the food?"

"Coming!" Tia Isa calls, walking into the kitchen with two plates in her hand and Papi close behind her.

"Sit, sit," Papi insists, setting down plates before running back to the kitchen.

"What a spread!" Mom says brightly as she looks down at

the food. When Papi comes back to drop a plate down in front of her, Mom flinches at the sight of it. "Oh, no, I can't eat all of that! I'd be rolling out of here."

"Just eat however much of it you want, Maite, it's fine," Papi says, and I can hear just the faintest edge of irritation in his voice. But he smiles that pleasant smile again and serves everyone some nonalcoholic sangria, which is really just fruit punch with cinnamon, in the end, and he sits down and we eat as a family, like it's the most normal thing in the world.

Mom asks Adrian about the dance last night, Papi laughs at the story Miguel tells about Ana Maria twisting her ankle while dancing, and the sound of forks scraping on plates and mouths chewing grows louder and louder. Mom laughs at something again, her sprinkle of a laugh, the laugh of a woman trapped in a black-and-white 1940s movie, a fake laugh used to endear herself to you. How can she just sit there and laugh when she's about to blow up our lives again? Finally, I've *had enough.*

"So," I say, loudly, cutting through the easygoing conversation at the table, "how's the divorce going?" I keep my eyes glued to my plate, still full of food and growing cold. I can't quite bring my eyes up to meet either of my parents', but I can speak.

"Valeria!" Miguel says in surprise at my outburst.

"That's not really something I want to talk about at the table," Tia Isa says, sounding confused and unsettled.

"Oh, Tia," I say, my voice dripping with apology, as I reach up to touch her arm, "I'm so sorry, I didn't mean *you.* I was talking about *their* divorce." I finally look up at my parents, my dad staring at me in horror and Mom watching me with a blank expression.

"Fuck off, Valeria," Adrian growls.

"Adrian, don't speak to your sister like that," Papi snaps automatically.

"What?" Adrian says defensively. "She's being a bitch for no reason—"

"Adrian!" Papi snaps again.

"Are you going to say anything, *Mom*?" I ask, going all in, ready to watch her house of cards fall down.

"Valeria, maybe we should—" Tia Isa says gently from my shoulder, but I ignore her, my focus entirely on my mom.

"Still waiting for him to sign the papers? You've been waiting for a few months, huh? Can't wait to drop us?"

"Valeria, what the fuck are you talking about—" Adrian starts.

"This is not how we are going to discuss this—" Papi says.

"Miguel, we are going downstairs," Tia Isa hisses. Miguel, confused and listless, picks up his plate of food and follows his mom back down to the basement without comment.

"What the fuck is going on?" Adrian asks, an edge of nervousness creeping into his voice.

"How did you find out?" Papi says to me, voice tired.

"I heard you last night," I say, losing my nerve a little and staring back down at my plate. The sound of my mom's voice last night, free of the sweetness that normally drips from it, echoes in my mind. *They're grown, I can go now.* But we weren't eighteen when she left, we were fifteen and confused. "The only reason she came back was to force him to sign the papers."

"Wait, what?" Adrian says, panicked. "She's not serious. You're not serious, Valeria."

"This is not how I wanted to do this with you kids—"

"No!" Adrian snaps, pushing back from the table so forcefully that the glasses rattle and Tia Isa's abandoned sangria topples, bright red liquid seeping into the one nice tablecloth without any stains. Ruined.

Mom's been silent this whole time, letting the whole scene play out before her. She pushes back from the table, but she doesn't stand up. I risk a glance at her and am surprised to find her eyes glittering with tears.

"This was incredibly inconsiderate of you, Valeria," she says, her voice wavering. "You spied on a private conversation, and then you tried to use that conversation as a weapon against your family?"

"You don't deserve to call us your family!" I scream, beyond the limit of controlling my temper, of holding back my emotions. "Where were you when Adrian broke his leg sophomore year? Where were you when I had to go to the doctor for my period cramps that were so painful I would end up sleeping on the bathroom floor? Where were you?" I roar, voice scraping my throat raw.

Mom's lips tremble, Adrian wavers by the threshold, and Papi sits at the head of the table, looking utterly lost.

I've had enough. I tear out of the room, out the front door, and down the street. I walk until I'm numb all over from the cold, until blisters form on the backs of my heels, until I can get the look of devastation on my brother's face out of my head.

CHAPTER TWENTY-NINE

I have no one left to turn to, not after the way I just left my family and the way I pushed Gage out of my car. Not after how mean and ugly I was at the breakfast table, handling the divorce news in the worst way possible. And especially not after years of keeping people at a distance. And instead of feeling safe in my manufactured solitude, that space I built between myself and others now feels like a boulder on my chest robbing me of breath.

When I return hours later, hungry and tired, the house is dark. Adrian's and Miguel's cars are missing from the driveway, and I can hear Leo howling from the basement. Not wanting to face my family, I go around the side of the house and climb the fence again.

I slip around to the basement patio, opening the sliding glass door to let Leo out. I throw his ball for him again, and he runs around energetically, unaffected by the Morales family drama.

When it gets too cold to stand outside anymore, I usher Leo inside and rummage through Tia Isa's kitchen.

After a meager dinner of microwave mac and cheese, I wash up in the bathroom, sneak into Miguel's room to steal pajamas, and settle into the couch.

When I wake up, it's not because a sound startled me or because light shone in my eyes, but because of the smell of citrus and soap, something both woody and bright. The bathroom door next to the couch pops open, and Tia Isa steps out, wrapped in a towel and with silicone eye patches on her undereyes. She must sense my eyes on her because she glances down at me and winces.

"Sorry, I was trying not to wake you up," she whispers in apology.

Leo is back on his new favorite spot, my legs, and it's still pitch dark in the basement. I glance at the clock on the microwave to check: 5:45 a.m.

"Go back to sleep," Tia Isa whispers, waving her hands at me like she's casting a magic spell.

Miraculously, I fall back asleep without issue, until someone else is shaking me awake.

"Hey, Valeria," Miguel says, trying to wake me up gently but doing a terrible job. I wince at the bright overhead light and try to focus on my cousin. "Do you think you're up for going to school today?" His voice is cautious, like he's afraid I might cause another scene.

"What's the alternative?" I croak, trying to free my legs from under Leo. He gives a huff of annoyance and hops off the couch before settling into his bed. "Do this all day?" I say, gesturing at my body covered in couch cushions and a blanket.

"I mean, you can," he says, "but I thought you might want to get away from the house."

"You're right, but I don't want to go up to my room," I tell him, letting him see how much of a coward I am.

"I can run up and grab your backpack? And there's a load of clean laundry in the basket, I'm pretty sure some of your stuff is in there."

"That sounds good," I tell him. "Thank you."

Miguel runs upstairs while I head into the small laundry room. Hanging up are some of Tia Isa's delicate shirts and sweaters, and in a laundry basket on top of the dryer is a whole load of folded clothes. I find everything I need, and although probably not an outfit I would think to put together—a pair of paint overalls and an old knit sweater—it'll work.

I'm brave enough to at least sneak up the stairs and out the front door to Miguel's car, eating the muffin he nabbed for me from the kitchen. We ride together in silence, Miguel heroically giving me the aux cord without saying anything. I play the angriest '90s girl rock that I can find, and Miguel and I scream out the lyrics to Meredith Brooks's classic hit "Bitch" together.

When we pull into the student lot, Miguel parks in his usual spot and then grabs hold of my hand before I can get out of the car.

"I'm here for you, you know that, right?" he says softly, his voice earnest. "Whatever you need, I have your back, Vale. Always."

I smile weakly at my cousin, feeling more teary and weary than I'd like to right before school.

"Thanks," I say, and it's just about the only thing I can get out before the threat of tears takes me out entirely.

Since we kept to Miguel's schedule this morning, we're running late, the bell already ringing by the time we're stepping off the student lot. We jog to class, Dean Winstead catching sight of us and rolling his eyes. I make it to first period with seconds to spare and slide into my seat. Classes pass in a blur, and I take up my usual role of uninterested student.

We get a pop quiz in English—*Use the following words in a sentence*—and I end up shattering the mug I've been working on in art class. My head feels like it's stuffed with cotton, and I can't bring myself to concentrate properly on anything all morning.

The bell rings for lunch, a reminder that I didn't grab any food before leaving the house. I reluctantly make my way to the cafeteria to buy something.

It's loud and overbearing the moment I step in. I can't tell if it's a good thing for the room to be so loud I can't think, but it's better than dwelling on what's happening at home.

I join the line for food and make sure to keep my back toward Adrian's table to avoid any accidental eye contact. I'm trying to peer over people's shoulders to see what's on the menu today—besides the usual too-greasy pizza and mystery chicken wraps—when I hear someone say my name.

"Valeria!" an out-of-breath Gage calls out from behind me, accompanied by the sound of shoes slapping against linoleum. He comes to a halt at my side, huffing for breath and looking at me desperately. "Do you have it?"

"What?" I sputter, conscious of the dozens of eyes that have turned our way.

"I know you probably want some space right now, and I totally respect that," he babbles, and I'm still struggling to catch up, "but you weren't responding to my texts, and my robotics project is due after lunch."

Oh, no.

My mouth gapes open like a fish, and I stare back at Gage in horror. He's watching me with wide, desperate eyes, and I wish I could give him what he wants, I wish that the answer I have for him isn't the last thing he wants to hear.

"Gage," I say, wincing at how I sound, embarrassed and afraid. "I didn't drive to school today."

Whatever hope was left in Gage evaporates in that moment. He looks confused first, his brows furrowing as he takes in this information, and once settled, his face goes stony. "But your stuff is still in my car," I assure him. "I bet I can call my dad and he can get it over to the school."

I reach for my phone, but my back pocket is empty. I try the other one, trying not to let my feelings show on my face, to spare Gage, but then I remember that I didn't bring my phone today. When I woke up on the couch in the basement, it was dead, and I saw no point.

"Fuck," I mutter, trying to think, trying to find the next best solution, but Gage has already made his decision about this moment.

"That thing is worth nearly half my grade, Valeria!" he cries out, his emotions getting the better of him. "You knew that! I'll never get valedictorian if I don't turn this in."

"I'm sorry, Gage!" I shout back. "We can still solve this, if we—"

"What 'we,' Valeria?" Gage says. "You've proven time and again that there is no 'we' between us." I flinch at his words, harsher than anything he has ever said to me before.

"We are not talking about that right now, Gage, we're talking about your project," I tell him evenly, trying to swallow back my hurt.

"It's all the same thing!" he snaps. "I had one goal this year, *one*, and the minute you step into my life, that all goes out the window—"

"Do not," I say, my voice sharp and dark. "Don't blame that on me. Be honest with yourself for once, Gage. Being valedictorian has never really mattered to *you*. You're just doing it because it's part of your parents' plan and you refuse to stand up to them."

We've slowly backed out of the food line during our confrontation, but we've done nothing to shield ourselves from the prying eyes of our peers. I'm so focused on Gage that I don't spare a thought to our audience.

Until I hear my brother's voice break into my bubble with Gage.

"Get out of my sister's face," Adrian snaps from behind me, stepping in close to protect me. Where was this Adrian this weekend when I actually needed him?

"Oh, great," Gage says, rolling his eyes at my brother. "Was this the plan all along, Valeria? String me along so your asshole twin would beat me?"

"I already beat you, dipshit," Adrian says.

"Adrian, please," I tell him, shoving his shoulder to get him to leave us. "Gage, can we please table whatever this is so we— "

"I can't believe I fell for this," Gage says. "I can't believe I fell for your bullshit— "

"Hey!" Adrian barks, pushing me aside and getting in Gage's face. "Don't talk to my sister like that."

"Adrian, don't do this— " I go to take a step forward, to pull my brother back from Gage, but Adrian's lackey is already at my shoulder, holding me back. "Let go of me, Lane!" I snap.

"You can't really believe you're at the top because you're smarter than me, right?" Gage says, nearly nose to nose with my brother.

"Oh, I'm sorry you were too busy crying last year to do your homework," Adrian says with false pity, giving Gage a push to the shoulder. "Must have really sucked to lose out on someone as hot as Ginger."

"Adrian!" I snarl, fighting against Lane's grip. I can't hear Gage's response, but I can see his eyes blaze with anger, I can see him step in close to Adrian to say something, to give him a push back. At this point half the cafeteria is surrounding us, shouting and spurring on the argument. "Miguel!" I scream, changing tactics, trying to get someone's help in stopping this fight before it escalates. "So help me, God, Lane, if you don't let me go right now, I will bite your ear off."

Lane rolls his eyes at my dramatics but lets go, and I go tearing out of the cafeteria and to Miguel's table. When I get there, he's already standing, attention caught by all the commotion.

"Gage and Adrian are fighting," I gasp out, and everyone at

the Debate Club table is struck silent for the first time in their lives. "Please help," I plead.

When we run back to the cafeteria, teachers have finally shown up, trying to dispel the crowd around the two guys.

"Go back to your tables!" Mr. Robertson shouts over a megaphone. Adrian has been pulled aside by one of his football coaches, and Gage is standing next to the dean, face white as a sheet. "You, too, Ms. Morales," Mr. Robertson says to me.

"My brother—" I start, but Mr. Robertson cuts me off with a sharp shake of his head.

"Unless you want detention, too, get back to your table," he says, voice hard, none of the jolly math teacher about him despite the bow tie he's wearing in the shape of pi.

"It looks like everything is settled," Miguel assures me, trying to pull me back out of the cafeteria.

"But—"

"*Go*, Ms. Morales. Now."

I throw my head back and groan, at a loss for what to do. I know I need to listen to Mr. Robertson, to turn around and leave Adrian and Gage to their fate, but it all feels like it's my fault, and I don't want them to face this without me.

"Come on," Miguel tries again, pulling me this time, and I finally give in.

CHAPTER THIRTY

Gage and Adrian are saved from being suspended because the fight never really turned physical. According to the people who hung around to watch, they didn't get past goading prods to the chest before the whole thing got broken up. Which is a good thing, too, because Adrian is eighteen, and with Gage's parents being lawyers, he could have ended up in real legal trouble.

Instead, word gets around that the two have been served detention and Saturday school for the week, and I feel *awful* about it, especially since I came out of the whole thing clean.

"Okay, you're coming with me," Ana Maria announces, finding me at my locker after school. "Miguel is going to drop the two of us off at the shop."

Normally, I would fight her on this, but considering how everything has been going with my life, this actually sounds like a great idea.

"Fine," I tell her, and her eyes go wide at my easy compliance.

"Damn," she says, "this all really *has* fucked you up."

"Ana, you don't even know the half of it," I tell her, picking up my bag and following her down the hallway.

"Well, you're in luck, because I'm working on some early recipe testing for the December specials," she says, linking arms with me and moving out toward the student parking lot. "And I have updates on Sofía's search for the person who got her on the homecoming ballot."

Miguel is waiting by his car when we approach, and he looks just as harried as I feel.

"Have you heard from either of them?" I ask him as we pack into the car.

Miguel sighs as he turns the car on.

"No, they were stuck in the office after lunch, and I assume they were sent straight to detention after last period, so I didn't catch sight of either of them."

"And the bag in my car?" I ask. I had Miguel text his mom—assuming my dad was dealing with the school calling him about Adrian—to see if she was home. I had hoped that she could take Gage's project from my trunk and drop it off at school for him, saving his grade and proving to him that none of this was on purpose or part of some grand plan to ruin him.

"Mom wasn't home," Miguel says, face pinched. "She was in Port Townsend for a job interview."

I throw my back against the headrest in frustration.

"The point of this afternoon was to get Valeria's mind off of everything," Ana Maria reminds my cousin from the passenger seat. "You're off to a terrible start."

"Go, then, please," I tell her. "Take my mind off of it."

"Okay, so, Sofía has turned her side of the bedroom into a

full murder board investigation," Ana Maria says, pulling out her phone to share pictures of it with us. She's not exaggerating; above Sofía's bed are dozens of notes and pictures tied together by red string, everything connecting to a piece of paper in the middle that just says "HOMECOMING COURT." "It's utter chaos. She's learning how to track people's IP addresses and keeps a notebook full of notes with her at all times. She's never been this passionate about *anything*."

"We have a budding detective on our hands," Miguel notes. "Do you think she's going to find the culprit?"

"Oh, absolutely," Ana Maria says confidently. "And then she's going to hatch an elaborate revenge scheme."

The ride to the bakery is short, and Ana Maria takes the time to detail the suspects in her sister's case. When Miguel pulls to a stop in front of the bakery, Ana Maria leans across the center console to give him a kiss, and I gag dramatically in the back seat.

We wave at Miguel from the sidewalk as he heads down Main Street, and as we turn to go inside the shop, I notice Ana Maria's eyes snag on a building across the street. I stop and turn to look with her at what used to be her family's bakery, Café y Más. The Ybarra family managed to lease out the old space to a new restaurant, a vegetarian Thai place with decent food. The Cuban tile inside has been replaced with bamboo paneling and decorative enamel paints.

It looks nothing like the bakery it used to be, but if you look close, the ghost of Café y Más is still there. The chipped blue paint on the outside is still the same, despite the sign changing, and the checkered black-and-white floor remains.

"How's it been?" I ask her gently. "With the shop, I mean."

Ana Maria sighs and turns her eyes away from the building to look back at me.

"Weird?" she says. "Our lives used to revolve around that place. I was afraid of what my family would look like without it, but it hasn't really changed. Whatever space was held by the shop has quickly been filled in by other things, like Mom's work at the bed-and-breakfast or Sofía's murder wall." She turns to look at the shop front for Morales Bakery, the white-and-gray-striped awning and the hand-lettered sign above it that reads "MORALES FAMILY BAKERY, SINCE 1975" and cute café curtains in the window. There's a bench outside with potted plants and a small tinajón on its side to honor my dad's side of the family from Camagüey. "And this place," she admits. "This has been nice to have."

"And our pastelitos were always better," I say with a crooked smile. "Just admit it."

"I will not," Ana Maria says, nose high as she pushes past me and into the restaurant.

"I know you switched over to Papi's recipe for the seasonal pastelitos!" I call out from behind her.

"I'm supposed to be nice to you today, Valeria!" Ana Maria snaps. "Don't test me!" She whips open the swing door to the kitchen, and I follow behind her, a smug smile on my face.

"Fine, fine," I relent. "I'll drop it for now. What are you baking today to cheer me up?"

Ana Maria stops and stares at me, and I can tell she's thinking about whether she should keep fighting with me or not. She finally just rolls her eyes and starts prepping to work in the kitchen. She puts on her apron, washes her hands, and begins to set up her station.

I sit down at a prep table across from her, far from the main activity in the kitchen, and watch as she buzzes about her space.

"For the December specials," she says finally, hauling up a tub of flour to her workbench. "I'm making brazo gitano with a pear-and-praline filling and a citrus olive oil cake with a pomegranate glaze."

"Thank God your deep love for my cousin ended this rivalry between our families," I tell her honestly. "Because getting to eat the concoctions that your little brain comes up with is truly a gift."

"Thank you?" Ana Maria says. She pauses for a moment in her work, considering. "So . . . lunch today."

"Oh God," I groan, dropping my head to the table. "I thought you were supposed to be taking my mind off of things."

"Remember when you gave me my come-to-Jesus talk to get my head out of my ass about Miguel?" she prods.

"Yes," I moan.

"I think it's finally my turn to tell you you're an idiot."

"I did not tell you that you were an idiot," I correct her, head snapping up. "I actually called you a coward." Ana Maria rolls her eyes at me.

"I feel like I can say this, as a certified third-party viewer of the whole situation, but you tend to keep people at arm's length, Valeria," Ana Maria says, her voice gentle, like I'm a wild animal that might get spooked upon hearing this dark truth.

"Yeah," I say, agreeing with her. "I do."

"And you don't see a problem with that? You don't see how

maybe that's fed into this whole"—she waves a giant whisk around in the air—"Gage situation?"

"This whole *situation*," I say, mimicking her with my hands, "has nothing to do with how close I get to people. This whole *situation* is just proof that I'm doing the right thing, that I *should* be staying away from people because no one, *no one*, is going to put me first," I hiss, and there's a hitch in my voice, along with a burning behind my eyes that I don't expect.

"Valeria," Ana Maria says softly, dropping her whisk and coming over to my side. "That's not true, and you must know that's not true, because you have Miguel. Your cousin is always going to be there for you, *always*. And you have me now, even though you're as prickly as a cactus."

"Did Miguel tell you what happened this weekend?" I ask her, my eyes boring into hers. Her eyes shutter closed, but just for a second I see that look of pity well up in them, and I want to scream. But my voice comes out small. "My built-in person who is supposed to love me unconditionally, who is supposed to care for me and look after me and listen to me cry about boys and school and whatever else, what does it mean when that person doesn't even want me?"

Ana Maria's eyes go sad, and her mouth drops open, at a loss for words. She was ready to give me a pep talk about the boy I like, and here I am breaking down in front of her because my mom doesn't love me. I can feel the pity coming off her in waves, and it's too much, I can't stand it.

"I'm getting out of here," I growl, swallowing back the tears and pushing past her and out to the back. The air is biting cold without my jacket on, and it's dark and damp in the alley, but at least it's quiet. At least there's no one here trying to feed me bullshit.

Ana Maria is right about one thing, though. This *is* my fault. I let myself care too much about things. I cared too much about Adrian's cold shoulder, and my grades fell. And then I turned to Gage, who was supposed to help me fix the first problem but only caused an even bigger problem for me. And then Mom . . .

"Jesus Christ," I sniff, trying to choke down the sobs. "Fuck!" I scream, kicking a dumpster and successfully stubbing my toe in the process. "Comemierda!" I howl at the pain. "Fuck!" I cry out again, just because it feels so good to scream. I keep screaming, because if I stop, I know I'll cry, and that's the last thing I want.

"Valeria!" Ana Maria calls out from behind me. "Someone is going to call the cops, please stop fighting that dumpster."

I scream again and give the dumpster another kick.

"Valeria, please, you're going to hurt yourself," Ana Maria says soothingly. "Please stop."

"I can't!" I cry out in frustration, feeling the bite of tears at the back of my throat.

"You've already dented it, the dumpster yields, come on," Ana Maria pulls me back by the shoulders. Ana is not small by any means, but I'm still bigger. If I really wanted to, I could throw her off, I could make her let go.

But I don't. The fight is draining out of me, and the sobs are starting to break through. I can't fight it off anymore. Ana Maria wraps her arms around me and tugs me in close. My knees give out and we crumple together to the asphalt, my breath choking on sobs and my nose and eyes leaking beyond my control. I cry into Ana Maria's neck and clutch on to her, like I'm lost at sea and she's the only mooring in sight.

I drag her in close, the warmth of her body radiating a kind of comfort. She's whispering soft things into my hair, words that get lost over the sound of my crying, but the gentle rhythm of them manages to be soothing. Ana Maria holds me just as tightly as I do her, and we stay like that, bound, until I run out of tears, until my throat is raw and my eyes are red and sore.

"I think you needed that," Ana Maria says softly, rubbing calming circles into my back. "How are you feeling now?" She leans back to look at me, her eyes soft and gentle.

"I don't know," I say. "There's just a lot happening right now, and I don't know what to do about any of it."

"Well, I think we have to take it step by step. Maybe we can tackle the easy things first. What would that be?" she asks.

"Get Gage's project to his teacher?" I suggest.

"Yeah," Ana agrees. "We can definitely do that. What else?"

"I still need to get my grade up in math," I add. "And I'm not sure Gage will be my tutor anymore after this."

"Okay," Ana says with a nod, considering this challenge. "We can find another tutor for you. And if you have to, you could do off-campus tutoring. I can help you with that."

"Gage kissed me," I admit suddenly. Ana's eyes goes wide at this surprise confession. "He told me he liked me, and he kissed me in my car, and it was magical. Until . . ."

I'm quiet for a moment.

"Until?" Ana prompts.

"Until I ruined it," I tell her. "Until I pushed him away. Like you said I do. Because I was scared. And then I went and made it even worse, and now he thinks it's all been part of a diabolical plan to take him down, and I don't know how to fix it."

"Baby steps," Ana reminds me. "Start with turning in his project and go from there. I'm sure Gage didn't entirely believe the things he was saying today. People do all kinds of things when emotions run high."

"Like fight dumpsters?"

Ana Maria laughs. "Exactly."

CHAPTER THIRTY-ONE

Soon the cold and the smell of the dumpster become too overwhelming to stay outside. Ana Maria heads back to the kitchen, and I go to the bathroom to wash up. Then I sit in the quiet office and pull out my math homework, taking everything one step at a time just like Ana Maria suggested.

Around five, she knocks on my door to present me with two dishes in her hands. On the left is the slice of brazo gitano, a delicate sponge cake rolled around a pear-and-praline filling, topped with crunchy candied hazelnuts and a decorative sprig of mint. In the other is a small cake, something almost muffin-sized, with a pink pomegranate glaze and dozens of bright red pomegranate seeds decorating the top.

"Time for a taste test," Ana Maria announces, dropping both plates in front of me. She hands me a fork, and I quickly bite into the little cake. It has the bright flavor of orange mixed with the almost grassy aroma of olive oil. The tangy icing is tasty, and I love the surprise of a pomegranate seed bursting in my mouth.

I turn to my notebook and hastily write out a score, making sure to hide my writing from Ana Maria. I flip the paper around and taste the next plate.

The sponge cake is light and fluffy, with the slightest hint of vanilla. The pear is baked but still firm, tart but mild, and the perfect complement to the nutty brilliance of the praline. All the textures of the cake play so well together, making for a perfect bite every time. I quickly scrawl out my second score on another piece of paper, fold both scores, and then hand them back to Ana Maria.

She opens the papers with a quirked brow.

"I'll take this into consideration," she says dryly, throwing my scores in the trash bin next to the desk.

"But really," I say, taking another bite of the brazo gitano, "this is really good. Best one yet."

"I hope you got your dad's taste buds, because I really want him to approve this menu," she says.

"I'm sure he will," I assure her.

"Thanks," she says with a smile. "I'm going to clean up, and then Miguel's going to come by and pick us up, okay?"

"Sure," I say with a nod, but just the idea of returning home fills me with dread. Time passes too quickly, Ana Maria cleaning the kitchen in record time and my cousin being punctual for the first time in his life.

Miguel ends up driving in the direction of our house instead of Ana Maria's, and considering I know how strict her dad tends to be about her schedule, I interrupt their conversation about Halloween plans.

"Are you not going home with me?" I ask Miguel anxiously,

desperately wanting my supportive cousin at my side before going into my house.

"Oh, uh, no," Miguel says. "I'm going to Ana Maria's for a little bit because her mom needs some camera help. She's shooting new pictures of the B&B for their website listings," he explains, and I want to yell that he can do that tomorrow, that I need him now, but I don't. I sink into the back seat and stay quiet.

"Text me if you need anything," Ana Maria says earnestly as I climb out of the car.

"Sure," I tell her, knowing I won't but appreciating the offer nonetheless.

Someone must have moved my car, because it's no longer in the spot I left it in on Saturday night. Tia Isa's car is also missing from the driveway, along with Mom's rental car. Which just leaves my car with Adrian's and Dad's, just how it used to be, before everything turned to shit.

I climb up the stairs to the front door and am nearly toppled over by an excited Leo as soon as I open the door. He's jumping up and down, twisting around my legs, yapping excitedly in greeting as I bend down to give him a pet. He smells freshly of roses, and he has a little kerchief tied around his neck.

I corral Leo back into the house and close the door behind me, hanging my coat up on the hooks by the door and dropping my backpack. The house is quiet, no smell of food cooking in the kitchen, and no sound of voices echoing down the halls.

"Hello?" I call out nervously.

"We're in here," Dad responds from the dining room.

Confused, I follow the sound of his voice, not knowing what to expect. I haven't really had a straightforward conversation with anyone all weekend, and now that all the dust is settled, I'm a little scared to start one.

In the dining room, Papi is in his usual seat at the head of the table, a cup of coffee in front of him. He looks tired and worn, his usual guayabera traded in for the grimiest white T-shirt he owns. Adrian is at the table with him, head in his hands and looking defeated. When I step into the room, he looks up at me with red-rimmed eyes.

"Adrian!" I gasp at the wretched sight of him and rush to his side. I pull him in for a tight hug, and he leans into me, arms wrapping around me in return. "I'm so sorry about today, I—"

"Mom left."

"What?" I ask, somehow surprised by this revelation, despite everything. "When?"

"This morning," Papi says. "As soon as I signed the papers."

Adrian breathes deeply, controlling his breaths as Papi breaks the news again.

"The divorce papers," I clarify.

"Yes," Papi says. "She was already packed and left as soon as it was done. I asked—" Papi's voice breaks off, the hard control wavering for a moment. "I asked her to wait until you were back from school, so she could say goodbye, but she said she had things to get back to. She—" He breaks off for a moment and sighs. "I always tried to protect you both from the truth, I thought it was better for you to not know everything. But that clearly didn't work. So, you should know, she's going back to Miami to live with her fiancé."

"Of course," I say, unable to stop the bitterness from creeping in. I hold my brother tighter, giving him a promise by touch alone that I will never leave him like she has.

"Your mother has her demons," Papi says evenly, "and she was never good at holding them back. I didn't want you two to see her that way, at her worst. I only wanted you to see her at her best, when she did her best to love you and care for you."

"I did everything," Adrian says, his voice hoarse. "I did everything to get her to come home."

"What do you mean?" I ask him, pulling back to look at his face.

"I did everything for her, and she didn't care. I'm top of the fucking class, I've been scouted by schools to play football, I have scholarships for college, I did everything *right*," he rasps, "to get her to come back."

"Adrian," I say in disbelief, "that's not how it works—"

"But that's how *she* works!" he explodes. "You said it, you already know, Mom only pays attention when you're the brightest star in her line of sight. As soon as you flicker, as soon as you falter just a little bit, she doesn't care. I'd text her every time I aced a test or won a game, and she always texted me back. But nothing else was worth noticing."

"Papi," Dad says, getting up from his seat and coming around to Adrian's side, squatting so they can be face-to-face. "The way your mom behaves has *nothing* to do with you," he says firmly. "This is *her* fault, not yours."

Mom's love has always been conditional. I learned from a young age that it was better *not* to be loved by her, because her attention ended up hurting more than it ever made me feel good.

Mom's love came with her expectations, and if you fall short, well, you're shit out of luck. Adrian learned the opposite lesson. He got trapped in the cycle of pleasing her, and even after she ran off, he was still working for her impossible love.

"I'm so sorry, mis niños," Papi says, his voice wavering. "I thought it was better to keep you in the dark, I didn't know—" A choked sob escapes him, and Adrian rushes to bring him into our tight hug. "I didn't know."

We hold each other, our little family unit, while Papi cries, setting off Adrian's tears, and then mine. We hold each other through it all, supporting each other as best we can.

Later, we order pizza and eat it in the living room together while watching *Scarface*. Papi and Adrian act out the scenes together in dramatic fashion.

"*Say hello to my little friend*," they say to each other, holding up breadsticks threateningly. The blood and the gore and the violence end up being a surprising balm to our souls that night.

I don't really fully process the whole day until I'm alone in my room. After I've washed my hair and slathered on a face mask I found at the bottom of a drawer, after I've turned off all the lights and tucked myself into bed, the realization starts rushing in.

I didn't get to say goodbye to my mom. I didn't get to look her in the face and call her out for all her shitty behavior. I didn't get to stand in front of her as the stronger person, the better person, to tell her how she hurt me and failed me. I'm not sure I ever will. I heard the promise she told my dad.

Te lo juro.

She's never coming back here. And I don't think I'll ever go looking for her.

But she'll stay with me, despite it all. She's everywhere. If Adrian tried his hardest to be the best, to be the shiniest thing in sight, then I did the opposite. I hid. I pushed people away. I decided that distance was the thing that would save me from pain, that indifference would be the thing that saved me from being hurt.

But Mom left, *again*, and it still hurt.

And the distance I put up between me and Gage, despite his best efforts, is the thing that ended up hurting me the most.

I hate that she's made me into this person. I could tell myself I chose to be like this independently of how she treated me, but if I'm honest, if I look deep into myself, I know it's because of her. She made me want to be this shadow of myself, so that her eye wouldn't turn to me and I wouldn't have to suffer under her attention. But I did that with everyone else, too.

I don't want that to be how I am anymore. I don't want her to control my relationships with people while she's thousands of miles away, not sparing a thought about me.

I'm going to start fixing that *now*. I've spent the last few months, the last *week* especially, resenting Adrian. And while my brother is not perfect, he doesn't deserve all this animosity I feel toward him. Because I know whatever pain I've felt the last few months, he's felt it too, and just like me, he didn't know how to deal with it. And we both handled it poorly.

Jumping out of bed, I creep into the hallway and knock on Adrian's door. It's silent on the other side, no murmur from the

TV or clacking of a video game controller. I knock again just in case and then push open the door.

Adrian is asleep, the worry drained from his face, a serene look of peace there instead.

"Adrian," I whisper from above him, giving his shoulders a little shake. "Adrian," I say again, leaning over to get closer to his ear.

He jolts awake at the sound of his name, eyes going wide as he takes in a deep breath. His room is dark, no night-lights or sleeping computer screens to illuminate it. It's just the moonlight and streetlamp from outside bleeding in to paint the outlines of everything in a subtle blue glow. I would think it'd be enough light to see by, considering I was able to walk up to him without tripping on the discarded books positioned like obstacles between his door and the bed, but maybe Adrian's vision is worse than mine.

Because as soon as his eyes take me in, the face looming above him whispering his name, *he screams.*

I slap a hand on his mouth immediately, hoping the thunderstorm sounds that Papi blares from a speaker while he sleeps is enough to drown out the pitiful wail that Adrian just let out.

"Jesus Christ," I hiss at him as he struggles for a second under my hand, "it's just me."

"Fuck, Valeria!" Adrian hisses back, throwing my hand off him and sitting up. "I thought the Green Goblin was coming to take me out. What the fuck is on your face?"

"Oh," I say in surprise, touching the dried green clay on my face. "It's a face mask."

"It's fucking terrifying is what it is," he says, still a little out of breath from the unwelcome surprise. "What are you doing?"

"I wanted to talk to you," I tell him, sitting down on the edge of the bed. "About everything."

"Fuck," he says again, wiping his face with his hands. "I can't take you seriously with that green shit on your face."

"Fine," I say, rolling my eyes. "I'll wash it off." I probably should have done that fifteen minutes ago, but my mind has been pretty distractible. I go across the hallway to the bathroom, checking under Papi's door to make sure no light has turned on. I splash water on my face, washing off every last bit of green before going back to Adrian's room.

I climb into his bed this time, resting my back against the wall with the window that has been cracked open, letting the cool breeze drift over me.

"We can't do this in the morning?" he asks once I'm settled.

"Will you even talk to me in the morning?" I ask. Adrian shakes his head like I'm being dramatic. "I don't want to keep doing this, Adrian. I want us to work past what happened this summer, to stick together through everything that's happening right now. I want my brother back."

"Oh yeah?" he says, laughing bitterly. I flinch at that sound, at the hurt burbling just underneath. "Where was that this summer when the whole family turned against me?"

"Adrian, you did a really shitty thing! Just because you were held accountable doesn't mean we don't love you."

"But that's what it felt like. Fine, I did something stupid, I shouldn't have taken Ana Maria's doughnut recipe. But you all dropped me like I didn't even matter." His voice is hard, like he's trying to pretend that this didn't hurt him as deeply as I know it did.

"Adrian, no," I say, my voice soft and compassionate as I lean across the bed and grab his hand. "I think it's because everyone loves you so much that we were so hurt by the whole thing. Papi thinks the world of you, and you tricked him, you told him the doughnuts were *your* idea. And Miguel trusted you! You hurt everyone with what you did, and instead of apologizing, you doubled down and got in a fight with Miguel."

"And what about you?" he asks, brushing over everything I just said. "The whole thing had nothing to do with you. It wasn't your recipe or your friend or your restaurant. You were just a bystander, and you dropped me, too."

"Just because I love you no matter what doesn't mean I have to agree with you no matter what," I explain. "You're always trying to live up to a standard that someone else set for you."

"You mean a standard Mom set," he says.

"Yeah," I say softly. "Are you still going to keep in contact with her?" I ask him.

"She's our *mom*," he says. "Of course. I hate what she did," he admits, "but I don't want to lose her because of it."

"Okay," I say, considering his words. I don't totally understand him or his reasoning, but at the end of the day, I have to accept it. We can choose our own paths. "Well, can you please stop giving me the cold shoulder? Because I miss you. I need you." My voice wobbles. Even though I thought I was out of tears to cry, I feel the burn of them returning.

"Okay." He pauses for a moment. "I miss you, too, you know."

"Good. Can I just ask one thing, though? Can we not go back *exactly* to how things used to be? As much as I've hated being without you this year," I tell him, "it has given me the opportunity to, I don't know, find myself? I always relied on you to do everything for us, to socialize for us and talk for us and move through school for us, and as soon as you left me behind, I realized I didn't have anything of my own. I've made friends—"

"About that," Adrian interrupts. "Your new *friend* landed me in detention today because he was being a little shit."

"Okay," I say, popping up from Adrian's bed. "I was *handling* that before you interrupted and made everything worse. Besides, I'm not discussing Gage with you."

"No, you made me sit down and talk about my feelings, it's your turn!" Adrian snaps at me.

"It's getting late!" I say brightly, cutting him off. "Don't you need your beauty sleep?"

Adrian jumps up from his bed, ready to pull me back into this conversation that I don't want to have, and I bolt out of his room and into mine. I lock the door behind me, his footsteps pounding down the hallway as he chases after me, but he can't reach me now.

"Valeria!" he says from the other side of the door, jiggling the doorknob.

"Good night, Adrian!" I say, jumping into bed and throwing the covers over my head.

CHAPTER THIRTY-TWO

With no one else awake to help me, I have to play car Tetris by myself, moving Miguel's car behind Adrian's to squeeze mine out from the driveway. I double-check that Gage's bag is still in my trunk and then head off.

When I pull into the parking lot, there are only a handful of student cars. I had to look on our school's website to see what teacher even teaches Marine Robotics, an elective I had no idea our school offered, and head straight to the classroom.

Walking down the empty corridors feels strange, since I almost never see these places without the hum of activity and dozens of students. The homecoming posters have been taken down, replaced by posters promoting the Halloween costume competition—first place gets a $100 gift card to Lacey's Diner—and posters promoting this weekend's band concert, where they will be performing the soundtrack for *The Nightmare Before Christmas.*

Ms. Wilson's classroom is in the back half of the school, over by the science block. Her door is propped open, the sound of some lo-fi radio leaking from the room.

Inside, a petite woman with dark skin and shiny black hair is sitting behind a large desk at the front of the room, her focus on an open notebook in front of her. From what I found on the website, she teaches the robotics classes as well as Engineering and Oceanography. I've never taken *any* of her classes, since they are all beyond me, but the look of her classroom kind of makes me wish I had. She has pictures of marine animals everywhere, beluga whales swimming across the wall with giant Pacific octopuses and schools of fish. There are pictures of that creepy robot dog from that one robotics company, and a table full of robotics projects from students.

Ms. Wilson's head pops up when I'm halfway into her classroom, and she looks at me curiously, dropping her pencil and pushing back from her desk.

"Can I help you?" she asks, her head cocked to the side.

"I was hoping to talk to you about this," I say, dropping Gage's bag on the desk in front of her. She looks at it with some trepidation, but relaxes when I pull out Gage's robot.

"Did you find that somewhere?" she asks.

"This is Gage Magnussen's project," I explain. "He left it in my car this weekend, and I promised to bring it to school yesterday, but—" I cut myself off, not sure how to explain myself in this moment. "We had something, um . . . bad happen in the family, and I didn't drive myself to school that day and I didn't have my phone on me and so Gage couldn't turn it in—"

"Slow down, slow down," Ms. Wilson says calmly. "Are you Valeria Morales?" she asks, and I want to melt into the floor.

"Yes," I say weakly.

"Ah, I see," she says.

"So it was my fault Gage didn't have his project, and it was my fault my brother got in a fight with him, and I don't want any of that to be held against him because he worked so hard on this Tupperware robot thing, the app he made to control it looks so good, and I really don't want his grade to be impacted by me and the things I've done. Please, please, I hope you can accept this project late."

Ms. Wilson crosses her arms over her chest and regards me silently, but as much as I want to turn tail and run, I need to stand firm for Gage. To make up for my mistakes with him and to make sure he knows that I would never do anything to get between him and being valedictorian.

"Thank you for bringing this in, Ms. Morales," Ms. Wilson says, picking up the robot and setting it down on the table behind her. "But since he was held up in the principal's office yesterday afternoon, he was given an extension for today. I appreciate the backstory, nonetheless."

"Oh!" I say in surprise.

"Is that all?" she asks.

"Um, yeah," I say. "Thank you."

I duck out of her classroom quickly and speed toward the library, where I work on the gala presentation until the bell rings for class. As much as I meant it when I told my brother that I was ready to get out of his shadow and start doing things on my own, I spend the whole day at school hidden away as much as possible. During lunch, I set up at a computer in a corner of the library *far* from Gage's usual spot. Now that I've been by more often this semester, the librarians don't look at me like I'm about to make off with half the stacks anymore, and they instead welcome me with a smile.

I work on details for the gala, emailing the donors to finalize details about their donations and coordinating with the assistant the Magnussens hired to stage-manage the event. After school, I run around town to gather some of the auction items.

I drive over to the art store downtown and pick up a donation from a local artist, a gorgeous oil painting of the Hoh Rain Forest featuring the giant mossy trees and a tranquil elk staring at the viewer. I go to the bed-and-breakfast where Ana Maria's mom works and pick up a self-care basket that she prepared, featuring the line of soaps and lotions made specifically for the property, dried lavender from their garden, candles from a local maker, two chocolate bars, and one of their famed robes.

I drop everything off at the Magnussen law office, where Ginger Davis has to accept my packages with a sour look on her face. We don't say anything to each other, and I don't run into either of Gage's parents on any of my visits.

Gage hasn't reached out to me since the fight with my brother, and I've been too scared to text him. There are so many things I want to say to him, and despite my best efforts, that kiss we shared plays in the back of my head every night on some kind of forbidden loop.

It hurts that some small part of Gage really thought that I would use him, tank his grades to ensure my brother beats him out, that what was budding between us wasn't real to me, too. That fake dating him wasn't one of the best things I've ever done.

But I'm hoping someday soon I'll be able to prove that to him.

CHAPTER THIRTY-THREE

Are you sure this looks okay?" I ask Tia Isa though the mirror, pulling on the loose hairs around my face.

"You look great, cariño," she says before spraying another blast of hairspray over my hair. Tia Isa has done me up to the nines for the gala tonight. She helped me apply false eyelashes, she went shopping with me to find the perfect cocktail dress, and she painted my nails a vibrant red.

At first when she offered to take me shopping, I was scared to go, with flashbacks of going to the mall with my mom and being forced into clothes that made me itchy and uncomfortable. But Tia Isa was easygoing and helpful the whole time. She understood what I was comfortable in and didn't force me into body con dresses with slits or tight bodices that wrapped my torso like a vise.

We ended up picking something that managed to be comfortable but formal, a strapless dress in a gorgeous green floral pattern that looks like an old painting, draped over the body and gathered over the hip so that the skirt cascades down from one side. Tia Isa picked out a pair of block heels for me with a sturdy enough base that I would feel comfortable in them all night.

She finished the look by lending me a necklace that had belonged to my abuela, a beautiful double strand of saltwater pearls with a delicate clasp dotted with emeralds. I kept on my usual small gold hoops and generously applied the red lipstick Tia Isa let me borrow.

After everything that happened the last couple of weeks, Tia Isa has remained a pillar of strength for our little family. She is always keeping us fed, making sure Papi doesn't work himself to death, and providing Adrian and me with the kind of motherly support that was frankly foreign to us. It had felt invasive at first, but I can see now that she was only ever trying to help us.

It hurt to know that this is what I had been missing all along, the mother that the game of life *could* have dealt me, if things had gone differently. But I'm just glad I have Tia now, helping us all even though she's going through her own painful life transition.

I have a long list of regrets about the last couple of months, and at the top of that list is how I've been treating my aunt. Someone was trying to show me unconditional love, and I snapped at her, because I hated that someone could see the gaping hole inside me that my mother left.

"Thanks for your help, Tia," I tell her as she swats my hands away from the loose hairs around my face and grabs the curling iron to style them properly into place.

"Anytime."

And I know she means it.

With all the prep done, I step back from the dining room table–turned-salon and pick up my small clutch. Papi comes out from the kitchen at that moment, where he was hard at work soldering something to "fix" the blender, and catches sight of me.

"¡Mi niña!" he cries out in joy at the sight of me all done up. "¡Qué linda estás!"

"Yeah, yeah," I say as he hurries up to stand beside me.

"That's Mami's necklace!" he says in delight when he notices it around my throat. "I haven't seen that in years. You know, she wore that on her wedding day in Cuba. She snuck it out of the country by sewing some of her jewelry into the lining of her jacket."

"I had no idea," I say in surprise, my hand rising up to touch the necklace.

"We'll send Dad a picture," Papi says to his sister. "He'd love to see Valeria wearing it." My grandmother died when I was in middle school, after her cancer had returned. She hadn't wanted to go through treatment the second time, and Abuelo wanted to take her somewhere relaxing for whatever time they had left. They moved out to the Oregon coast, where they had always loved to vacation, and bought a small cottage in the middle of nowhere near the water. After she passed away, Abuelo stayed, having fallen in love with the small community they had built for themselves there. His arthritis makes it difficult for him to travel, so we usually drive down to spend the winter holidays with him in his cottage.

"Oh, my little girl," Papi says, tearing up as he takes a picture of me.

"Stop it!" I shout at him, slapping the phone away. "Don't

cry, I'm literally just going to help run a charity auction. There is no need for waterworks."

"But you look so grown-up! Doesn't she, Isa?" he asks.

"She does." Tia Isa smiles.

"Okay, okay, this is as much sappiness as I can take," I say, pushing Papi away and clomping in my heels to the front door. "I'm heading out now, please hold your tears until I leave!"

I pull on my nylon raincoat, which really ruins the vibe of the whole look, and run out the door to my car.

The Magnussen Charity Gala is being held at a venue near town that used to be a barn and is now used for weddings during the summer. In the off season, it usually sits empty, hosting a rare winter wedding or an event for some local company.

The barn is still painted the classic red with white trim, with an open field nearby that boasts wildflower blooms in the summer but by this time of year is just a field of muddy sludge. There is a paved entrance leading to the front door, decorated with string lights and lanterns, leading everyone inside into the dry warmth.

I park my car in the gravel lot next to the venue and try to walk across in heels without falling. There's an attendant standing outside the barn in a neat suit, holding a clipboard and walkie-talkie.

"Name," he says briskly, not looking up from his clipboard.

"Valeria Morales," I say. "I'm working with Gage on the fundraiser."

His eyes slide down the list, flipping the paper over to continue searching.

"There you are," he says, making a mark next to my name.

"Here is your name tag." He picks up a tag from a neatly organized pile on the table next to him.

I nod and say thank you before stepping into the venue. It's massive inside, high ceilings made of timber with glittering chandeliers. The wood floor has been replaced by poured concrete, and the mezzanine is decorated with swags of green chiffon. Dozens of round tables take up most of the space, with thoughtfully decorated place settings and dramatic floral centerpieces.

A stage has been made up at one end of the barn, complete with red velvet curtains and stage lights. There's a podium on the lip of the stage, where Gage will be emceeing the auction.

"There you are!" a voice cries out from behind me, and I turn to find Mrs. Magnussen, decked out in a floor-length sparkling green dress and earrings so heavy with gold and diamonds that her lobes are stretched out in a very painful-looking way.

"Hi, Mrs. Magnussen," I greet her politely.

"Oh, dear, please call me Nicole," she says with the friendliest smile she has ever given me. "You did such a marvelous job putting together all these donations for the auction," she says, sweeping her hands toward the table where some of the items are on display.

Her tone is free of the passive-aggressiveness from the last time we spoke, and I try not to let my eyes grow wide and take the compliment in stride.

"You got Olympic Wellness to donate some *oxygen facials*? Amazing!"

"Oh, Cece was so happy to donate to such a great cause. Honestly, everyone I spoke to told me how much they loved being a part of this gala this year."

"My husband and I firmly believe that we have a duty not only to uplift our own community, but communities around the world," she says, and the way she says it is a little like patting herself on the back for being such a good person. She's a bit of a snob, but at least she's putting her money where her mouth is. "Have you gotten anything to eat yet? There are some waiters walking around with these delicious little arancini, they're divine. Oh, David, there you are! I'm so sorry, Valeria, I have to run, make sure you snag one of those arancini before they're all gone!"

Mrs. Magnussen darts away before I can say anything, and I'm left alone to explore the gala. I snag a glass of sparkling apple cider from the bar and try to find the elusive waiter carrying the arancini, but before I can find him, I run into more local business owners. Diana from the bookstore catches me and tells me that she's planning to outbid everyone for the trail ride with the "most handsome rancher she's ever seen," and Carla Simpson, who owns a lot of real estate in town, chases me down to ask about donating to the gala for next year.

I'm suddenly the center of attention for cocktail hour, with people slinging compliments my way, and instead of shying away like I might have a couple of months ago, I soak it all in. I worked hard on this, and despite my life kind of imploding in the middle of it all, everything still turned out great. *I* made it great.

"Distinguished guests, please make your way to your seats as we prepare to welcome tonight's speaker to the stage." Everyone shuffles over to the tables and sits down. I end up at a table toward the back with the high school principal and some people I don't recognize. The food is bland at best and served by waiters who all place the plate down as though it were part of a choreographed dance.

I try to listen to the speech about global vaccines, but my attention keeps skipping around the crowd, trying to spot Gage. He's not at the table at the front with his parents, he's not onstage, and I'm not sure where else he would be.

By the time dinner is served, the guests are a few glasses of wine deep and ready to put down some money for the auction. I start tapping my leg anxiously, not even nervous to see how my donations perform, just anxious from the anticipation of finally getting to see Gage, albeit on the stage.

My heart starts racing, a pounding so powerful I swear you could see it through my skin. We haven't talked, *really* talked, since I kicked him out of my car that night. And to be fair, he was really the only one talking that night. I had been spiraling, afraid of the space between us closing in, of letting someone in close. I have a lot to say now, though, and I need to tell him how I feel.

But when the curtain opens back up, it's not Gage at center stage, but Ginger. She has her hair in a stately updo, and she's wearing a red strapless dress with a huge bow at the back, the tails of the bow so long they nearly touch the ground. Honestly, she looks *resplendent*, and I get why Gage just carried on dating her for so long despite not feeling all that romantically interested.

"Good evening, folks," Ginger says into the mic, her words clear and well enunciated. "I'm so thrilled to be taking you through the evening's auction."

Wait, she's leading the auction? I glance around, confused, and I notice that Gage's parents are doing the same at their table. Even from this far, I can see that his mother's lips are pursed in disappointment and his father's brow is drawn down in a look of what I can best describe as polite anger.

Despite what seems to be a last-minute changeup, Ginger does an excellent job leading the auction. She throws in just enough jokes to capture the audience's favor and keeps things moving at a good pace.

The presentation I prepared for the auction blinks on behind her, and the chaos starts. Paddles start flying up, fighting for the chance to snag the two-night stay at the bed-and-breakfast. The named bookshelf donation from the bookstore ends up being surprisingly popular, as two old men fight each other back and forth until one finally wins out with a surprising twelve-hundred-dollar bid. Gage's mom does end up winning the oxygen facial from Olympic Wellness, and an older gentleman has the winning bid for Michelle's ikebana floral arranging classes.

We're getting toward the tail end of the auction when a slide pops up on the screen that I did not prepare. It's pictures from the inside of Morales Bakery, of the mural I painted last year.

The mural is a wall of vibrant florals of all kinds, wisteria dripping from the crown molding and roses blooming from climbing vines. If you look closely, you can spot bees perched on petals and limes growing on branches and hummingbirds snacking on a hibiscus. It's now a popular corner in the shop where everyone poses for their pictures. This project was what got me interested in doing murals, but our shop didn't have any other walls for me to paint on, and I'm not sure Papi would want me taking my art to the walls at home.

But how the hell did it end up in my gala presentation?

"Next up we have the mural services of Valeria Morales,

whose work many of you might recognize from Morales Bakery."

An electric shock runs through my body at the sound of my name coming out of Ginger's mouth.

"This item includes one twenty-by-thirty mural, which can be used to advertise your business or add some flair to commercial real estate with a stunning work of art on exterior walls, or even for a splash of character on the interior. The bidding will start at seven hundred dollars."

Before I can even register what's happening, a bidding war begins. Paddles go flying up as business owners vie for the opportunity to get *my art* painted on their walls. I watch, mouth agape, as the number climbs higher and higher. Finally, the paddles slow down, the bidding war down to a final three until Carla Simpson shuts down the bid with a stunning *three-thousand-dollar bid.*

The auction moves on to the next item, but I'm still in shock. My work is worth three thousand dollars to someone? My work, which wasn't even supposed to be an item up for auction?

I'm having such a hard time processing all this that I nearly jump out of my skin when someone taps on my shoulder. I'm even more surprised when I turn to find Gage standing behind me.

He's wearing a tux, complete with black bow tie and little white handkerchief in the pocket of his jacket. His hands are in his pockets as he watches me warily, a faint smile on his lips. I sit there silently, afraid of what he might do or say.

"Can we talk?" he asks gently.

I must look a little silly, my jaw still hanging open from the shock of the mural bid, so I just nod slowly. Gage offers me his hand to help me out of my chair and leads me toward the back of the venue.

We're nearly to the back door when a hand slams down on Gage's shoulder and stops him in his tracks.

Mrs. Magnussen is standing behind us, looking incandescently angry.

"Where have you *been*?" she hisses at her son.

Gage steps in front of me subtly, blocking me from his mom and taking the brunt of her anger full on.

"I let Ginger take over the emcee duties," Gage tells his mom levelly.

"That was *your* job, Gage," his mother says.

"And I didn't want it. So I didn't do it," he says, his voice not wavering one bit. He sounds confident and sure. "I gave it to someone who *did* want it and who has been doing an excellent job. Better than I've ever done it, honestly. You've been asking me to let Ginger help with the auction, so I did."

"That decision wasn't yours to make," his mom snaps.

"Darling," Mr. Magnussen cuts in, bright veneer smile plastered on as he tugs on his wife's arm. "This is not the time."

Mrs. Magnussen looks around to see if anyone is listening in on this awkward conversation before collecting herself.

"We will discuss this later," Mrs. Magnussen says, turning away sharply and following her husband back to the table.

Gage doesn't waste a second after their departure, grabbing my hand in his and leading us out into the cold afternoon, the sun already starting to set. He pulls me out to the field, away from the venue, laughing, as I am pulled along in stunned silence.

"What is going on?!" I finally cry out, confused and delighted by this turn of events.

"I'm celebrating!" he shouts, dropping my hands and turning his face toward the clear sky. "I'm free, for now, at least."

"Congrats?" I say, unsure how to respond to this unrestrained version of Gage.

"Thank you," he says, dropping his head down to look at me, his eyes warm and earnest, so different from the last time he looked at me. "For everything."

"I'm not sure what I did. And honestly, you shouldn't be thanking me for anything," I say hesitantly. Now is my moment. No more being afraid. No more hiding. "I owe you a huge apology. I'm so sorry I almost ruined your grade and got you detention, but you have to know I would never—"

"Valeria, it's okay."

"No, it's not, and I shouldn't have said those things I did about you just wanting valedictorian because of your parents. It wasn't fair, and—"

"Valeria." Gage puts his hands on my shoulders, grounding me. I stop babbling and find the nerve to look him in the eyes. "I should be the one apologizing to you. I said some shitty things that day, too. Miguel told me about what happened that weekend," he says. "I had no idea you were going through that."

"Oh, that?" I say, a little flippantly. "I wanted to talk to you, after it happened, but I had just thrown you out of my car, and then the cafeteria happened and . . ." I trail off, shrugging my shoulders. "It would have been nice to listen to some Latin."

"I'm sorry I wasn't there for you, Valeria. I hate that you felt like you couldn't come to me."

"You were giving me space, which I needed," I tell him with a wan smile. I don't know where we stand now, but it feels good being so honest and straightforward with him, after weeks of lying and holding back. "And I thought . . . maybe you needed some space from me, too."

"God, Valeria, that's the last thing I want. I hate that I made you think you're to blame for *anything* bad in my life. You're so fierce and so determined, and I've never met anyone like you. You're the reason I was finally able to stand up to my parents." He smiles this big, open smile, so full of joy.

"*Me?*" I squeak out in shock.

"You're the best thing that's happened to me in a long time, and I just want you to know how great you are, and I thought seeing people go crazy for your art would—"

"Wait, you added my mural to the auction?" I ask, being the one to interrupt this time. Gage grins sheepishly.

"I hope that was okay. After you gave that impassioned speech to Ms. Wilson about my robot, I had to come up with my own grand gesture."

"She told you about that?" I ask, embarrassed.

"She did," Gage says, taking a step closer, and I find myself being drawn to him, just like always, the gravity of him pulling me in.

"Thank you for the mural," I say, suddenly feeling shy. The fact that that's what he chose to do shows just how much Gage *sees* me. He's seen me since that first day in the library when he called me out for being lost without Adrian. And not only that, but he believes in me. That I can do big things. It's not something I'm used to, and honestly, it feels a little uncomfortable, but it also feels good. And I want to hold on to that feeling.

"I wish I hadn't pushed you away that night," I admit, my eyes focused on the laces of his dress shoes. "I was just scared."

"Of what?" Gage asks, closing the last bit of distance between us to thread my hands with his.

"Of everything," I whisper. "Of the future. Of what you might expect of me. Of the hurt you might cause me if I let this thing between us go any further."

"But what about all the good things that could happen?" he asks, his breath fluttering the hairs around my face. He squeezes my hands and lets out a pained sigh. "Valeria, do you know how many times I've thought about that kiss?"

He drops his forehead against mine and sighs again, and something in me burns at the sound of longing in his voice.

"That was my first kiss," I admit in a whisper. "I was worried I didn't know what I was doing."

"You figured it out very quickly, trust me," Gage assures me. "And, you know, it gets easier. The more you do it."

"Is that an invitation?"

"Only if you want it. Only if you want me, for real this time," he offers. "No deals, no fakes. The real thing. I'm yours if you want it, if you're ready."

A drop of something cold lands on my cheek, then another. I glance up at the sky to see tiny snowflakes glittering as they fall around us. They flutter in the air, light and small, getting caught in Gage's eyelashes, melting on the tip of his nose. But his eyes are still focused on me, not on the early snow falling around us.

I reach a hand up to Gage's cheek, wiping away the dot of melted snow there, sweeping my thumb across his bottom lashes to catch another snowflake. He's wound tight under my touch, frozen, waiting for my answer. I sweep his hair off his forehead and gaze into his eyes, and I find my resolve melting under his focus.

"I want it," I whisper, my lips a breath away from his.

He comes alive at my words, his arms wrapping around me and pressing his body to mine. He doesn't kiss me, not at first, he just holds me close and presses his face into the crook of my neck, inhaling deeply before pulling away with what I can only describe as a giggle. Gage Magnussen giggling is not something I'd ever thought I'd see, but it's already become one of my favorite sounds.

His hand reaches up to my face, his fingers grazing my jaw as he turns my face up to his.

I can't stand the wait any longer, and I press my lips to his, my hands reaching around his neck to pull him closer to me. It feels better than the first time, my hands more confident on him, our bodies free from the confines of the front seat of my car.

Everything about Gage fits, my body sinking into his like I've found my missing puzzle piece. There are no parts of myself I need to cut or bend or shape for him. It's easy, like breathing, and I can't get enough.

CHAPTER THIRTY-FOUR

We need more boxes!" I holler up the stairs, taping shut the box I just finished packing.

"There's no way!" Miguel shouts back from upstairs, where he has been hauling boxes from downstairs to the front door. "We just bought more!"

"I just used the last box!" Adrian calls out from behind me, busy filling up one with things from the basement kitchen.

"I'm going to lose my hearing being around your family," Gage complains, covering his ears in what I am sure is an overly dramatic response to the volume of our voices. "You should get one of those house PA systems."

"Screaming works fine," Adrian says, and I smile at Gage in triumph.

Gage and Adrian are by no means *friends* at this point, but since they both care about me, they've settled on a kind of truce. Especially since Gage has taken himself formally out of the running for valedictorian. The race was costing him something it wasn't worth, and after a lengthy fight with his parents, he withdrew, leaving Adrian in the lead. There might still be a surprise upset next semester, some dark horse come to take it all away from Adrian, but for now it's not a cause for concern.

Tia Isa ended up getting that job in Port Townsend working at a nursing home facility. The sign-on bonus was enough for her to put a deposit down on her own place, and she and Miguel were finally on their way out of the house. They found a duplex a couple of miles out of town that sits on a hill, with a deck that has a stunning view of the sound.

Miguel clomps down the stairs, grumbling in frustration.

"How are we out of boxes?" he complains, looking around at the living room. Miguel and his mom didn't bring much with them up here, so we didn't really need that many boxes to start. But as Adrian and I started going through the living room, we started finding some of Mom's old things. Her CDs, an old blow-dryer, her high school yearbooks. She is never coming back, and these things would just end up collecting dust.

Adrian decided to pack them, picking out what was garbage and could be donated. Now that the basement is getting clear of things, there is a big, blank wall calling to me.

Papi already agreed to let me paint it. I've mapped it all out in a digital rendering for him to approve, a finalized version of the Cuban tile design I had worked on before. I want the mural to look like wallpaper, something busy but not distracting. Between this and Carla Simpson's winning bid, I'm on my way to my own mural business.

But more than that, this mural will be a small step toward healing, toward reclaiming our home and making it truly ours, painting over the colors Mom chose years ago.

"Valeria and I could run to the hardware store and buy some more boxes?" Gage offers.

"No!" Miguel and Adrian bark at the same time, united in their dislike of me dating someone and me being *alone* with that someone.

"Actually," I say, standing up, "I think that sounds like a great idea." I hook my arm around Gage's and pull him away from his packing project.

"No funny business, Gage!" Miguel shouts at our back. "That's my little cousin!"

"We are not your *little* cousins, Miguel," Adrian says, his ire getting redirected. "I'm bigger than you."

"And I'm *older*," Miguel points out as I push Gage up the stairs.

"And *I'm* stronger. I could take you any day—"

"Oh, yeah?" Miguel asks. "Prove it, let's arm wrestle, then."

I smile at the sound of their back-and-forth, because even though it sounds like they're at each other's throats, to me it sounds like how we used to be. There's still some resentment from this summer that hangs between Adrian and Miguel, but we're all working on it.

"Where are you heading off to?" Tia Isa asks from the kitchen, where she's packing up some of the stuff Papi is gifting to her. Her husband is still being an asshole about the divorce, and Tia Isa will need to go back to California soon to settle everything, but in the meantime they don't have much to start fresh with.

The furniture in the basement will help them out for now, along with all the surplus kitchen equipment that has been taking up space.

"We ran out of boxes," I explain. "So we're going to go run out to get more."

"Oh!" Tia Isa says. "I know where they are, I set aside a bunch and put them over—"

"What's that?" I say, backing away toward the front door, pushing Gage behind me. "I can't hear you, Tia! Text me if you need more packing tape or something!"

As we slip out the front door together, I can hear my aunt laughing. I reach for Gage's hand giddily and run toward his car. We're out of breath and laughing by the time we're inside, the windows quickly fogging up from our breath. Gage turns on the heater and waits for the car to warm up.

"You know," I say, my fingers drumming on the dashboard in front of me, "I actually have a surprise for you. I wanted to wait until we were alone."

"Oh yeah?" Gage says, his eyebrows climbing up and his mouth quirking in the corner.

"Here," I say, taking out a folded-up piece of paper from my back pocket, a secret that I've been carrying with me since school ended on Friday. I've been keeping it to myself for days now, basking in it, letting myself enjoy it, and letting the truth settle in before I share it with anyone else.

Gage takes the paper, eyeing me curiously before unfolding it carefully. As soon as he opens it, he quickly recognizes what he's holding. His eyes glance over it, taking in everything, before landing on the most important line printed:

Algebra II

Quarter 1: C 74

Quarter 2: B+ 89

My future is wide open, full of possibility and opportunity. I've proved to myself that I can do things, that I can set my mind to something and *do it*. Fate isn't determined, a future isn't set in stone, and I can do more than I ever thought possible.

"Valeria!" Gage cries out, dropping the paper and pulling me in for a hug. "This is amazing! You're amazing!"

"I couldn't have done it without you," I whisper, wrapping my arms around him and holding him tight.

"Knowing you, I think you would have figured it out," Gage says proudly. "I'm going to see you in that stupid cap and gown in the spring."

"And I'm going to see you in all those elaborate tassels high-achieving weirdos like you wear," I tell him, poking him in the rib for good measure.

"Does this mean we get to celebrate?" he asks, pulling back to look at me, a goofy smile still spread across his face.

"The guys will eventually realize that Tia Isa has more boxes," I say, "so we don't *actually* need to go out and buy any."

"Perfect," Gage says, sliding the tip of his nose along mine, his breath warming up my cheeks.

"Stupendous," I say, my lips teasing his.

I'd be lying if I said that kissing Gage wasn't scary anymore. It definitely is. It is scary when I remember that he is more experienced than I am. It is scary when I think of where he might end up next fall. And it's scary how much my feelings for him have grown, how they've expanded and taken over and there seems to be no end in sight.

Every day there is something new about Gage to fall in love with, something new to learn. But as scary as that feeling is, I can't help but feel excited about the road ahead of us. I want to see how big this feeling can grow.

COQUITO FRENCH TOAST

At this point, coming up with a recipe to go with my book has become my favorite part of my process. It's my little reward once the book is mostly finished, a treat for myself and (hopefully) future readers. To me, it seems like this book has even MORE food than *Guava and Grudges* did, and every time I read back through it, I became hungrier and hungrier for the dishes I had thought up. Like the Morales family, food and cooking are my favorite vehicle for expressing love. So think of this dish as a thank-you to all my readers, who deserve a sweet treat and a calm Sunday morning.

INGREDIENTS

4 tablespoons butter

½ cup brown sugar

1 loaf of bread (preferably Cuban bread, but any enriched bread like brioche or challah works great)

5.4 fl. oz. can of coconut cream

12 fl. oz. can of evaporated milk

6 fl. oz. (half of a 12 fl. oz. can) condensed milk

5 eggs

¼ teaspoon cloves

¼ teaspoon nutmeg

¼ teaspoon cinnamon

1 teaspoon vanilla

1 teaspoon rum extract (optional)

1 teaspoon salt

INSTRUCTIONS

1. Add butter to a small saucepan on medium heat until melted, stirring gently as you go. The liquid should start to boil as the milk solids begin to turn from white to brown. Continue to stir for about five minutes, making sure not to let the butter get too dark. Once the liquid is a toasty brown color, remove from heat.
2. Stir the brown sugar into your butter mixture.
3. Spread the butter-and-sugar mixture evenly on the bottom of a 9" x 13" pan.
4. Cut your loaf of bread into chunks. If you cut bigger pieces, you'll get drier tops that get crunchy when baked. If you cut smaller, more even pieces, you won't get a craggy, crunchy top. I love the added texture, but you might want something smoother!
5. Add the chunks to the pan, on top of the butter-and-brown-sugar mixture.
6. In a blender, combine coconut cream, evaporated milk, condensed milk, eggs, spices, vanilla and rum extracts,

and salt. Blend until all the spices and the salt are well incorporated into the liquid.

7. Pour your liquid over the bread, making sure to cover every piece as you pour.
8. Cover with foil or plastic wrap and let rest in the refrigerator for at least five hours or overnight.
9. When ready to bake, take the pan out, remove the cover, and preheat your oven to 350°F.
10. Bake for 45–60 minutes, until the liquid has set and only a slight jiggle remains when you move the pan.
11. Let rest for 5–10 minutes and serve hot!

TIPS:

- I like to serve this French toast with a mix of berries, whipped cream, and warm maple syrup.
- I know being left with half a can of something can be really annoying! If you like your French toast to be sweeter, you can add more condensed milk to the custard, but the full can would just make it way too sweet. Instead, you can use the rest of that can to make Vietnamese iced coffee, drizzle it on top of the warm French toast instead of maple syrup, or eat it by the spoonful from the fridge like I did as a child…

ACKNOWLEDGMENTS

I've dreamt of being an author since I was little, hogging the family computer to type up stories at every opportunity. The fact that I get to do it for real now, that my stories reach new readers every day, never ceases to amaze me. So, thank you, reader, for picking this book up and taking a trip to Port Murphy.

Thank you to my amazing agent, Marietta Zacker, who has my back at every turn. You make being an author a dream. And to my editor, who I will follow into the ends of the earth, Alex Borbolla. You simply *get* my stories and what I'm trying to do, even when I'm not sure what's going on. You make writing books so much fun. And to Ashley Burdin, who is simply integral to my plotting process. Your instinct for storytelling is incomparable and I am so lucky to call you my friend.

To the team at Bloomsbury: thank you, Faye Bi, for trusting me and sending me across the country to yap about my books, those trips are some of the best parts of this career; to Lily and Phoebe, marketers extraordinaire who are willing to collaborate and brainstorm with me, thanks for being at my side; to the design team at Bloomsbury, who reached out and asked if I wanted to illustrate my new covers (daunting, terrifying, exciting), thank you for this opportunity; to my designer, John Candell, who helped bring it all together, thank you for your insight and guidance; and to the dozens of other people who all play a part of bringing this book to readers, thank you all for your hard work!

To the best coworkers in the world: Allison, Erin, Sasha, Jaime, Nabeeha, Bryce, Kelly, Meg, Julia, Olivia, and Becca. Y'all are the most talented people in this industry, hands down, not to mention kind, funny, thoughtful, etc., etc. You're always first in line in meetings to plug my books for me and I'm so grateful for your support. Especially when I get off topic in meetings and talk your heads off about MSDS sheets. Safety first!!!!

To my incredible group of writing friends, who make publishing a less scary place: Akshaya Raman, Amanda Foody, Amanda Haas, Axie Oh, Charlie Lynn Herman, Claribel Ortega, Janella Angeles, Kat Cho, Katy Rose Pool, Maddy Colis, Mara Fitzgerald, Meg RK, Melody Simpson, and Tara Sim.

And to my family, who insists my books need this warning label: EAT BEFORE READING. Your support of my art is invaluable, and your constant chaos is like perennial inspiration for comedic fodder. Keep it coming.

JANSSEN SOLBERG

ALEXIS CASTELLANOS was born and raised in Florida, where she enjoyed sunny days, dramatic thunderstorms, and delicious Cuban food. After graduating from college, she moved to New York City and worked as a scenic artist, bringing theatrical sets to life with a little bit of paint and a whole lot of ingenuity. She currently works as a graphic designer by day and spends her nights dreaming up stories. She is the author of the graphic novel *Isla to Island* and YA novel *Guava and Grudges*. She lives in Los Angeles with her partner and two cats. Connect with her on Instagram, Twitter, and TikTok @alexisc_art and on her website, alexiscastellanos.com.